MW01073654

THE NAMES

THE NAMES

Florence Knapp

PAMELA DORMAN BOOKS | VIKING

VIKING

An imprint of Penguin Random House LLC

1745 Broadway, New York, NY 10019

Simultaneously published in hardcover in Great Britain by Phoenix Books,
an imprint of Hachette UK Ltd., London, in 2025

Copyright © 2025 by Florence Knapp

Penguin Random House values and supports copyright. Copyright fuels
creativity, encourages diverse voices, promotes free speech, and
creates a vibrant culture. Thank you for buying an authorized edition
of this book and for complying with copyright laws by not reproducing,
scanning, or distributing any part of it in any form without permission.
You are supporting writers and allowing Penguin Random House to
continue to publish books for every reader. Please note that no part of this
book may be used or reproduced in any manner for the purpose of training
artificial intelligence technologies or systems.

A Pamela Dorman Book/Viking

The PGD colophon is a registered trademark of Penguin
Random House LLC.

VIKING is a registered trademark of Penguin Random House LLC.

All internal illustrations © Sam Scales.

Designed by Cassandra Garruzzo Mueller

ISBN 9780593833902

Printed in the United States of America

For my husband, Ian—
with love

THE NAMES

Prologue

October 1987

Cora's mother always used to say children were whipped up by the wind, that even the quiet ones would come in after playtime made wild by it. Cora feels it in herself now, that restlessness. Outside, gusts lever at the fir trees behind the house and burst down the side passage to hurl themselves at the gate. Inside, too, worries skitter and eddy. Because tomorrow—if morning comes, if the storm stops raging—Cora will register the name of her son. Or perhaps, and this is her real concern, she'll formalize who he will become.

Cora has never liked the name Gordon. The way it starts with a splintering sound that makes her think of cracked boiled sweets, and then ends with a thud like someone slamming down a sports bag. *Gord*on. But what disturbs her more is that she must now pour the goodness of her son into its mold, hoping he'll be strong enough to find his own shape within it. Because Gordon is a name passed down through the men in her husband's family, and it seems impossible it could be any other way. But this doesn't stop her arguing back and forth with herself, considering all the times she's felt a person's name might have influenced the course of their life. Amelia Earhart. The Lumière brothers. Only last week, she'd noticed a book on her husband's bedside table, *Clinical Neurology* by Lord Walter Russell Brain.

"Doesn't that strike you as odd?" she'd asked.

"Coincidence," Gordon had replied. "Although you wouldn't believe the number of urologists called Burns, Cox, and Ball. And, actually, Mr. Legg is pretty common in orthopedics."

Do you not see the risk? she'd wanted to say. *Do you not see that calling our son Gordon might mean he ends up like you?* But she couldn't. Because surely that was the point.

She rests the crook of a bent finger against the warmth of the baby's cheek as though his skin might transmit some vital message. Of what he wants. Of who he might be. But before anything can be divined, something crashes against the back wall of the house—a sound both heard and felt. She draws the baby closer as the security light flickers on outside, illuminating the roiling silhouettes of the firs. Vast and looming, then receding, before being made large again. She hears Gordon emerge from the next room and belt down the stairs, pictures him striding pajamaed across the dark of the living room toward the patio doors, then standing in the spotlight, squinting without his contact lenses, trying to determine what's out of place. She imagines him reduced by the looming threat of the trees, the immensity of the storm.

A few minutes later he opens the door to the nursery, and Cora feels a draft of cold air, as though it's attached itself to his clothing and followed him up the stairs. "It was just the watering can," he says. "Come back to bed now."

"Soon," she agrees. But she doesn't want to leave the baby alone and so she lets him sleep on, his head heavy against her arm as the sounds of the storm meter out the minutes of night unraveling into day.

GORDON IS ON the phone to a colleague already at the practice. Cora overhears them discussing the lack of warning in the previous night's weather report, then the possibility of canceled appointments and staff not getting in. She makes breakfast one-handed, the baby pre-occupying her other, as she helps Maia tune in to a local radio station to listen as names of schools closed by storm damage are read out. Maia's comes halfway down a roll call of unfamiliar primaries, eliciting a small, delighted smile and a silent thumbs-up, which falls to her side as her father enters the room.

Reaching for a slice of toast before he heads off, Gordon says, "My parents are coming on Sunday. Make sure you get to the registrar's today." Two statements, side by side, delivered as though one justifies the other. "And don't cut across the common," he adds. Flashers, murderers, and, today, trees that might still come down in the aftermath.

THE HOUSES ON their street are all stucco-pillared fake grandeur, front gardens composed of neat, low-lying shrubs, overlooked by identikit blank windows. When they step outside, there's little evidence of the storm. But beyond the cul-de-sac, the landscape has that same blinking unreality of emerging from a cinema in daylight.

Trees lean at odd angles. Flattened fence panels leave gaping invitations into back gardens. A rotary washing line lies collapsed across the pavement. A few doors up, a man's shirt is caught on a privet hedge, pegs still pinched at its shoulders. Maia's eyes flit about, their town suddenly a spot-the-difference puzzle.

They walk along the edge of the common, steering the pram around fallen branches, stopping to look at an oak's vast, wormy rootball, dripping with clods of mud. Maia crouches in the hollow beneath. "Careful not to get your coat dirty," Cora says. *His words.* Her own instinct is to encourage Maia to lie down, to breathe in the rich, musky scent of the earth, to imagine herself as a fox cub curled up nose to tail. She's nine, on the cusp of being too old to want to do these things.

Maia clambers out and dusts off her coat. At the zebra crossing, where the amber globe of a Belisha beacon lies decapitated beside the road, they wait for the cars to stop. Maia looks toward the pram and says, "Why don't I have your name, if he'll have Dad's?"

Cora raises a hand to thank a driver. "Ah, but you do. It's just something no one else knows about," she says as they cross. "Maia means *mother.* I can show you in my book of baby names when we get home."

"Does it actually?" Cora is surprised at how happy this makes her daughter. "So why aren't we calling him something that just means *Dad*?"

Cora looks at the baby, whose full-moon face peeps out from his oversized snowsuit. She stops pushing for a moment and leans into his cocoon of talc-scented air. His eyes flutter with excitement on meeting hers, his swaddled limbs cycling frantically in celebration. He is not a Gordon. She blinks *I love you*, then straightens back up. "You know, I did actually look at which names mean *father* and the one I liked was Julian, which is *sky father*."

To Cora, it implies transcending a long line of troubled earth fathers, and for a while she'd wondered if it might be a name Gordon would compromise on. If it *means* father, if it's still a tribute to him, surely that's almost as good? But home early one evening, the book of names open face-down on the sofa, he'd picked it up, scanned the splayed pages for a moment. *Just the girls' names, remember, Cora. We have Gordon for a boy.* And when he'd snapped the book shut and placed it back on the shelf, the idea of a conversation was somehow put away too.

"I like Julian," Maia says.

"Me too. What would *you* call him though?" Cora asks. "If you could choose anything?"

"Well," she says, and Cora can tell by the way she stretches out the word that she's already thought about it. "It's not a very normal sort of name, but I like Bear."

"Bear?" Cora asks, smiling.

"Yes. It sounds all soft and cuddly and kind," Maia says, opening and closing her fingers as though she's scrunching sweetness in her hands. "But also, brave and strong."

Cora looks at the baby and imagines him being all those things. She wants that for him.

Closer to town, the clear-up has already begun. Two men with chainsaws cut fallen lime trees into transportable chunks, leaving only shorn stumps in the pavement's tree pits.

Maia gives a shy wave to a small blonde girl whose hello is lost to the noise of machinery. And once they've passed, she tells Cora, "That's Jasmine. From ballet."

"Oh, yes, the one with the older sister at—"

"Sadler Swells. But I have a question," Maia says, finding her way back to their conversation before Cora has a chance to correct her. She takes a breath, as though she's about to ask something forbidden, and then says, "Why does it matter? To Dad, I mean. The same-name thing."

Cora wants to say it matters because sometimes big men feel small inside. Because some people—like Gordon's father—travel through life believing themselves so far beyond improvement, they come to think their children, and their children's children, should all be made in their name. Because sometimes their need to please previous generations is greater than their need to love future ones. To Cora, it feels like a chest-beating, tribal thing. But she doesn't say any of this to Maia. She already picks up on enough. The morning after a disagreement, no matter how silently Cora has endured it, Maia will seek her out at the kitchen sink, wrap her narrow arms around her waist, and say, "My lovely mummy," her cheek resting against Cora's back. At those times, Cora feels the commiseration, the shared sadness. And once, the dampness on the fabric at the back of her dress where Maia's face had been moments earlier.

"Tradition is just important to some people," she says instead.

"Having your own name is too, though. Sometimes? Maybe even Dad would've liked having his own one."

Cora takes a hand off the pram to wrap her arm around Maia's shoulder. "Wise girl."

She wonders again if she is doing this right. Any of it, all of it. If it's even the right thing for Gordon himself to be carrying on this tradition. Maybe consenting to live in the shadow of his father and his father's father is only perpetuating the likeness, increasing the weight of it for him. Perhaps calling their child something different would be a liberation. Not at first, but later.

And Maia. Isn't she just teaching her daughter that keeping the peace is more important than doing what's right? Cora wonders what Maia thinks of her for agreeing to give her brother this name that will tie him to generations of domineering men. And it dawns on her that while Maia's name was originally intended as a silent bond between them, in revealing its meaning, that, too, may be a burden. Perhaps she has unwittingly sent a message that their lives are destined to follow the same path, when her real hope is for her children to tread their own.

1987

Bear

Cora watches as the letters form, each one emerging like some magical and extraordinary thing from the nib of the registrar's pen as it moves across the page. Bear Atkin. Bear. Just four letters, B-E-A-R, but each one feels charged, no longer just consonants and vowels. A great surge of—what is this thing?—joy, yes, that's it, joy—courses through Cora's being. A whole-body dizzying happiness. She glances at Maia, who stands beside her chair, and sees the surprise on her face.

As the registrar hands Cora the certificate, she tells her she's been doing this job for twenty-two years and has never had a Bear before. She cranes over the desk and looks into his pram. "But it's just perfect for you, isn't it?" And then to Maia, "You look like a very proud big sister. Take good care of this little Bear of yours, won't you?"

Outside the office, Maia is giddy. "I can't believe you chose my name—I just—I just never thought you'd call him *my* name!" Cora kisses her forehead and puts the envelope into her bag, as Maia wheels Bear onto the street.

At first, Cora feels as though she is floating above the paving and, catching sight of her reflection in a shop window, she's surprised to find she's a solid, grounded thing. Maia is a few steps ahead, but Cora hears her stream of chatter, observes her lovely back as she bends over the handle to bring her face closer to her brother's, and is elated. She knows this will be a defining moment in Maia's life, a moment when she was given a voice and wasn't asked to fit into the shadow of her parents' marriage. But then, before they've even reached the top of the hill, comes the knotty realization of what she's done. If Gordon were to discover the name was Maia's choice . . . She blinks and tries to push the thought away. He's never hurt Maia. But perhaps that's because Maia has been good and small and shown herself only in the places where Cora has sensed it won't put her in harm's way, always calling her back, sending her off for a bath, or to fetch some unneeded thing if she's felt her stepping too close to the fire.

Beneath Cora's autumn layers, her top begins to dampen. Her sanitary pad becomes a heavy wodge between her legs, while a cold sweat mottles her forehead and prickles at the back of her neck. It's as if every fluid part of her is attempting to escape her body. To make a run for it.

What has she done? How could she have been so stupid? And *Bear.* Without it being the choice of a nine-year-old—because he can never know that it was—how can she possibly explain this name? A name that will seem like she's chosen it to humiliate, to say that his family tradition, his father's approval, means so little, she didn't even confine her betrayal to something ordinary. Something like Julian, perhaps.

She thinks of repeating Maia's words, of telling him that a boy called Bear is someone who will be soft and cuddly but also brave and strong. But she knows he will find little value in these qualities. That they will only make him more furious. And *how* will she tell him? What possible time or place will soften this news? Catching him in the right mood, cooking his favorite dinner, none of these things will help. And the goodwill he's shown toward her recently, through her pregnancy and the early weeks with the baby, when he's treated her with the professional consideration he extends to all new mothers in his practice . . . that won't withstand this. What was she thinking? She will have to change it. She'll have to go back to the registrar and apologize. It can't be too late; the ink is barely dry. She'll understand that it's the turbulence of the storm; of being awake all night after weeks of broken sleep. It's not a normal time. But as Maia reaches the zebra crossing, she turns, her face open in a way Cora has rarely seen, the tension that usually shapes her features momentarily lifted. "Mama—" And that name, she hasn't called her that for years, long since replaced by *Mum*. "Thank you, Mama. This is just one of the most special things that's ever happened to me."

Cora checks her watch as they walk along the edge of the common. There are five hours until Gordon comes in from work, which seems both an eternity and not nearly long enough. She must make some kind of plan. Cora has only just remembered Maia is meant to have swimming tonight and wonders if the sports center will be open. Mehri has taken her since the baby was born. Can she ask again, just one more week, if she'll be going anyway? Perhaps she could take Maia home for tea afterward too—their girls don't know one another that well, but they live nearby, are the same age; it can't be that much of an imposition, can it? If she can keep Maia out of the house until seven, that would give her half an hour between Gordon getting home from the practice and Maia arriving back.

When they get in, Cora parks the sleeping baby in the hallway, fixes Maia a snack, then makes the phone call. The pool is closed. But Mehri offers—Cora doesn't even have to ask—to have Maia over for tea with Fern instead. And for a moment this gives her some confidence, as though this small piece of the jigsaw fitting so neatly into place is a sign that things might be okay. She goes into the bathroom and piles her damp clothes into the laundry basket, changes her underwear, and pulls a clean top from the drawer as she thinks through what to do with Bear. And despite her anxiety, she realizes she has thought of him as *Bear* effortlessly, as though this has always been his name. As though he's just been waiting to slip into it, and now only needs her to make it real—to break the news to Gordon—and this drives her on.

She wonders how she might keep Bear safe. Considers stringing out his milk, so that by six she can feed him into that state of slack-armed slumber where she can safely lower him into the Moses basket without him waking. But then what? She goes to the closet, starts to move shoeboxes from the floor, stacking them out of sight beside the chest of drawers. When the space is big enough, she swipes away dust with the side of her hand, then fetches the little bed and positions it in the cupboard to check it fits. She sees the madness in what she's doing. He wouldn't hurt their baby, would he? But because of Cora's moment of impetuousness, Bear's existence is now a personal affront to Gordon and his family. She can almost hear his voice. *My son? Bear? Have you lost your mind?* No, she thinks, as she moves things into place around the basket, she must keep him safe.

She runs a finger down the narrow gap between the closed doors but can't judge how much air it might let in, so she opens them again, steps into the Moses basket, and shuts herself inside the closet. There is a line of vertical light, and when she puts her eye to it, she sees a slice of bedroom. She stands, sinking into the darkness, observing this sliver of her own life from a new angle. The bed she shares with Gordon, its floral duvet cover a wedding gift chosen by his parents. Twin nightstands. Just a clock on her side. A lamp, a notepad, a stack of books on his. She realizes there is nothing of her own self impressed on this space, no trace of her physical presence. Really, there is only the *feeling* of her hanging over the stillness of the room.

She hears the muffled sound of Bear beginning to stir in his pram, but before she's opened the closet doors, she hears Maia go to him, her voice soothing, cajoling him from crying out. Cora imagines her unzipping his snowsuit and carefully lifting his warm body out, and when she can no longer hear them, she decides Maia must have taken him through to the living room. Cora stays a while longer in the cupboard, feeling as though she has temporarily stepped out of her own life and pressed pause.

At six-thirty, Cora hears Gordon's key in the lock. She thinks she may be sick. She moves through to the hallway, where he greets her, kisses her cheek, and hands her his suit jacket. She brushes her fingers across the warm grain of the fabric before hanging it up, wanting to slow everything down, to feel these tangible things, to savor the moments when she can choose where to focus her mind.

She follows him through to the kitchen and, unable to continue holding the tension she's been carrying all day, hears herself blurting out, "Gordon, I've done something."

He turns then, leans back against the countertop, not taking his eyes from her, and she knows he won't ask, will not help to draw it from her. He loosens his tie, not dropping his gaze. And when she speaks, she hears herself as he will: pathetic, weak.

"I went to register the birth like you asked, and I—I hope you won't mind, but I've called him something else. Not Gordon. You know I've never really wanted to call him that and I—I—"

She stops because he hasn't blinked; his eyes haven't left her face. And this part, it's like someone with a fear of heights, someone at the top of a ladder, so sure they're about to fall, they have the impulse to jump and get it over with. It takes all her strength not to sink to his feet and let him kick her, to not even try to escape its inevitability, but to submit, because this anticipation only delays what she knows is coming. But then she thinks of Bear up in the bedroom closet, and Maia eating dinner in Mehri's kitchen, and straightens: "I've called him Bear."

He smiles and she sees his demeanor shift, sees him shake his head, reach for a drink. She realizes he doesn't believe her. "No," she says, "no, it's the truth." And she takes out the envelope from where it's hidden between two cookbooks. He turns then, one hand still on the water filter as he surveys the certificate. He spends longer than he needs to, staring, and her hand begins to shake as she continues to hold out the paper for him, its audible wackering filling the seconds as they tick by. He looks up and, holding her gaze, lets the jug drop, hard, so that it smashes against the kitchen tiles. She feels water soak into her socks and knows she should have thought to put on shoes.

He reaches out, grabs a clump of hair near the crown of her head and pulls it backward, his face just inches above hers. For a moment she's confused, thinks he may be about to kiss her, but instead he hurls her head against the side of the refrigerator.

Even though she'd promised herself she wouldn't, she cries out in shock, then quickly closes her mouth, not wanting to risk waking Bear. She must not drag his presence into Gordon's thoughts.

"You're my wife," he hisses. "I asked you to do one thing for me"—her head slams against the fridge once more—"and you couldn't do it. Just one"—*thud*—"damn"—*thud*—"thing."

Some part of her realizes he's only just beginning; that there are only so many times she will feel the flux of brain, skull, and flesh against metal before she does not. And so she overrides her wish not to disturb Bear, and does something she's never done before: she screams for help. Not just once, but over and over, knowing the small window in the pantry is open, that the door is ajar, that it will be impossible for someone in the cul-de-sac not to hear. When he covers her mouth, she clamps her teeth down hard on the side of his hand, sinking into flesh and wiry hairs. He recoils, surprised. But it's only a moment's relief, because now there are a few feet between them and she realizes he will use this as a run-up, that he's about to charge.

She springs sideways and feels the midwife's careful stitches pop. But there is no pain, just a rush of adrenaline, as he chases her through to the living room. He grasps her hair again, but she jerks away and is freed, a prickle of white heat at her scalp.

He lunges, pulls her to the ground, and although she hasn't heard the shatter of glass or the front door open, someone—who?—is in the room with them. It is the man from two doors down, who only moved in a few months ago; the man she sometimes sees walking his dog back from the park on the afternoons when she's set out to meet Maia at the halfway point from school, the man who has smiled at her pregnant belly and who one day said something about it being *nice weather for ducks*, as they sloshed past one another. This man, he is pulling Gordon from her, and for a moment it feels as though this is an end, of sorts, that whatever happens next will be a de-escalation. But then Gordon is shouting, "What the hell are you doing in my house?" as the man's dog yaps at his ankles, its trailing lead caught up around the legs of the coffee table. The man puts up his hands, as if to say, *I don't want any trouble, I don't want to fight*, as Gordon places flat palms firmly against his chest and then pushes with such force, Cora can only watch as the man falls backward, smashing through the glazing of the patio doors.

LATER, AND NOT necessarily in this order, a police officer—young, maybe not even twenty-two—will dial the digits of Mehri's number that he finds written out by the phone and arrange for Maia to stay overnight. Then, he will go upstairs and retrieve Bear from the closet, and Cora will wonder how he knows to jig the baby just so and to pat his back until his cries ebb into occasional shuddering sighs. But she won't think to ask, because the words have disappeared from her head; the path between thought and voice temporarily broken. She will keep a hand over her right ear, trying to silence the ringing inside her head, not comprehending why it's there or that it has anything to do with the scene in the kitchen just forty-five minutes earlier. She will notice when the flashing blue lights slide from the living-room walls as the ambulance outside pulls away. She will watch as an older police officer cuffs Gordon's hands behind his back and, although she cannot hear the man's words, she will understand he is a patient, that there is something in his manner that tells her he is uncomfortable to be cast in this role, leading away the man who perhaps officiated his own mother's death; diagnosed his wife's depression; said, *Don't worry, I've seen it all before*, as he felt the man's enlarged prostate. Because Gordon is a man well-liked by his patients. He is a good doctor, no matter what his surgeon father thinks of general practice. Cora will nod and point to the back of the chair as the young police officer gathers up her things, slipping his hand into the front of her bag to check her keys are there. He will leave the room momentarily to lead through a second set of paramedics when he hears them in the hall. And they will smile and treat her with such tender kindness that she feels it's this—of all things—that may break her. She watches the medic's lips, can't decipher the words, but senses their warmth, notices how she keeps her eyes on Cora's own, not returning the anxious glances of her more junior colleague. All these people, so many of them young, dragged into the horror of their evening, into the messiness of their lives, which have been unfolding year by year, month by month, week by week, day by day, hour by hour, to bring them to this moment.

Julian

Afterward, Cora is unsure what made her say it, only that she did and it felt right. Now, as this baby lies in his pram—Julian, *sky father*, ethereal, transcendent—Cora has a feeling of being more rooted than she has for years. As though, feet planted, she holds the two kite strings of her children's lives safe in her palm.

As she walks, there's a new certainty in her step, an awareness of the extension and contraction of her muscles. As though something inside has woken. She turns to cut through the common unthinkingly, only noticing when Maia pauses. *But Dad said . . .* A trainered foot hovering above the ground, as though her mother is asking her to step into another world.

"We'll be okay," Cora says. "We'll stick to the main path. There are hardly any big trees right next to it and there'll be so much to look at." Surprise registers on Maia's face, but her foot falls, and then she is off, quietly exploring the new landscape.

Cora has never wanted Maia's freedom of movement to become constrained, yet she recalls how years earlier, as a ballet dancer, her own body had been alive, alert, attuned to music, intuiting any flicker of emotion—a nerve, a hesitation—just through the quality of her partner's grip. And now, she experiences that same heightened sensibility, aware of the kinetic energy in the things around her. She notices the bump and spin of the pram wheels as they pass over the windswept ground of the common. The scent of damp air penetrating the sandstone boulders. How her pupils react as the October light makes brilliant the white of the cricket pavilion. The way her ears receive the muffle of Maia's footsteps and the flattening of twigs as she pads along the dirt path ahead. *Feel the floor,* every teacher since she was five years old had called out, vowels melding into the piano music that ricocheted around the walls of a church hall, a community center, a studio. And now, all these years later, she feels the floor again. She feels all of it. She recognizes its grip, its support, and knows the floor—this earth—has her. That it rises imperceptibly to meet her, and will catch her if she falls, because she has done the right thing.

Cora is used to sudden explosions that come at a light being left on, or realizing too late she's been overly friendly in the way she's spoken to a tradesman. She lives trying not to set a match to Gordon's anger, but still she spills petrol about her, dripping it over shoes she has forgotten to polish, sloshing it across a particular shirt not washed in time. She races from thing to thing, tending to whatever might spark, but it's always something behind her, just out of sight that she hadn't thought of. But today is different. She gets to choose how it's revealed, what the conditions are, the way it's presented. And she feels fearless. Yes, he might—*will*—be furious, but the consequences won't be pointless this time. She will have got what she wants: for her son to grow up with his own name.

When Maia drops back and falls into step with her, she is humming, a low, frantic sound, full of erratic key changes. Cora takes a hand from the pram and squeezes Maia's mittened palm. "You don't need to worry. He might be cross for a little while, but he'll get over it."

"But you said it was because of what *I* said before we went in. It'll all be my fault."

"No, I said you were my inspiration. There's a difference. Van Gogh might inspire me to paint a picture, but that doesn't mean it's his fault when my sunflowers look like a jar of yellow Chupa Chups, does it? You reminded me how important it is for everyone to have their own name, but it was completely my decision to call him something different."

"Sunflowers would never look like Chupa Chups."

"Well, you don't know that; you haven't seen mine. But listen, Julian was a name I'd picked out long before today, so the idea must have already been floating around in my head. And look at him," she says, nodding toward the pram, "doesn't he look like a Julian to you? There's nothing else he could have been. Can you imagine him as a Gordon? Really?" Maia laughs, a quiet, nervous laugh. She glances sideways, as if to check it's really her mother. "You don't even need to be there when I tell him, but let's think about how to make tonight special."

"What will you cook? Maybe lasagne?" Maia asks, and Cora knows, again, that she has done the right thing, because no child should ever be so used to fitting around a parent that they will suggest the food they like least themselves.

When Maia was younger, Cora had cut open a piece of penne one lunchtime when it was just the two of them. "Look, like a pirate's scroll," she'd said, "completely flat once it's rolled out. That's all a lasagne sheet is."

But Maia had pursed her lips. "Flat pasta tastes different. More chewy and fat."

Cora had picked a tube of penne from Maia's plate. "Maybe you're right," she'd said, biting into it, "they're probably not quite the same."

But still, the next time they'd had lasagne, as she'd set the dish onto the table and Gordon had proclaimed it his favorite, Cora and Maia had caught one another's eye momentarily—unintentionally—and Maia had looked away and said, "Yes, nice sauce," and her goodness had scrunched at Cora's heart.

Maia always seemed attuned to the undercurrents in a room. Cora saw it in the stiff set of her small frame, as though someone had placed narrow rods beneath the shoulder seams of her T-shirt. She saw it in the way her eyes moved between them, tracking their interactions, while being careful to avoid anything that could hint at an alliance. She saw it in the way Maia rushed for kitchen roll to mop up a spill Cora might be blamed for. In the way she watched television with a plate held beneath a breadstick to catch its crumbs.

One day, Cora had taken something into school for Maia— something forgotten, a packed lunch or gym bag—and the receptionist had said, "You might be best taking it down to make sure she gets it in time, if you don't mind." Cora had walked along empty lesson-time corridors and when she'd reached the right classroom, she'd looked in through the glass panel, about to open the door, and then stopped. Because there was a girl. Pausing in her work to say something to the friend sitting beside her, which made them both laugh. And for a moment, Cora had not recognized her daughter. But even when she had, still the two Maias did not perfectly align. This Maia's laughter reached all the way to her eyes, her smile fractionally wider and easier than the one she knew.

Maia had looked up then, as though aware of being watched, and she'd smiled and given a thumbs-up as Cora held the forgotten item up to the glass. But the Maia she'd witnessed had already vanished. And on the way home, Cora had felt a scooped-out hollow at her core with the realization that, however much she might have imagined she could exist in isolation, just *Mum*—warm, supportive, encouraging—in her daughter's mind, she and Gordon were packaged together, two inseparable halves. It didn't matter what their different roles might be, Cora was an equal impediment—something to be protected and worried over. Just as Gordon was a presence to be minded and feared.

AT HOME, MAIA cuts stars and moons from colored paper and strings them together with yellow ribbon. "These can go around our plates," she tells Cora, who's chopping vegetables in the kitchen, while Julian sleeps in his pram in the hallway. Cora smiles and feels almost optimistic. She hopes she's not misguided and that she'll find a way to lead Gordon to see it this way too.

Cora wonders aloud if swimming will still be on after the storm. "I hope not," Maia says, screwing up her face.

Cora pictures Maia in the changing room pulling clothes back onto her still-wet body and then emerging, damp-haired, into the cold night air. "You're probably right, I can't imagine the pool will be open today."

In the late afternoon, Cora puts Julian in his bouncy chair and sets it in the center of the kitchen table where she can talk to him as she layers sheets of pasta and béchamel sauce into the lasagne dish. Every now and then, she looks at him and thinks, *Julian*, and then, *sky father.* And they feel like strong, talismanic words.

"Do you like your new name, Jules?" Maia asks.

"*Jules*," Cora says, testing how the word feels in her mouth for the first time. "I hadn't thought of how it would sound shortened. It's nice. Although careful not to say his name until I've told Dad, okay?"

At six-thirty, she hears Gordon's key in the lock, pictures him hanging up his suit jacket in the hall. *Feel the floor,* she tells herself, heels gravitating to first position. She can hear the approval in his voice when he calls out, "Lasagne! I could smell it the moment I opened the door." As he passes the dining table on his way through to the kitchen, he says, "And decorations too. Well done, Maia." But then, "Come on, Cora, it's not safe to put the bouncer up here." He lifts it down smoothly, so he doesn't wake the baby. "It's not as if I haven't told you enough horror stories from the practice. Try to think."

Cora apologizes, then asks Maia to lay the table.

Maia comes through from the living room and gathers knives and forks from the drawer. Out of the corner of her eye, Cora can see she's been flustered by Gordon's change in tone. But before she can take over, the cutlery is clattering to the floor and Julian startles, clutching at the air around him with shaky hands, frowning in his sleep. For a moment Cora freezes. *Don't cry, please don't cry. Julian, sky father, grounded,* she thinks. And miraculously, the frown disappears and, moments later, his face has resettled, and he is asleep again.

"Butterfingers," Gordon says to Maia, and Cora turns toward the cookbooks for a moment to breathe silent thanks, where the spines of Prue Leith and Mary Berry seem to almost vibrate with the pressure of the birth certificate pressed between them. *Please make this okay, Mary,* Cora pleads inwardly. She imagines lemon pie with billowy meringue frosting, its peaks toasted evenly, believing if she can make the image perfect enough, everything will be fine. She wonders at this trust she's placing in random things—the scent of damp sandstone, a vision of a well-turned-out pudding—but what else does she have?

Cora places a hand on each of Maia's shoulders, hoping to channel comfort into her small, anxious body, which feels rigid beneath her palms. Perhaps she should have rung Mehri, asked if swimming was on. "Don't worry about the table. I can do it," she tells her.

Over dinner, they talk about the practice, about a new scheme Gordon is piloting to recruit patients with depression to work as outreach volunteers, delivering prescriptions to those who are housebound. But then the question comes. "Did you register the birth?"

"Mm," Cora says. She is mid-mouthful and holds up a hand to show she has more to say. She finishes chewing, and swallows. "I was

going to mention that. I wanted to do something special. It's a celebration. Of you, really. But, well, I'd been looking into names, and
realized that Julian—" And she stops for a moment because Gordon
has put down his knife and fork. "Well, I realized that Julian, it
means *father*. And I know Gordon is your family name, but I liked
the idea of something more personal, that honors you. Just you. And
so, well, I hope you don't mind, but that's the name I registered."

The room is quiet.

"You—You've called him Julian? Not Gordon?" Gordon asks, and
she can see he is struggling to take in what she's said. She wants to
fill the space with words but can't think of any, and so she nods. And
then nods again, as though he has asked the question twice. "What
the—"

But then Maia is talking over him, brightly, with confidence, as
though she does this all the time, as though she's used to interrupting her father. "That's what the moon and stars around your plate
are for," she is saying. "Julian means *sky father*. I traced around your
paperweight for the moons and did the stars the way you showed me:
two triangles. I rubbed them out afterward, but you can still see the
lines a bit, on the back. Turn them over," she says. And she gets up
from her place and goes to stand by his side, lifting the chain of
shapes. "Look," she says, tracing the faint pencil lines with her finger. "Do you like it? The name? What it means?"

"Julian," he says.

"*Father*," Maia translates again.

And Cora realizes her daughter has learned what to do. How to
soothe, to placate. That just through watching, the first time she's
stepped into this role, she is already accomplished. If it doesn't stop,

Cora thinks, this pattern will repeat unendingly, the destiny of each generation set on the same course.

And despite how impossible it feels—the unscalable obstacles of where they'll go, how she'll get money, who'll even believe her, how she'll stop him taking the children from her—a switch is tripped. Cora knows she must make a plan.

"Do you like it?" Maia is asking again.

Gordon smiles and says, "So, tell me, Big Sister, was this your clever idea? Or your mother's?"

"Mainly Mum's," Maia says, sitting down at the table again, "but I like it too."

There is only the scrape of cutlery on plates. Julian's wispy breath as he sleeps in the bouncer at their feet. And then the penny-drop of Maia's jerky hum as her father's silence lasts too long. Cora is crushed for her. She has the sensation of her throat closing as she goes to swallow, and it is like drowning, and so she mimes eating, balancing tiny morsels on the fork tines, as Gordon—slowly, neatly, with his usual meticulousness—chews each mouthful, until his plate is clear, still saying nothing. The room is an overtightened violin string. It is just a question of when it will snap.

"Go and run yourself a bath," Gordon says to Maia eventually. Cora sees her blink, unable to look at them, sees her touch the ends of her knife and fork together on her plate, push in her chair, and walk from the room. Cora wants to hug her small rod-bar shoulders.

Gordon stands, and although Cora does not turn to look, she can sense him behind her chair. Feels the flat of his palm pressed lightly against the back of her head. Waiting. It is only when they hear the pipes groan overhead, when the bathwater begins to run, that he pushes her face down into the uneaten lasagne, the plate hard against her nose, sauce covering her lashes, stray hairs sticking to her cheeks.

His words come quiet, but clear. "A name that goes back generations and you really thought I wouldn't mind?" He laughs, a dinner-party laugh, a laugh for friends. Then he pulls her face from the plate using her hair as a lever. She stills her hands, which instinctively move to wipe away the food, and instead rests them in her lap. Holds her head high. Blinks. "I won't be letting this go," he says. "Understood?"

She nods, a slight inclination of the head, as she tells herself this will be the last time. That she will never again sit with a dinner she has made dripping down her face. That she will never again watch her daughter try to mollify this man. That she will not change their son's name. Everything—*everything*—has already changed. She sits, spine straight, neck long, feet planted firmly on the carpet. She feels the floor, and still, even now, it has her.

"Now eat your dinner," Gordon says, and releases her hair with a jerk.

She waits as he strides from the room and climbs the stairs. And when she hears nothing but the noises of the house, the click of the boiler, the quiet hiss of the radiator, she reaches for a napkin and wipes the sauce from her skin in swift, decisive movements. She looks down and sees Julian's eyes—wide, blue, clear—fixed on her. As though he has witnessed it all and, inexplicably, is not scared. But, instead, believes in her. Julian, *sky father*, she thinks, knowing he will transcend the one upstairs.

Gordon

Coming back from the registrar's office, it's as though a cloud has descended. Cora looks down at the baby and feels she has broken something. Less than an hour ago, walking in the opposite direction, his small form seemed filled with hope and possibility. But now, that's tainted. Where earlier she'd seen only the peach blush of his cheeks and the delicacy of blue-veined lids, now she sees a chin dribbled red and lips pinched in popeish judgment. She could have refused to follow Gordon's instructions, told the registrar some other name. Julian. Bear, even. But she didn't. And although her real resentment is with herself—with her husband—somehow, it seems easier to let it fall to this newborn lying in his pram.

Maia has run ahead to walk along the church wall, raising into relevé, extending her left leg, arms out for balance, the bulk of her autumn layers shrouding any grace in her movements. Cora is relieved she does not have to talk. She's cold and tired when they arrive home. She leaves the baby asleep in the hallway and crawls into bed with her coat still on. She doesn't know how much time has passed when she's stirred by Maia calling up the stairs that he's awake, but she sits on the edge of the bed for a minute longer, listening to him cry and trying to muster the energy to stand, only forcing herself to move when Maia calls again.

Downstairs, having wrested him from his snowsuit, Cora sinks onto the sofa, lifts her jumper and . . . stops. Repulsed. As though nothing could be more alien. The baby bangs his head against her chest in frustration until he finds his own way to nourishment, and she turns away and stares at the wall as he feeds.

A FEW DAYS later, as Cora and Gordon brush their teeth before bed, she bends to spit out the paste and then says, "I wondered if I could have money to buy formula?"

When he doesn't reply, she looks up and their eyes meet in the mirror. He continues to move his brush in careful circles, one tooth at a time. She has never known anyone to brush with such diligence, gums preserved in pristine arches. She looks away, not wanting to appear captive to this pause in time, and opens her side of the bathroom cabinet, pretending she has not cleansed her face already. She squeezes a blob of soft-pink lotion onto a cotton pad.

He rinses and spits, rinses and spits, and only then says, "Why?" A word—a question—that seems to steal the air from the room.

"Oh, I don't know. I'm just not getting on with it so well this time," she says, trying to sound casual.

"Not getting on with it?" He repeats her words as though they're incomprehensible.

Perhaps if she'd said, *With Maia it felt natural, but this time it feels different. Do you ever hear this from your patients?* Then, he might have listened in that careful, doctorly way of his, discussed it with her, then come to the idea of formula himself. But she didn't.

"So you want to just give up?" He is staring at her in the mirror. "Do you know nothing about how important this time is? The nutrients and antibodies? It isn't just this week or this month. It's the rest of his life—it's protection from cardiovascular disease, diabetes, everything. But, instead, you want to give our son some man-made rubbish from a tin? Exactly what else is it I ask of you, other than to be a mother to our children? But that's too much?" he says. He takes the cotton-wool pad from her hand and crams it into her half-open mouth. "Well, it's not happening, Cora. You can damn well get on with it."

He walks from the room, and she stands for a moment, dumb.

Cora removes the pad, hooks a finger inside her cheek, trying not to gag as she sweeps the web of loose fibers from her tongue, the roof of her mouth. Then she bends and places the sodden wad into the bin, careful not to let the metal lid clang against the wall.

When they'd met over a decade ago, what had struck Cora first was his kindness. In a café on the Strand, putting her wallet back into the zippered pocket of her bag, she'd dropped her sandwich packet and, forgetting the surgical boot she wore, nearly overbalanced as she'd gone to pick it up. "Here, let me get that for you," he'd said, gathering up her lunch and moving to open the door for her as he brushed off her apologies. "What's the injury?" he'd asked, motioning to the white boot once they were outside.

"Oh, I've just had a small bone removed from my foot. It's less dramatic than it looks."

"Which one?"

"Sesamoid?" she replied, more of a question than a statement, because so few people seemed to have heard of it.

"Tibial or fibular?"

"Both. You're a surgeon?"

"GP. Both is unusual," he replied, appraising her, before reaching his conclusion: "You're a dancer."

"Maybe, maybe not. It depends on my recovery."

"Listen, I was going to Embankment Gardens to enjoy the sunshine. Will you join me?"

And because it felt like the first day of spring, and because he was a doctor who seemed kind and trustworthy, and because he was still holding her lunch and she had nothing else to do, she agreed.

In the park, they sat on his jacket, laid out on just-damp grass. "You haven't got anything to eat," she said, realizing he'd left the café empty-handed.

"It's okay, I've come straight from a conference with good biscuits."

He handed her the sandwich, and as she ate, she found herself telling him about the excruciating wait. Of knowing the removal of these tiny bones might have destroyed her balance, her ability to land jumps; how she worried her big toe might quickly deform without the sesamoid beneath. He'd listened with a medic's ear, asking thoughtful, precise questions about her pain, her recovery. And when he'd crossed off a checklist of physical issues, he moved on to how it affected her as a person.

She'd told him how it felt like the slow, messy ending of an all-consuming love affair. One she'd left her family in Ireland for as a young teenager, and now found herself being abandoned by.

"It's all I've been focused on for so long, I'm not sure who I am without it. But I can see now, even if it's not this that ends it, some-thing will. I may have another six months, a year, before some other part of my body gives out. And it's like"—she gestured to the air with both hands—"everything."

The details of that day come back easily. Their socks peeled off, winter-white feet sunk into the grass: his decorated with a smattering of dark hair, nails perfectly trimmed; hers calloused and battered, still red in places, even after a few months away. *Working feet,* he said kindly when she apologized for the one on show. He'd leaned for-ward to brush black sock fluff from one of her toes and it had felt both surprising and right for him to touch her.

She remembers how they'd passed an apple between them, turn-ing it to take polite bites from opposite sides, until two narrow strips of shiny green skin where they met was all that was left. She'd told him about her last performance. How it had been set to Betjeman; how, as the poet's words boomed through the vast auditorium, they were as metronomic as any music. She'd beat out the first line of "A Subaltern's Love Song" on the ground to show him, three rows of tutus rising and falling with the words, and he'd surprised her by supplying the next line. She'd always divided people into Science or

Arts, but here was someone who was both. By the time they stood to leave the park at dusk, his hand at her waist as her booted foot prickled back to life, she also felt the unexpected tingle of . . . love? She'd not imagined that just five months later she would be pregnant with their child.

When had things changed? Was it that night at dinner with his parents, when he'd dug his nails into her thigh beneath the tablecloth to stop her from speaking? Probably, although she hadn't realized it at the time. Nor did she see it when, one Sunday, irritated by something she'd said, he'd thrown a half-eaten pear across the room at her—hard—its irregular shape sending it off course and bringing it to land on the sofa beside her. She'd glared at him and said, "If that was meant to hit me, you're going to have to improve your aim," and they'd laughed, and he'd apologized. She does not remember him ever apologizing again, and she does not remember them laughing about it after that either. Would things have been different if she hadn't laughed? If she'd threatened to leave?

When Cora comes out of the bathroom, Gordon is sitting in bed reading a thick hardback. He looks up from the book and smiles and she knows the argument about formula is over, but so, too, is any possibility of discussion.

"It's about a guy working in Lebanon around the same time I was there," he says. "He went on to help in the Falklands, San Salvador after the earthquake. I wonder if he's in Somalia now . . ."

In a parallel life where she and Maia hadn't come along, he, too, would have gone to help in those places—humanitarian sabbaticals in between his work as a GP. She knows she's meant to acknowledge this, but she just wants to sleep before the baby wakes again, so only nods and makes some noise intended to approximate interest. Since coming home from the registrar's office three days ago, she's found it hard to play her role. Her face feels like hardened wax, smile lines fixed in repose, impossible to reanimate.

IN THE MIDDLE of the night, she wakes to feel Gordon's foot jabbing her ankle. "For goodness' sake, Cora. I've got to work in the morning! How can you not hear him crying when I can?" Cora switches off the monitor and the baby's cries are muted to a distant wail. "And don't do that with the covers—you can get out without letting all that cold air into the bed. Show some consideration."

She opens the door to the nursery and sound bludgeons her senses, as though someone has turned the volume on a stereo to maximum without warning. She wants to turn away. Instead, she takes the baby from his cot, sits down in the rocking chair with him, his sobs gradually receding to tiny shudders. She looks out into the blue-black darkness where she'd forgotten to pull the blind over at bedtime and an image from childhood drifts into her mind. She cannot remember why she was there or who was with her, but she recalls standing just outside Mr. Barry's milking barn, looking in through a crack where the door had been left ajar. There, the vast, bony hindquarters of black-and-white Friesians were lined up, metal suction cups hanging from swollen udders, the air filled with the rhythmic thrum of milk being pumped. She remembers how the animals stood there, pliant and accepting, and wonders now why they didn't object, why they didn't kick their hooves as Mr. Barry bent for their udders. Did he hit them? Is that why they accepted it? Was it fear? Perhaps, she thinks, because here she sits in the baby's milk parlor, in bovine suppliance, breasts fed through the gaps of a sleep bra. She wants to pull her flesh from the baby's mouth. To stand and let him fall from her lap. To let Gordon deal with his namesake's indignant howls. She wants to stride from the room, descend the stairs, go out into the street, where she would grand jeté in giant leaps down the center of the road, feeling cold air and moonlight on her unencumbered body, a herd of cows lolloping along behind, making their own ungainly break for freedom. She is exhilarated and appalled by the violence of these images. But she is not like her husband; she would never act on these impulses. The baby pats at her collarbone as he feeds. She can feel his eyes on her, seeking her out, willing her to look down at him. She rests her head back against the chair and squeezes his hand gently between her thumb and forefinger. It's as much as she can give.

The following day, the midwife calls with a form for Cora to fill in, apparently intended to diagnose postnatal depression: *I have looked forward with enjoyment to things: a) As much as I ever did, b) Rather less than I used to, c) Definitely less than I used to, d) Hardly at all.* How can this piece of paper hope to crack open the complexity of her life? Of anyone's life? She doesn't even attempt any nuance in her responses and ticks the full-joy option every time.

"Goodness, we are feeling perky, aren't we?" the midwife says as she looks over Cora's answers.

Earlier that morning, Gordon had appeared behind Cora, moving her unwashed hair aside to nuzzle her. "You know, if you're having problems, there's no need to involve any madwives. You can come straight to me, and I can have someone at work prescribe for you."

And she'd closed her eyes as he kissed down the side of her neck, not because she was enjoying it, but because she was tired and with her eyes shut, she could switch off and leave her body almost entirely.

"Now get into that shower and make yourself presentable. It's just a practice meeting this morning, so I can mind Gordon for a few minutes," he'd said, patting her bottom lightly.

And so here she sits: washed, blow-dried, clean-clothed. *Not that one, Cora, there's vomit on the shoulder.*

The midwife plunges a biscuit into her tea, tongue hoovering crumbs from her lips as she speaks. "To be honest, I should probably check your stitches before I sign you off, but we're two down right now and I don't know if I'm going to get to all my babies today as it is. Are you okay to just mention it to your husband if you have any problems, what with him being a doctor? Or should I come back later in the week?"

The midwife finishes her digestive and, even though she says not to get up, Cora walks her into the hallway and closes the door on her brief chapter of at-home care. She watches herself as she does this. She's spent a lot of time like this recently—viewing herself from above as she moves around the house, changing nappies, ironing Gordon's shirts, cooking for his parents. Almost as though it's some-one else doing these things. Only with Maia does she occasionally feel herself reinhabiting her body.

Cora sits down next to her as she watches television and Maia snuggles into her side and says, "Mm, smells like you," before turn-ing back to the screen.

It feels to Cora as though she has left something unspoken, dangling: *It smells like you . . . but is somehow not you.*

"What do I smell like?" Cora asks.

"Mum, of course."

Later, Cora wonders if she'd imagined it, but either way, it pulls her to the surface. She stares at the screen, telling herself she'll do better tomorrow. Just like she had once done with Maia, she will blow raspberries onto the baby's skin, she will read aloud to him from one of her husband's books, lulling him to sleep with the sound of her voice, his cheek turning hot and pink against her skin as the afternoon hours pass. And later, when she puts away the washing, she will carry him from room to room in his Moses basket, talking to him as she folds clothes into drawers. Together, they will meet Maia after school and buy gingerbread men and they will sit on the shelf in the sandstone near Pig Rock, and the bubble around her, which has contained only herself these past few weeks, will expand to gather her two children in beside her. Then everywhere they go, they will move as one. The bubble stretching as Maia runs ahead, reshaping as Cora pauses to step away from the baby's pram for a moment, but always contracting back to hold the three of them close in its safety.

But when morning comes, she finds she does not have the energy for these things, that she cannot pull back the dullness that blankets her. It is the same the next day. And the next. She feeds the baby staring out through the patio doors, looking toward the fir trees at the end of the garden, which somehow give the illusion it's raining even when the sky is bright. Then, she carries him upstairs and places him gently into his cot, and when she hears him wake after only twenty minutes, she moves quickly through to the kitchen and turns on the radio, pretending she has not heard, because he was meant to sleep for longer. Waking so soon was not part of the plan. She loads the washing machine, turns on the dishwasher, the hum of appliances helping to drown out the baby's cries. It is a surprise when, some time later, kneeling on the kitchen floor, clearing out the bag of plastic bags so it will fit more easily on the inside of the pantry door, she sees Gordon's hand out of the corner of her eye, feels his fingers gripping her upper arm. She lets out a little scream, shocked to find him—anybody—in the house with her.

"For goodness' sake, Cora," he says, releasing her to snap off the radio. "Thank God I came home. Can you not hear him up there? What are you even doing?" he asks, taking in the bags scattered across the kitchen floor.

She looks up at him, one hand suspended mid-fold, and motions dumbly with the other, her words lost. Because, really, even she doesn't know what she's doing.

"You don't deserve children if this is how you look after them," he says. "This is neglect, Cora. It's actual neglect."

He turns and leaves the room, and she stands, letting plastic bags fall down around her. She runs up the stairs behind him. "I'm sorry." She's already crying, half hysterical. "Gordon, I'm sorry." He ignores her, takes the last few steps two at a time. He is lifting Gordon from his cot when she enters the room and she sees that their son is red-faced, tear-streaked. That curdy vomit covers his babygro and the cot sheets.

"Please," she says, reaching for him. "Please, give him to me," her hands out, needing to make it right. But Gordon turns from her and when she tries to stretch around him, he elbows her away and holds the baby higher on his shoulder.

"You're an unfit mother," he says over the baby's cries.

"I didn't mean to, please, just give him to me, please," she says, and for the first time since he was named, she feels a pull toward her baby. A primitive need to give comfort, to feel his cries subside in her arms. She moves for him again, and Gordon lifts the baby, holds him high in the air to keep him out of her reach. "No, don't do that," she says, hearing the intensity of the child's wail step up. "I'll be good, I'll be good." She doesn't know where these words come from, only that they are intended to make it stop. An offer of her immediate and total submission.

The baby's feet are dangling near Gordon's forehead, its frantic screams filling the air. Cora backs away, sits in the rocking chair, her hands gripping its arms to stop herself from lunging for him again. And when Gordon has waited long enough to be sure she will stay there, he lowers the baby to his shoulder, his eyes fixed on Cora's. He pats the infant's heaving back, as it smacks its face impotently across its father's lapels, smearing them with bubbles of drool and tears.

"If I ever come home to find him like this again, I will take both of them from you, and you will never see them again. Do you understand?"

Cora nods, desperate, still clutching the arms of the chair as tears track down her face. The room feels charged, as though a bomb has gone off, as though bits of debris are still falling around them, floating through air that rings with an echo of what's just played out here.

"Now do your job and feed our son," Gordon says. He shakes his head, watching her. And then, "I'll sort things out downstairs."

A minute later, she hears the front door open and the clang of something heavy hitting the inside of their just-emptied rubbish bin. "No, sadly not," she hears him say, his voice raised, speaking to a neighbor. "It's given up the ghost." And she knows he's thrown away her radio, a wood-encased Roberts her mother had sent over from Ireland the Christmas before last. There is a pain in her chest and images flicker through her mind: her mother shopping for it; wrapping the box in brown paper on the dining-room table, soft, liver-spotted hands smoothing the end creases into place; packing it into the car to post once the school day has finished. *You did this. This is your fault*, she tells herself.

For a few days, Cora feels a shift. A conviction to rework the threads of connection with her son. The will is there, the want is there, but something in the child has changed. Where once he'd turned toward her, now he turns away.

"I don't think he's getting any milk," she tells Gordon a few nights later as they sit in bed. He looks away from his book, touches a hand to the infant's sunken fontanelle. The next day, after morning surgery, he places six bottles and a box of formula wordlessly on the kitchen counter.

But it is not the relief Cora had hoped for. The bottles are her neglect, they are her turning up the radio to block out his cries; they are his howls as Gordon held him out of reach. She feels self-loathing in her pathetic attempts to mother him. In her desperation for him not to be heard crying in the moments before she can get to him. In how he no longer seems comforted just to be held in the crook of her arm. She cannot see a way back to good.

By the time the baby is six months old, every week Mehri still says, "Would Maia like to come for dinner with Fern after swimming? It's no trouble," and Cora accepts, grateful Mehri seems to understand the invitation can only work in one direction.

"Where's that beautiful boy of yours," she says when she drops Maia home, reaching for the baby, who seems to almost vibrate with excitement, a charged atom in Cora's arms at the prospect of being handed over for a few moments.

One day, they bump into each other outside the bakery and, after leaning into Gordon's pram to coo over him, Mehri puts a hand on Cora's arm. "I've been meaning to say," she says, locking her eyes on Cora's as though she is trying to plumb her depths for what she keeps hidden, "you can talk to me, you know, if you ever need to."

Cora thanks her, and wonders what Maia might have said and if it's time to start collecting her from swimming herself. She raises a shielding hand to her brow and squints into imagined sunlight.

When she walks away, back straight, with what she hopes looks like composure, she thinks she can feel Mehri's eyes on her, although when she presses the button to cross at the traffic lights, she glances back and sees she's already gone. Cora feels her stomach lurch, as though she's jumped from a plane with no parachute, the ground rushing toward her too fast. But before she can be overwhelmed by the sensation, the green man appears, and she crosses the road, grateful she has the pram to hold on to.

Seven Years Later

1994

Bear

Bear runs down the street, arms outstretched, bag banging against his side, brown curls pulled almost straight by the wind. His mouth is a roaring O of delight. When he reaches Maia, he lets his bag, lunchbox, and a robot made from tin foil and toilet rolls fall to the ground as he throws his arms around her waist.

"Beeeees!" he shouts. "You're back," as she laughs and tries to stay upright. Fern says living with Bear must be like having a dog; no matter what mood Maia is in, he still thinks she's the best thing in the world.

When she'd let herself into the flat half an hour earlier, she'd put down her duffle bag of unwashed clothes and fruit caramels, bought with her last francs at the duty-free in Calais, and felt relieved to be home. Tired from being a guest in someone else's house all week. From trying to hide her waning enthusiasm for communicating with Valerié, who set Maia's nerves on edge by smoking her father's

Gauloises through lips painted red with makeup stolen from the pharmacie at the end of the road. Beforehand, she'd imagined they might be like sisters, or that Valerié might even be her first romance. She'd conjured soulful conversations sitting on the harbor wall at dusk, conducted with more French vocab, confidence, and fashionable clothes than she possessed at home. But then she'd realized French girls were just like English ones. And worse, that *she* was exactly the same person in France too. But now, with Bear, those thoughts disappear. She is just Bees, and there is something welcome and uncomplicated in that.

Maia has been Bees since Bear found his first words. As a baby, he would crawl around the house, palms slapping at the floor as she chased after him, *I'm coming for your honey, Bear! The bees are after you! Bzzz!* And he would squeal with delight, until speed outpaced coordination, and he'd collapse over his own arms, face planted against the floor, laughing, as she bent across him. *I'm going to sting you with kisses, Bear!* smothering his apple cheeks, only just stopping short of biting them. He was delicious to her.

Once, when he was three or four, in a rare and awkward visit from their father's parents, their grandmother had said to no one, "Don't you think it's time he called her by her proper name." And then loudly, as though Bear was hard of hearing, "You know she's called Maia!"

But Bear had leaned into his sister's side where they sat on the sofa and said, "We're creatures. I'm Bear, she's Bees."

Her grandmother had let out an exaggerated sigh and said, "Well, if you must call her by that ridiculous name, at least make it just one bee."

And Bear had replied, as though stating a fact: "She's a swarm."

Maia felt elated to be included in his wildness. She saw how adults responded to him. "And what's your name?" someone would ask, leaning over the counter in a shop, something in the set of their face softening when they heard. Instant fondness. Delight. He was a buttercup held beneath the chin: *Do you like butter?* Yes, always yes. There was no one it didn't work on. And Maia would bathe in the warmth of his glow.

Sometimes Fern would say, "Oh, God, you're so lucky. Mother, why didn't we have one of these!"

And Mehri would laugh and say, "The world can only have so many bears in it. Don't you think they deserved one more than we did?"

"Ugh, don't be so reasonable. Come here, Bear, I need you. Hug me like you hug Bees. I want you to crush my bones." Other times, she would pull him to her and trace the heart-shaped birthmark on his forearm. "Look at this, *a bear-heart*! A perfect, squashy little bear-heart!"

To Bear, it has always been like this. But to Maia, life is split into two halves. Before. And after. In the after, there has always been Mehri and Fern. It is funny to think they were once just people from her swimming class, but now they are family, or feel like it, at least. Fern's dad is on tour for months at a time and when he's away, it seems to Maia as though their life is a cocoon of warmth, intimacies, laughter, cooking. Mehri holds out a spoon and they taste-test whatever stew or sauce she's making. A little more cumin? More chili, more lemon, more salt; together they decide on the flavor of the food, and their life together. They talk over one another, share clothes, and even mothers and daughters seem interchangeable at times—Cora and Fern, Mehri and Maia—they move around one another effortlessly. Bear gives his love as easily as he is loved, but all of them know his heart belongs to Maia.

Fern's dad is nice. He brings things back for both girls: matching kimonos from Japan; gumnut babies with little felt hats from Australia; Milka bars in lilac wrappers from Switzerland. And always something for Bear too. But Mehri and Fern's house feels different when Roland is there, and Maia stops putting her feet up on the sofa or helping herself from the fridge.

"You don't have to be weird just because he's here," Fern tells her.

"I'm not."

"Yes, you are. Most dads aren't like yours was, you know." Maia knows that. But there's a difference between knowing and feeling.

Sometimes, in lessons, she looks out of the window and imagines what life would have been like if the *Before* had carried on, and when the teacher shouts "Maia!" to bring her attention back, she jumps and, in that instant, knows. Blood thrumming in her ears as she furiously blinks away tears that appear from nowhere. It's a *fight-or-flight reaction*, Peggy had said. But being able to name it doesn't take it away. At their next session, she'd told Peggy she didn't think it was either of those things for her, that it was more like *freeze*. And Peggy had said, "You're right—I should have said that. It can be *fight, flight, freeze* . . . also *fawn*. That's the fourth response. The one you might have had to rely on when you were living with your father."

Maia knew what she meant, but somehow it was the literal image of a baby deer—quiver-legged, dapple-spotted, vulnerable—that left her sitting with a tissue disintegrating in her hands, tiny white lint balls sticking to the wool of her school skirt. When the time was up, Peggy hugged her. "Next week, maybe you can tell me what you were thinking about just now." And then she'd reached into a desk drawer and brought out a freshly ironed handkerchief. "One for the road. Sometimes tissues aren't up to the big snotter cries, are they?"

Maia made sure the hanky was washed and smoothed flat for their next session. She kept it in the inside breast pocket of her blazer, and when she told Peggy about the fawn, she didn't let herself cry, but her hand hovered above where the hanky rested. Only when she stood to leave did she make herself say, "Oh, I nearly forgot—"

But before she could take it out, Peggy said, "My handkerchief? I should have said, you can keep it," and for the first time all week, Maia had felt her body loosen. She still carries it with her now, even though she only sees Peggy once or twice a year, just to check in.

Once the boys notice how jumpy she is, they delight in touching her on the shoulder or pulling the end of her ponytail when she's least expecting it. "Leave her alone," Fern tells them. But it's too much fun, they can't help themselves.

"Idiots," Mehri says. "They're just trying to get a reaction because they all fancy you."

Fern rolls her eyes. "That's what you say whenever a boy does *anything* annoying."

"Because it's true! Look at you both!"

"Ugh, you're blinded by love for us, Mother. We're like two ugly peas in a pod," and they press their faces together and puff out their cheeks, laughing. And then Fern says, "Anyway, Bees is into girls."

Maia's cheeks flush red, but Mehri acts like she's just been told Bees likes sultanas over raisins. "Sadly, that won't stop the boys from thinking they're God's gift."

Maia doesn't know when she first realized she was gay. Perhaps the year after her father left. She remembers their swimming teacher dividing them into As and Bs. The Bs left on the side, while the As were sent into the pool. She can still picture Fern jumping in, then reemerging. Head back, treading water. Fern had beamed up at her, a semi-circle of smooth black hair fanning out on the surface. And Maia's stomach had flipped, her chest expanding with something that felt glorious and surprising. Like a balloon being blown up. She'd had to look away. Had known, even then, that Fern loved her, but not like that.

Now, Maia and Bear recover his things from the pavement and walk up the hill toward home as he asks questions about France, and listens to half an answer, before interrupting with another. "Is the Mama Bear home?" he says when they reach their door, and Maia tells him not yet. She's left a note on the table saying she'll try to finish work by five and will collect pizza.

"Yum. I hope she gets Sprite too. What about Mehri?" he asks, and Maia reminds him that Roland is arriving back from Japan tonight, so she and Fern won't be around.

"What d'you think he'll have brought for us?" he asks. Maia says she doesn't know and that they mustn't expect anything, even though she's been wondering this herself.

In the kitchen, Maia makes milkshakes, plunging the frother up and down in the jug until all the strawberry powder is mixed in and bubbles start to form. "Harder, Bees, we want it really froffy," Bear says, standing on tiptoes to watch.

"Fro-th."

"Fro-th," Bear repeats back.

"Eeee," she says as she begins to pour.

"Eeee," he echoes, his eyes traveling up the glass with the rising line of the milk.

When he's licked away a strawberry mustache, Maia remembers the fruit caramels and lets Bear pick out one of each flavor, and he sits on her bed chewing while she unpacks. She sorts her clothes into lights and darks and empties a loose centime from her jeans pocket before putting them in the washing pile too.

"Here you go, this one's French," she tells Bear, and he holds the coin close to his nose and breathes in, before running off to his own room to fetch his money box. He jangles it upside down until a two-pence piece slips back through the slot, then puts the coins side by side and sniffs from one to the other.

"The same," he concludes. "The money smell is funny, though. When you smell it, you know exactly how it'd taste, don't you?"

Maia nods. "Dirty."

"Like pavement grime mixed with the standing-up toilets at school."

"The urinals?"

"And also," he says, breathing in again, "metally. Can we taste, just to check?"

"You want to lick a coin after saying it smells like urinals?"

"Yes!" he says, and Maia soaks up the sound of his laughter. She's missed it.

CORA REACHES INTO the dense foliage of the forsythia, checking for nesting birds before choosing a few branches to strip out near its heart. She overhears the end-of-day conversations as visitors wander back to the car park, their voices drawing close, then fading away. She's never sure—as she walks through town or crosses the common—if people might recognize her and remember. Her photo didn't appear in the press and, as Mehri says, *Tell me, azizam, how might someone pick you out when you barely left the house?* But even so, Cora likes that here people rarely notice her; talking unchecked, as though she and the stately home's other gardeners hear as little as the plants they tend. This, Cora thinks, is partly true. She can lose whole hours deadheading the rose garden or reshaping shrubs into neat domes, oblivious to even her own thoughts. But then she will look up and realize she's been mulling over something one of the children has told her, some new thing in their life. Or a memory from before.

Barren, he'd said. It had been years between Maia's birth and Bear finally coming along. Her fault. Her failure to conceive. Although had she ever allowed herself to wonder if the issue might have been with him? Her memory is hazy. Perhaps her way of enduring it back then had simply been not to think, not to feel. She snips at the outer branches and wonders now if he'd been right. If it had been of her making. If, at some deep, subconscious level, it was a form of self-protection. For herself, for an unborn child. Sometimes, even now, she hears his voice in her head, the things he might say if he could hear her thoughts. *What utter tosh. Listen to you, trying to make out it was all some bit of supreme cleverness on your part, when the fact is, you were barren.* The word has lost its sting. And with the early evening sun on her back, her hands smudged with earth, she thinks, once again, how different life is now.

She begins to gather up the cut branches, keen to get home to Maia and Bear; to Mehri and Fern. Then remembers Roland is also coming back today. Even after all this time, she still feels a slight wobble at the idea of manning her ship alone. It's not that she doesn't see Mehri during Roland's homecomings, just that Cora senses her being less available.

In the early days, after Gordon was taken away, they'd drifted from room to room, as though looking for some unnamed thing that couldn't be found. Images from the television screen passed before their eyes without meaning and the days blurred, punctuated by a stream of visitors. Police officers, social workers, a woman from a domestic-abuse charity, someone from the CPS. All spokes on some giant wheel that had been set in motion behind the scenes. She'd had no idea so many people were standing in the wings waiting to step forward. Some visited regularly, while others turned up unannounced, holding out a photocard on a lanyard by way of introduction. Cora's mother, Sílbhe, moved around the house quietly, making cups of tea, washing clothes, conjuring up meals that left no trace on the kitchen. Each night she camped at the foot of the bed where Cora and the children slept, a silver-haired protector who placed herself between them and the door.

"He's locked up," Cora told her. "We're safe now." But she recognized a new fierceness in her mother and knew she wouldn't leave them to sleep alone. Not at first.

"I'm so sorry, I didn't know; I just never saw it," Sílbhe whispered, her soft, freckled hand on Cora's one night as she sat up in bed feeding Bear.

"Because I didn't let you—it was too risky to ask for help. No one could have known."

"But I'm your *mother*. It was my job to know."

As the weeks passed, the bruise covering one side of Cora's face worked its way through a petrol puddle of colors until finally it paled to yellow, then faded into her skin. The alarm bell of tinnitus ringing in her ears lessened too, revealing the sound of silence; her own breath; of tiny bones shifting and crunching somewhere inside her ear as she chewed.

The patio doors were reglazed, and where they'd been boarded up, light flooded the room again. The day before she returned to Ireland, Sílbhe scrubbed at the patio with a coarse brush and endless washing-up bowls of soapy water, until a neighbor, who must have seen her from an upstairs window, took over with his pressure washer. Cora sat in Maia's room at the front of the house, Bear asleep on her shoulder, unable to witness the effort it took to erase the stain of Vihaan's blood. She thought of Lady Macbeth and wondered if her neighbors did too; the washing-away of blood somehow synonymous with a woman's guilt. Even now, an anonymous quote in an article run by the local newspaper replays in her head: *Dr. Atkin was such a gentle man, couldn't do enough for people. If it was murder, you have to wonder what drove him to it. It beggars belief.*

The morning a taxi arrived to take her to the airport, Sílbhe said, "Don't be waving me off. It'll make it too hard to leave."

And so they'd sat in the living room—Cora, Maia, and Bear—and listened as the car pulled away, leaving them in eerie silence, the quiet somehow bigger than the space her mother had taken up. And even though Cora hadn't wanted her to go, she'd needed to know she was capable of doing this alone. Whatever *this* may be.

"Okay, you two," she'd said, wanting to do something—anything—to be taking that first step. "Let's bake. You can oversee," she told Bear, placing his bouncer on the kitchen table. "And you, my lovely big girl, can be chief stirrer, quality control, and taste tester."

As they'd weighed flour, sugar, and too-cold butter straight from the fridge, Cora's anxiety began to dissipate. She watched as Maia ushered mixture into cake tins, spilling batter down their sides, and realized this was all she needed to do. Just keep following one step with another.

The months before Gordon's conviction had felt like a pause in time. Even though Cora felt sure of the outcome, she was somehow unable to move their lives forward, to settle and say to herself—to Maia, to Bear—*so this is how it will be.* She had a sense of rootlessness, almost as though they were on holiday, where the rules and patterns that once regulated their days had been temporarily left behind. The bits of routine that did remain—school, mealtimes, swimming lessons—felt surprising; things they must navigate around. But once they were back inside with the door locked and the chain across, the hours were formless, open to possibility. They found themselves taking baths at four o'clock in the afternoon and learning times tables during Bear's night feeds. On Saturdays, Cora and Maia ate toast spread with golden syrup and sprinkled with Rice Krispies, spilling crumbs over the duvet cover and Bear's babygro. "This is health food," Maia told Bear, "every Krispie fortified with frolic acid!" and Bear kicked his legs and rewarded her with gummy smiles.

There was an ease in doing things as they came to them, and Cora wondered at the structure that had metered out their days to that point. At how, in Gordon going, they'd also cast off all the other strictures that ordered their lives. For the first time in over a decade, Cora began to dance again, just for the sheer, private joy of it. Tentatively at first. When Maia was out at school, she sometimes pushed back the table and pirouetted around the kitchen, as Bear sat looking on from his bouncer, laughing. A hearty sound that made her insides fizz; some long-repressed part of herself bubbling back to life again.

And throughout that time, Mehri arrived with home-cooked food. At first, Cora noticed how the texture of another woman's mashed potato, or the creaminess of her cheese sauce, was somehow distinctly different from her own. But then these things became familiar, beloved even, and they often ended up sharing meals.

The girls had been so young then, only nine. They're sixteen now. Fern the more outwardly confident of the two—*mouthy*, Mehri likes to say, proudly. And Maia is breathtakingly capable. In the beginning, Cora had tried to stop her from always helping with Bear, but the counselor said people often did instinctively what was needed to heal. "You'll see if it's too much for her."

WHEN CORA ARRIVES home with pizza, she is bone tired. But in a way that feels good. She hugs Maia hello, then washes the dirt from beneath her fingernails, while Maia gets out glasses and waits for the tap to come free and fills Cora in on the French trip, pausing to remind Bear to use his fractions to divvy up the slices he's sharing out.

Cora dries her hands. "Hang on," she says, leaning in to snip at a string of mozzarella trailing between box and plate. But Bear carries the dish away, laughing, watching to see how far he can go before the cheese boings apart. It's in these moments—domestic, cramped, the three of them bustling about their flat's small kitchen—that Cora feels most amazed. *Oh. We're actually doing it. We're all here, and we're doing okay.*

Julian

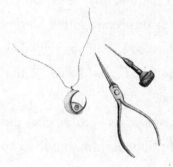

J ulian crouches over the bead tin, hunting for a crystal the same
color as the wine his grandmother drinks once he and Maia are
in bed at night. He lets them spill through his fingers like a soft
rain of tiny treasures until he sees what he's looking for. "Got it."

"Ah, good," Eileen says from the table. He likes Eileen; he's known
her ever since they arrived in Ireland, two years ago. She's their
nearest neighbor and the person he's left with if his grandmother has
errands to run. They mostly sit in silence, neither feeling the need to
fill the space with chatter. His job is to assemble loops of beads; a
decorative weight that dangles from the end of each bobbin to keep
the tension of Eileen's lace just right.

Up at the table, Eileen works with the bobbins he's completed on
previous visits, which make a subtle click-clacking sound as she
throws them gently across the green domed pillow. It looks to Julian

as though her movements are random, as though she is shuffling the bobbins between her fingers without order or care, but still, at the top of the pillow an intricate web of lacework grows, held in place by a raised bed of stainless-steel pins. Sometimes, at school, he takes a clutch of pencils from the box and lays them on his desk, although when he moves them against one another, they don't make the same satisfying noise. He'd asked Eileen about it once. "It's the echo from the hollows inside the wood," she'd said. "I like that you notice—there's not many who do."

He threads jewels onto brass wire, pinches the ends together, and holds it up to the light flooding through from the conservatory. He only shows Eileen the best combinations and when she's really taken with one, she tells him to make up another, because the bobbins always work in pairs and Eileen likes to give them matching spangles. That's the actual name. At first, Julian thought it was a word she'd made up for him, but one evening, he stayed later and when Eileen's lace group arrived, he heard them say the word, and felt oddly pleased to have been entrusted with the proper term. They pass around shortcake biscuits with a glinting layer of sugar granules dancing on top, because blessed are the lacemakers; that's what they say whenever they eat cake or biscuits. They laugh and then offer him the plate, because blessed are the spangle-makers too. He makes spangles for some of the others as well but keeps the best ones for Eileen. In the past, he would thread them onto the wire and leave it for Eileen to attach to the bobbin, but lately, she's handed him the pliers and the wire cutters. It's easy for his small fingers to double-thread the wire back through the final bead, to pull it tight, then clip the wire right at its base. Eileen says he's God's gift to her, what with her arthritic fingers.

When Maia and his grandmother arrive from counseling to collect him, it always feels as though it breaks the stillness that's settled over the room when it's just him and Eileen, and like he's putting down the lid on a part of himself as he closes the bead box. But he's also relieved. Even when he's absorbed in his task, he's aware of their absence. Images of them flicker through his mind: his grandmother's small car on the long, winding road that cuts between fields. Gray sky, blue car, green grass, yellow lichen, dark rock. His grandmother and Maia inside, the faint smell of petrol, and the leather of his grandma's driving gloves.

"Why do you wear gloves to drive?" he'd asked her once.

"In the olden days—even older than my days," she'd said, smiling in the rearview mirror, "steering wheels were made of metal or wood. You needed to protect your hands from the cold. Or splinters."

He remembers his father's hands on the steering wheel, big and firm, a smattering of hair on the backs of them. He blinks the image away.

"Why did Mummy never learn to drive?" he'd asked recently. He saw his grandmother's shoulders rise and fall in the front seat in that way they always do whenever he asks a question that has an uncomfortable answer to do with his mum.

"Well, she was in London from fourteen, so she missed out on that time when I might have taught her. And later, I don't think he wanted her to." And then she'd corrected herself. "No, that's not right. He didn't let her."

She'd blinked at him in the mirror then, both eyes pressed shut for just a moment, in the same way her cat, Thistle, does. "It's a cat's way of saying *I love you*. She only does it to people she really likes," she'd explained when they'd first arrived. His grandmother says she loves him out loud all the time, but he likes her silent cat blinks even more.

He didn't let her. They never call his dad by his name. They call him *he* or *him*. Julian notices that people talk about God in the same way. Not Grandma Sílbhe—she doesn't believe in him anymore—but at school, when they go across the road to morning church, Julian hears the priest say the Hes and the Hims. There is Father this and Father that, and it feels like a muddle of fathers that Julian can't quite unpick. He hasn't done the Sacrament of Penance yet, but they talk about it in the playground and the other boys are almost giddy with what will be their first confession.

"I'm gonna say a stolen pencil!" says Reggie. "You should tell about the money you take from your mammy's purse for ice creams," goads another. Their eyes are wide. They all agree the sins have to be not so bad they could get in trouble, but bad enough to justify confessing.

"Did Mummy talk to anyone when she picked you up today?" he remembers his father asking back then, when he was in his first year at school, and they still lived in England. "No one? You wouldn't lie for her, would you?" his voice like a fingernail prying open the ends of a staple. "Has she been using the phone again? I'll know if you don't tell the truth, Julian."

Now, the idea of telling the priest his sins makes his breath feel like it's being sucked from his body. Grandma Sílbhe says they won't be doing any of that. That he just needs to keep his head down and try to fit in at school. But still, the words he hears in lessons swirl around in Julian's mind, dark and ominous like the low sky that settles over the fields around the house before a storm. *O, my God, I am heartily sorry for having offended You. I detest all my sins because of Your punishment . . . I dread the loss of heaven and the pains of hell . . .*

Julian doesn't want the pains of hell. But even more, he doesn't want to be the one inflicting the hurt. When they play hide-and-seek, Julian can only stay hidden for a moment or two once Maia's come into the room. Somehow, watching as she peers behind the sofa or the door makes her seem too vulnerable. And even though he knows that's the game, it is unbearable. He doesn't want to feel her surprise; to see her jump and be momentarily afraid. So he tries to pitch his voice just right—not too loud, not too quiet—"Maia, I'm over here."

He watches Maia when she sits working at the kitchen table, hair trailing over her schoolbooks, a face that says she's gone into herself. It makes him feel wavery inside when she's distracted; there-but-not-there. *Maia*, he says, under his breath when the feeling of being alone gets too much, *Maia*.

And she'll exhale, her fringe rising in a gentle sigh. "I'm concentrating, Jules." And even though a moment later she might reach across the pages, give his hand a squeeze, she doesn't look up, her pen still poised over a diagram, labeling the parts of a plant cell or a human heart.

He's overheard Grandma Sílbhe talking to Eileen. Saying that he—Julian—will be all right; that he can barely remember the night his mother died. It's Maia she really worries about. And he realizes the wavery feeling isn't something other people can see.

SOME NIGHTS, ONCE Julian has finally fallen asleep, Maia gets up and joins her grandmother in the living room, where they talk in hushed voices and her grandmother pours her some wine—just an inch at the bottom of a glass, *to be companionable.*

One evening, Maia builds up her courage and says, "I know Mum didn't like me doing it, and I know you probably won't either, but could I carry on with ballet? Could we find a class here?"

"Why ever would you want to do that?" Sílbhe asks. "I thought you only went because he insisted?"

"I did, but—"

"Sorry, you can say it. I know you'll have your reasons."

"Mum never wanted me to dance because of the stress it can put on your body. And I guess because she could see I never loved it the way she did. But I miss it now. It's like a—a connection with her." She stops. There are other things she could say, but already her grandmother is nodding, suggesting they find a class and drive down into town one night a week.

"But no leaving before you're eighteen," her grandmother cautions. As soon as she's said the words, her face drops, and for a moment, it looks like it may crumple entirely. But then she touches a finger to her eyes. "Will you listen to me, clucking over you with all my regrets. As if someone can't go to a dance lesson without leaving the country." She takes Maia's hand across the side table and squeezes it in apology, although she doesn't look at her. Nor when she adds, "But she was too young; I can see that now. She needed more care. She needed *parents*. I don't know what we were thinking, letting her go out into the world like that." Maia understands the subtext of what she's saying and pictures her mum in the chair where she sits now. Before she and Jules were born, their existence not even imagined.

After a while, Maia breaks the silence. "You know I'd never even want to leave this town, let alone Ireland." And as she speaks, she feels the truth of her words.

AT BALLET CLASS, the other girls watch her, only warming when they've sized up her jetés and the angle of her brisé. A smile, a shared complaint as they extract sore feet from slippers. She sees her mother all around her. In the other girls with their necks long, in her teacher's habit of standing stock still, heels joined in first position when she wants their attention. Her mother gravitated toward this pose at the kitchen sink washing up, or waiting for Maia at the school gates. Maia always thought she'd renounced ballet completely, but now she sees it was there all along.

"Your mother is very jealous," he used to say, the hardness of his gaze demanding Maia look up, as though, with eyes locked, he might overwrite her thoughts with his own. "She can't bear to see you get what she could never have. But it's not your fault her body gave up; you shouldn't have to pay the price for that."

She hadn't enjoyed dancing back then, in England. She danced because he wrote the checks and insisted Cora take her each week. Maia knew she could never reach the level her mother had. She didn't have that drive, that natural pull to it. It was a duty, something to please her father. But now, in Ireland, it has changed shape, morphed into something else. And she yearns for it. To inhabit the same intangible space her mother once did. She feels her in her own calves and quads held taut, in the balls of her feet pressed against the floor.

Sometimes, in the middle of the night, Julian climbs into bed with Maia, snuggling his small body against her. He falls asleep twirling her hair around his fingers in the dark, his soft, wispy breath on the back of her neck. On those nights, she stays awake as long as she can, and only when she feels her eyes beginning to close against her will does she carry Julian back to his own bed. She lays him down, covers him over, then returns to her crinkling waterproof sheets. Each morning, she strips her bed, loads the linens into the washing machine and when she gets home from school, they have been blown crisp by the wind, and Grandma Sílbhe has put them back on her bed again. Her shame is held wordlessly between them, even though she knows she isn't judged for it. "Who wouldn't after what you've been through?" her grandmother said the first time. But still, Julian is nine years younger and keeps his bedsheets dry. Sometimes, she runs her hand across his mattress to check, and then feels bad for being disappointed.

It's NOT THE RETIREMENT Sílbhe had planned. She'd imagined a slow winding-down into the penultimate stage of life. Wasn't that how it went? Childhood, early adulthood, marriage, children, midlife, retirement, until finally . . . But that was before the children arrived. Would she have used that time differently had she known? Sewn more quilts, read more books, gone to Venice? Found love again, she thinks, in more honest moments.

She'd known Cian since school. There was always something between them. She can still remember his soft, boyish lips at sixteen,
simultaneously eager and gentle. But then she'd met Hugh, and Cian
had met . . . She can't remember her name now. It was so long ago, or
perhaps she was just too taken with Hugh to care. They'd lost touch.
But then, a few years ago, in the aftermath of torrential rain, she'd
taken a different route home when the bridge was closed, and her car
had hiccupped to a stop on the unfamiliar ribbon of gray tarmac that
threaded its way through the craggy land. She'd sat for a while,
let the engine click and sigh as it cooled, but when she turned the
key, there was still nothing, so she set off on foot.

A mile up the road, the light beginning to fade, she'd seen the sil-
houette of a house emerging from behind a hill as she drew closer. It
was unlit, but still, she'd walked around its side, hoping she might
find someone who could help. There was a small studio, separate
from the main building, a glow at the window. She'd knocked, and
when Cian came to the door she'd felt relief, surprise. But also something else: like an expectation being met, as though somewhere in the
background of those years since Hugh had passed she'd known their
paths would cross again. Cian had smiled, opened his arms—a
gesture both passive and confident—requiring her to choose to step
into them.

"Well, if I didn't always know you'd be turning up at my door like
this someday. What took you so long?" he said. "Will we go over to
the house? I'll turn off the soldering iron and we can go over and
have a drink."

He unplugged the iron, a black whisper of smoke fading from its
tip, and she noticed the stack of small, cream boxes embossed with

his last name then. She recognized them from the window of the jewelers down in the town, but she'd never made the connection; Brennan isn't an uncommon name around here.

She'd seen him a few more times. Cian was interested and interesting, with things to say about books and art and politics, and when he asked her about her life with Hugh—about her daughter in England—he did so with warmth and generosity. Meeting Cian again felt like cracking open an oyster and finding a pearl inside.

Dropping her home after dinner one night, he reached across the space between their seats, and she found herself leaning toward him too. His kiss felt familiar, and when she went inside, she stood with her back against the closed door, giddy, like a teenager again. That night, she sat at her dresser, ran a finger across her lips, then turned toward the photo of Hugh, gone over twenty years. His smile in the picture always seemed to be encouraging her. *Go on, do it. What have you got to lose?* Maybe she was just seeing what she wanted to see, she told herself. Foolish old woman. But still, she found herself gently twisting the rings from her finger and placing them in the small ceramic dish he'd bought her one Christmas. There.

But then, only a few days later, she received the call. A call that had seen her frantically throwing things into a suitcase, forgetting what she really needed; she'd had to buy underwear at the airport. When they returned a few weeks later, she was overwhelmed. By the loss of her own beloved daughter. By caring for two children newly afraid of the dark, who flinched when a log popped and hissed on the fire, and flew together like magnets if she dropped a saucepan lid. And the idea of Cian Brennan . . . well, she'd barely stopped to consider it.

He'd come over late one evening when Maia and Julian were finally asleep. She'd stood in the doorway, him in the cold. She only realizes now, all this time later, that he was in shirtsleeves, his coat probably in the car; he'd expected to be invited in. She told him in short, halting sentences what had happened, trying to choose words and phrases that wouldn't conjure images in his head. But still, it was enough. He opened his arms to her, but she stayed in the doorway.

"Cian, about—" She knew *us* was the right word to use, but she couldn't. She felt for her wedding ring and his gaze dropped to her hands.

"Us?" he asked. And then, palms up in submission, he said, "I understand. It's not our time." She nodded, grateful he'd said it for her. "But if you need me. For anything. Anything at all," and she bent her head again and he knew he'd said enough. He touched her arm, his rough hand crackling against the static fibers of her wool sweater, and then he'd turned to get back in his car. A part of her wanted to stay on the threshold between two worlds and watch him go, but the open door was letting cold air into the house, and she didn't want to risk the children waking and not finding her where they expected. She doesn't resent them, even now, two years on. Only him—their father. And God.

She feels such a ferocious need to inhabit her current life that it dispels tiredness, casts off any idea of impending retirement, of self-interest, of following her own path. She's all they have. Her life was not set up for having young children again. She's forty-five minutes from the nearest secondary school and although Maia could catch the bus the last leg of the journey, it would only save twenty minutes and Sílbhe doesn't seek shortcuts. Not where they're concerned. Their evenings are taken up with ballet, an art club for Julian. Counseling for each of them. Her included, although she fits her own sessions in during the day while they're at school, taking an early morning slot so they don't have to witness her looking puffy-eyed at pickup. *Heroic, brave,* some young woman on the radio called her when she'd interviewed Sílbhe about domestic homicide, but that wasn't how it felt. She feels like she's been spun around in the washer, then hung out to be blown dry with Maia's sheets on the line. But she's also energized, forced into an unasked-for second youth. What else could she do? What else would anyone do?

Gordon

Gordon sits at his desk and rifles through his new pencil case for the right color. The case has a monkey's face on it, its eyes large and quizzical as though someone has just told a joke. He chose it with his dad, *just boys together,* because his mum can't be trusted to go shopping. Afterward, they'd gone to Pizza Express and sat opposite each other at one of the gray marble tables, cutlery resting neatly on napkins bearing the swirly logo.

Gordon had wanted to be entertaining, to say the kinds of things his dad might want to hear, so he'd told him a joke he remembered from his *Knock, Knock* book, and when that didn't work, he relayed an episode of *Dogtanian and the Three Muskehounds* where Dogtanian's sword broke.

"I don't know how he'll protect himself without it," Gordon told his father. His stomach had felt wobbly ever since it had happened, and two episodes later, Dogtanian still hadn't managed to get it properly fixed.

His father nodded, and leaned in, lowering his head to Gordon's level. "So, tell me, what has Mummy been up to while I've been at work over the summer holidays?"

"Oh, I don't know," he'd said, disappointed they weren't going to discuss the sword. He tried to think what kind of stuff his mum did, but it was hard; she was just *there*. "Erm, cooking, mopping the floor, watering the plants." His father had folded his arms and sat back in his chair and Gordon had found himself desperate to say something that might draw him back in. "And one time, she said a bad word," he offered, and just as he'd hoped, his father stopped looking bored and leaned in again.

"Go on."

It was such a good feeling, a rushy, headlong feeling, like riding his bike over a hump in the pavement, making his stomach leap. He racked his brain for more indiscretions, things that seemed to make his father's face lighter, more engaged, as though he was drinking up Gordon's words. He found himself embellishing, confusing what had happened with what *might* have happened, or even what he wished had happened: ". . . and after we'd stroked the cat for a while, Mum said, 'He doesn't have a collar, so let's take him home and keep him under your bed and Dad will never know!'"

He sensed this as the moment he'd pushed it too far. "The bill, please," his father had said to the waiter. And then he'd sat staring into space and it was as though a shutter had come down.

"Knock, knock," Gordon said, trying to find his way back in. His father didn't answer, so he played both parts, trailing off before the punchline.

In the street outside, he'd had to race to keep up with his father's long strides. But still, at dinner that night, his dad had brought up some of the things Gordon had told him. Not about the cat, which he must have known wasn't true, but other things. He sounded pleased by the details, almost like he was teasing his mum, and Gordon had felt vindicated. Especially when his mum didn't say those things were made up, but only looked at her plate, blinking, leaving Gordon wondering if she really did sneak bags of Monster Munch while he and Maia were at school; if she actually had used up his birthday bubble bath.

Later, Maia had appeared at his bedroom door. "Do you have to be such a little—" Gordon wasn't sure what word she'd been about to say, only that it was a bad one. And that the reason she hadn't said it was because they'd heard their dad coming upstairs. In bed, he had an odd gnawing feeling deep in his stomach. A bit like hunger but mixed with something ugly and sad. He turned over and buried his face in the pillow, trying to block out the memory of his mum blinking in that weird way. And Maia, glaring.

The teacher is putting down a rectangle of card in front of each child, telling them these will go on the front of the trays where they'll keep their workbooks and spelling diaries for the rest of the year. She tells them they should write their name and design a decorative border around it. Gordon sits for a moment, looking at what his classmates are doing, and then settles down to his own piece of card. Using his most careful handwriting, sounding out the letters in his head to make sure he gets it absolutely right, he writes

L-U-K-E in orange felt-tip. When he's happy with his printing, he sets to work on a border of rockets and spaceships, ringed planets, and shooting stars. His pens are so new and fresh that he takes extra care not to let the colors bleed into one another and dirty the nibs. He is thinking about the sky's velvety blackness, about astronauts in bubble helmets, about space food, and squeezing paste onto floating toothbrushes, when he becomes aware of the child at the next desk leaning toward him.

"Yeah, Miss! That's not his real name!" the boy is saying. Others are getting up from their chairs now, crowding in on him. Gordon covers his paper. But then there's the shadow of the teacher standing over him and Mrs. Bellamy tugs at the corner of his card and he sees his careful work smudge as it's pulled from beneath his arm.

The teacher looks at it, then tears it in half. Gordon feels his lip wobble, hears someone say, "Gordon's gonna cry!" He bites down hard to stop the tremor and feels the metallic tang of blood in his mouth.

"I know exactly who you are, Gordon." The teacher looks down at him, sees his watering eyes, and with a mixture of frustration and pity says, "Oh, for goodness' sake. Go and sit in the corridor until we've finished."

He wants to explain, but realizes he can't even explain it to himself, except that he has always wanted to be called Luke. Outside the classroom, he sits against the wall, pinching at the birthmark on his forearm, watching as its misshapen heart outline disappears and reforms, disappears and reforms.

Later, when she calls him back in, he glances at the bank of trays where the other children have taped their names in place. It's easy to spot his own in amongst the brightly decorated cards. The teacher has printed it in thick black indelible letters, G-O-R-D-O-N.

He finds himself trying to hold back tears again, and this time, he wins. He feels his sadness dry up and spark into anger. And as he makes his way to his chair, when a girl leans back, hair standing proud of her head like a horse's tail, he doesn't *purposely* knock into her, but neither does he make any effort to go around her. She wails, clutching at her skewed ponytail, as his name is bellowed across the room. He wishes he was somewhere else. He wishes he was some*one* else. But he is Gordon. In class 2C, at the beginning of a new school year. It will be *his* name that is muttered in the staffroom. Bloody Gordon. Gordon sodding Atkin. And he senses something of this, the feeling of being disliked.

That night over dinner, his father asks how his first day back was. "Good," he says, as he shovels forkfuls of macaroni into his mouth.

"Don't speak with your mouth full," his father tells him, and then looks pointedly at his raised elbows, stuck out at odd angles as he manhandles his cutlery. Gordon lowers them.

He notices his mother's drink and says, "Can I have a straw too?"

"No," Maia says.

"It's not up to you. Why does Mum get one and not me? She's not even a child."

"I'm just getting better from some dental work," she says. Maia sighs and their father gives her a sharp look. Gordon stops shoveling, stares at his mother's face and sees the fat swell of her left cheek, as though she's stuffed a ping-pong ball inside. And, not understanding quite why, he detects she isn't telling the truth and that the others are all in on the secret. It's always like this. The three of them, knowing something he doesn't. And he suddenly craves another outing with his dad, to be *just boys together* again, to pull him away from Maia and his mother and redefine allegiances. Ever since Pizza Express, he's been thinking of other things he could tell his dad, things that would please him. So now he's saving them up in his head, a *my-grandmother-went-to-market-and-she-bought*-style list of all the things his mother does wrong.

MAIA SITS ON THE SOFA, the plate of biscuits Mrs. Radley left out for her half empty. She likes babysitting for the Radleys. They only live a few streets away, but where Maia's house has faux pillars flanked by neat planters, theirs has a path of old tiles that look like they've always been there, bordered by riotous plants that tickle at your ankles as you make your way to the front door. Inside, there is the mess of everyday life. Of people leaving things where they put them down, and then not picking them up again until Mrs. Radley announces it's time for *a blitz*. There is something cozy and not unclean about their mess, and Maia sinks into it, takes her textbooks from her bag the minute the children are in bed, spreading them out on the coffee table, placing one at a casual angle on the floor, wanting to integrate her things with theirs.

At home, the cushions are always plumped, the work surfaces wiped down, as though an orderly veneer will purify the reality of their lives. But somehow it doesn't work. The tidier it is, the more it looks like they're hiding something.

"Blimey, Maia! It's like a show home," a girl from her year had said once when she'd stopped by unannounced to borrow her tutu for a recital. "Where's all your stuff?" she'd asked, glancing into the living room as Maia ran upstairs to get the skirt. "Oh, we keep a lot of junk in the garage," she'd said, hoping she wouldn't ask to see.

When the Radleys arrive home, she hears them on the path outside before their key is in the lock. They are always talking or giggling over something and when Mrs. Radley calls him a bloody idiot for dropping his keys, he only laughs. As Mrs. Radley searches in her handbag for the babysitting money, Mr. Radley chats to Maia, but his eyes are drawn back to his wife as though she is a slice of chocolate cake and he is politely waiting for the moment when Maia leaves, and he will be free to tuck in. She imagines them like the characters in the sex education video at school, where a cartoon couple chase one another around the bedroom trying to tickle each other with feathers, looking happy and excited. She knows sex isn't about feathers, but Mr. and Mrs. Radley seem as though they'd have fun like that. Sometimes she hears her own father grunting through the wall. She pulls the covers up over her head, but it's habit to want to know if her mother's all right. She strains to listen from beneath the duvet but hears nothing. It makes her think sex is probably something her father does *to* her mother. Not the reciprocal act they talked about in part two of the periods chat at school last year.

Maia isn't interested in boys. Sometimes, when her friend Sadie is talking, she finds herself transfixed by the soft pink of her lips and imagines what it would be like to lean in and kiss them. But she doesn't do anything, because it feels complicated. All her focus is on getting to university to study medicine.

It seems odd to be following in her father's footsteps, but when she's witnessed him in professional mode, the fear she often feels is overshadowed by something close to admiration. She's in awe of the reassuring voice he uses with patients; the way he shakes the ther- mometer before reading the mercury, his face never betraying alarm no matter how high her fever; the calm precision with which he'd administered a shot of adrenaline the time Gordon had been stung by a wasp. For a moment that day, it had seemed as though he might die right there at the picnic table in his Batman costume, but then her father had donned the invisible cape of medic and saved him. A hero, fleetingly. She longs to possess that kind of competence and control.

Even though they have the thick UCAS book in the sixth-form common room, Cora clocks a noticeboard at parents' evening and in the days after makes suggestions of where Maia might apply. "It says you need to write a personal statement. Do you know what that is?" Maia reminds her that she's only in the lower sixth and doesn't need to do it until the start of the next year. Her mother looks panicked, as though they might somehow forget in the meantime. Maia looks at the places she's suggested on a map. Manchester, Leeds, Cardiff, Edinburgh, even one in Ireland where Grandma Sylvia lives. They are all far, far away.

Maia knows her mum rarely speaks to Grandma Sylvia. Dad doesn't like her to make long-distance phone calls and they never visit. Sometimes, Grandma Sylvia sends checks for Christmas or birthdays that their father deposits into a bank account, along with Maia's babysitting money. "Mum," she'd asked once, "why is Grand- ma's name *Sílbhe* on here?"

"Oh, that's her name. It's the Irish version of Sylvia."

"So why don't we call her that?" She saw her mother pause, open her mouth, and then close it again. "Well, how do you pronounce it then? Properly I mean?"

"It's *Shilva*," her mother told her, and her face had softened as she'd said the word. Maia knew then why her father wanted to erase any connection with Ireland.

Maia says the name in her head, lets it swirl around in her thoughts at the dinner table like an act of defiance. Sílbhe. She enjoys the little flick above the í, like the flame of a candle that refuses to be blown out. At school, she starts writing her own name as Maía, a change so subtle no one notices but her.

Gradually, Grandma Sílbhe comes to seem their only potential savior. Maia imagines turning up on her doorstep or calling from a telephone box and asking if she can reverse the charges. But in the end, she writes a letter, paying for a stamp with money she finds on the ground. It only takes a week or two of walking with her eyes down on the way to and from school. People don't drop money in the streets near home, but by the small parade of shops, the park, the ticket machine at the train station, she finds coppers everywhere. She wants to tell her mum this, so she'll have money of her own, but knows her mother—the doctor's wife—can't be seen hunting for change in the dandelions that grow up around the glass bottle bank like some kind of bag lady. Maia thinks about this and is shocked to realize how little separates them. Her mother lives in a warm house and is bought clothes to wear, but she has no more money or freedom than the woman who pushes a shopping trolley of scavenged treasures around town.

Late one night, she'd come downstairs for a glass of water. The light in the living room was off, and so Maia had stood in the darkness, unseen, as her father knelt over her mother, wrists held behind her back, as she ate from a bowl on the kitchen floor, his voice low and calm beside her. "Maybe now you'll think twice about making us live like animals, Cora. It's not nice, is it? I hope this will help you to remember to clean out the fridge next time. No one wants to have to eat rotten food like this."

Maia had turned, silently carried what she'd seen up the stairs with her, and then vomited it across the landing carpet. She had stood for a moment, looking at the walls splattered with chunks of carrot she couldn't remember eating, wondering what to do. And then she'd called out weakly from the top of the stairs, "I've been sick," and moments later her parents had appeared, no trace in their faces of what she'd just seen in the kitchen.

The next morning, she'd written the letter in the school library on pages torn carefully from the back of her exercise book.

It's a Tuesday morning when Sílbhe calls. Cora is scrubbing the grates on the hob and working through the "Dance of the Sugar Plum Fairy" in her head. Some sequences she remembers instinctively, others she is less sure of and wonders if she's adding her own bits of choreography to fill the gaps in her memory.

"Cora, are you alone?" The voice on the other end of the phone is so familiar, even though they rarely talk. Cora avoids making outgoing calls that will show up on the bill, but her mum seems to have taken her lack of communication as a cue not to ring too often. And somehow, it's easier that way. "Can you speak?" Cora looks about, as if her mother might know something she doesn't.

"Yes?" she replies, almost a question.

"I've had a letter from Maia, darling. I know what's going on."

Cora sits on the arm of the sofa, winded. And then reflexively stands, glancing through to the kitchen window to check he's not coming back in a gap between patients.

"Mum, I don't think—I'm not sure I can do this right now."

"Is it true?" Cora says nothing and the silence stretches out across the telephone wires that connect them. "I wish I'd known." Still Cora says nothing. She wonders how much Maia has said. Wonders how much Sílbhe knows. "I know you can't access your bank account, so I'm going to send a check for Maia. She can get the cash out for you, and I want you to use the money to buy tickets to come here."

Cora laughs, a quick, sharp burst of disbelief she hadn't intended to escape her. "The children don't have access to their accounts, Mum. He takes care of all that."

"You mean they've never got it? The money I send for them."

"I'm sure it's probably all safely tucked away somewhere for when they're older. But they can't just go into a bank and withdraw it. They don't have bank cards or anything like that."

The line goes quiet for a moment. "But I could send you cash in the post? And you'd get that? He's at work when the morning post arrives, yes?"

Cora sighs. "It's not that easy. If I tried to leave, I'd lose the children. He gets someone at the practice to prescribe for me, it's all over my records—antipsychotics or something."

"You're psychotic?"

"No, of course not. But if even my own mother has to ask . . . It's his insurance policy. He's made it look like I'm mad so I wouldn't get the children. He's told me." Her mother is silent. "But none of this matters; it's really not that bad. I don't know what Maia's told you, but I'm fine and the children are well looked after. They have clean clothes, plenty to eat, after-school clubs, ballet . . ." Cora falters at her distortion; the lessons aren't Maia's choice. But then she presses on. "He doesn't touch them. They have everything they could wish for. Some children are living in poverty, you know?"

"But it's not right, Cora." She is still looking out of the window. The longer the phone call goes on, the more convinced she is that he's about to round the corner and come into view. Sometimes he puts his key in the lock silently, hoping to catch her out. She imagines him standing just inside the front door, listening now, without her even knowing he's there.

"Just a second," she says, and places the receiver on the table, while she peeks into the hallway. When she picks up again, she's firmer. She should never have let herself be drawn in like this. The shock of her mother knowing, of realizing Maia had told her, the Irish lilt of home, have all caught her off-guard. "Mum, I'm sorry Maia's worried you. She should never have said anything. Everything is fine."

"Think about it Cora, please."

Cora thinks about it all the time. About Gordon turning eighteen. It's only eleven years away and she's lived like this far longer than that already. But she doesn't tell her mother any of this.

WHEN MAIA GETS HOME from school, Cora puts on a cartoon for Gordon to watch, fixes him a snack, and then follows Maia up to her room. She's sitting on her bed, using a corner of almost-smooth sandpaper taken from the design and technology workroom at school to buff her nails to a glassy shine.

"You wrote to Grandma?"

Maia stops polishing and looks up, her face expectant. "Will she help us?"

Cora kneels on the floor in front of her. "I know things could be better," she says, "but do you understand what might happen if you start involving other people like that?"

Maia looks down, fingers the sandpaper. "What?"

"I wouldn't be allowed to keep you. No one would believe me. Dad's a doctor. He'd make things look a certain way and the courts would award him custody. I might not even be allowed to see you." Maia doesn't say anything. "Nothing he can do to me would be worse than that."

Maia thinks of her mother crouching over the bowl on the kitchen floor.

"What?" Cora asks, seeing the look that passes across her daughter's face.

"I saw. The night I was sick. I saw."

Cora feels as though she may crumple, but instead she straightens her spine, draws in her core, elongates her breath, feels her diaphragm rise.

"Don't do that," Maia says.

"What?"

"That. The ballet thing. It's meant to help you perform on stage, not to fool your own daughter."

Cora slumps, softly. "Is there anything you don't notice?"

Their eyes meet for a moment, and the same sad, closed-mouth smile passes between them. Maia traces over a smoothed nail with her fingertip. She sees her mother tilt her wrist to check the time and Maia looks out of her bedroom window, craning to glimpse the end of the cul-de-sac. "He's not coming yet," she says.

"It would always be worse—the *worst* thing—to lose you and Gordon. To not be here for you. I have a choice," she says, "and this is my choice." Maia raises her eyebrows. "I do. I know it's not much, but I do. This is my choice. Every time."

"But couldn't we just say what he's like? Tell them we want to be with you. Surely, we'd get a say?"

Cora shakes her head. "He'd say I was an unfit mother. They can't let you stay with someone they think might harm you or who might not take proper care. And your brother . . . he might not even *want* to stay with me," she says, her voice barely a whisper. She blinks, trying not to let it show how much it hurts to admit this. Maia squeezes her hand. "I'm sorry. This isn't how I wanted things to be. I never wanted you to grow up having to see things like—" She stops, because saying it out loud makes it more real, more awful. "I hope you won't hate me for it. When you're older. I hope you won't think I was weak or—"

"Mum!" Gordon's voice interrupts, calling up the stairs. Cora stands, joints clicking where she's been kneeling. "Mum!" louder this time, his impatience obscuring her reply.

HER MOTHER CALLS every day that week, even though Cora has stopped answering and lets the phone ring out into the quiet house, ready to pick up only if it's Gordon's voice on the answering machine. She knows her mother will not put her at risk by leaving a message and she's grateful. She doesn't want to hear the things that will undermine the careful scaffold she's erected around her existence. Without anyone to question it, she can almost let herself believe it's normal. But her mother's words threaten the nuts and bolts, leaving her feeling that scaffold could all come crashing down. And where would she be then? Still in the same place, in the same predicament, with no route out.

Five days after she last picked up the phone to her mother, there is a knock at the door and when Cora opens it, she sees a police officer, his hat beneath his arm. She notices this detail and feels relieved, recalling something her father once said. About how they only leave their hat on if they've come to tell you someone has died.

The police officer's hair is cropped close to his head, and she can almost hear the buzz of the clippers he must use each morning, eyes tracking the razor's progress in the mirror, the sink below lined with a thin veil of fuzz. He is shuffley-footed as he tells her why he's there, and it's only when Cora says that her mother has dementia, explains how she is prone to making things up, that his face eases.

"Oh, thank God," he laughs and then catches himself. "Sorry, no offense. I didn't mean it like that. It's just it would have been really awkward if it was true. He's my doctor. We had to draw straws down at the station to see who'd come out to this one," he says. "I'm the new boy. I think I'll always draw the short one until someone else comes along."

She watches for a moment as he walks back up the drive. When he reaches the end, he returns his hat to his head. And she feels it then. The quiet death of something.

Seven Years Later

2001

Bear

The child at the table across the aisle is three or four years old. Her wails compete with the noise of the train and seep in around the edges of Bear's earphones, drowning out the White Stripes. He waits until the girl looks his way, ready to catch her eye. It takes a moment or two, but it stops her mid-wail, mouth ajar, as she watches him send a caterpillar of movement wiggling through his eyebrows, first one, then the other.

She stares and he takes out his earbuds and says, "You want to see it again?" The child nods almost imperceptibly, uncertain, but not dropping her gaze. "Are you looking?" he says, even though he can see her eyes are fixed on him. The child's mum is looking too. Suspicious; she hadn't seen what caught the girl's attention.

Bear leans forward across the aisle. "Ready then." He smiles and repeats the eyebrow trick and this time the child laughs and he sees the mum relax, release her protective grip. "One more time?" he says. The girl nods and a few of the other passengers turn to look, grateful to this boy who's coaxed the child from her caterwauling.

He slides across the aisle into the empty seat opposite them. "Hey," he says, "want to see something else?"

"Yes, please," the mum says. Bear waits until the girl nods, and then unzips his rucksack and takes a sheet of A4 paper from the sheaf inside.

"Okay, you can have a swan, you know, with a reeaallly long neck. A butterfly. Or a bear," he says, holding out his arms and giving a little roar.

The child giggles. "Bear," she says.

"Bear. Good choice. That's my name too. I'm Bear. What's yours?" he asks as he starts to fold the paper, smoothing creases with the side of his hand.

"Robyn," she says.

"No way! Like the bird?"

When he's done, he walks the bear across the table toward the child, shifting the weight between its triangular feet.

"Want me to make you a robin to go with it?" he says, and the girl nods, her hand on the animal, eyes darting from Bear's face only momentarily. "It's more of a generic bird, really, but maybe if you have some felt-tips at home, you can color its belly in red."

When the train reaches the end of the line at Brighton, Maia watches from the ticket barriers as Bear waves goodbye to a woman and child, the girl's hands filled with what Maia knows will be paper animals. He turns and sees her then and his face is full beam as he lopes along the platform, arms outstretched the last few steps, embracing her across the barrier before he's even on the other side. "Bees," he says, "I've missed you." Maia's whole body fills with warmth.

They stop at a fish and chip shop, then walk along the seafront and cover the preliminary topics: Mum, school, Bear's latest geography field trip, Maia's homeopathy training, and then into the easy back and forth of everything and nothing.

"So, what's she like?" Maia asks, when Bear tells her he's asked someone out.

"Kind of quiet, but also, like, really confident and kind. Smart too. We'll be discussing some book in English and everyone will be coming out with all the usual lame stuff and then she'll say something and the whole class will be kind of, I don't know, like you can tell she's in a different league. But it's not like she does it to show us all up. It's just who she is." He doesn't mention that their surnames are almost the same—only she's Atkins with an *s*—or that he also sits next to her in maths, which she's less good at; he wants to keep some details for himself. A seagull missing a toe hops toward them, and Bear breaks one of his chips in half and throws it for the bird, who snaps it up hungrily and then flies off.

"Who does she hang out with then?"

"Lily? She's not one of the popular kids," Bear says, understanding what she's really asking, "but everyone's cool with her."

Fern once said Bear is one of those kids who could be in the popular crowd, but then chooses some other, more obscure group, and Mehri had smiled in agreement. Maia realized it was true, that Bear could glide effortlessly across the unseen lines that define most children's school days. And that it was never like that for her.

"She has this hair. Always makes me think of licorice toffee or something . . ." and he trails off, embarrassed by himself.

"Like Grandma Sílbhe's sweets? Oh, Bear, you've got it bad," Maia says, and they laugh, and he nudges her shoulder with his own as they sit looking out to sea from one of the rusted turquoise benches. "What color are her eyes then?" Maia asks, teasing.

Back in Maia's flat, they drink hot chocolate sitting cross-legged on a sofa draped in a throw he doesn't recognize. Bear wonders if Maia and her girlfriend choose these things together, or if the living room is a merging of both their possessions. He decides that later he'll use some of the money he earns from his newspaper round to buy her something from one of the shops in the Lanes, a cushion maybe.

"I had this weird thing in class," he says. "I can't even remember how we got to it, but we must've been talking about *The Canterbury Tales*, how the men are defined by what they do, but the only women— Well, it's more about who they are in relation to a man. Like the Wife of Bath, or even the nun in a way."

"I can't remember the stories, but I'd say definitely the nun."

"Anyway, somehow it ended up with the teacher asking us, if we had to give our life a title where we were defined by someone else, what it would be. And I realized—"

"Oh," Maia says, grasping where he's going with this. Because until she moved away, it was always there hovering in the back of her own mind.

"You know what I was thinking?"

"Yeah, I think so. After it happened, I always thought people in shops, teachers, our neighbors . . . Well, that I'd pass them in the street, and they'd be thinking, *Oh, there goes . . .*" She pauses for a moment, and then begins again. "*Oh, there goes the murderer's daughter.*"

They sit in silence. Maia moves her feet so they meet Bear's where the sofa cushions join. And for a while they stare at the tips of their toes.

"What's weird is that it's taken me fourteen years to have that thought. That I'm the murderer's son."

"Do you actually feel related to him like that, though? When you've barely met him?"

"I guess not. Most of the time I don't really think of myself as having a dad. Do you?"

"Yes, but in a different life. Like I had one, but now, in this life, I don't."

"D'you reckon he thinks about us? Like we're his?"

Maia goes back to looking at their socks. At the stripes of hers and the faded black of his. She's wondered about this often but doesn't share her thoughts: that she believes he probably still thinks of her as his daughter, but perhaps not Bear as his son. She wishes she had that same anonymity in their father's mind. "I don't know," she says eventually.

"It's next year, isn't it? That he's getting out of prison?"

Maia wants to sweep the conversation away. To stop it polluting Bear's mind or their time together. But she knows she has to give him a little. That it will only make him more hungry if she denies this is a part of his history too. "If he's good," she says.

"Will he be, d'you think? Good, I mean."

"Yes," Maia says, her spine running cold. "Me and Mum have been surprised he hasn't been let out earlier. He was incredibly charming. I don't think anyone would have believed how he treated Mum, if it hadn't been for what he did to Vihaan."

They speak his name as though they knew him. But it's not familiarity; it's a point of honor, an acknowledgment of what he sacrificed for them. "We mustn't ever forget that we only have our freedom because he died for us," Cora says. To Maia, it's always sounded like he was their own personal Jesus. They don't go to church, but every year on October 16, even now, they go to Vihaan's grave and lay flowers for him. Sometimes there are already flowers there, just starting to wilt. It's only as they've grown older that she's recognized the choices—crocuses, daffodils, peonies, dahlias, cyclamens—as their mum's favorites and realized she must come more often.

"Do you think he'll, you know, come after her? Or us?"

"Oh, Bear," Maia says. "It was all such a long time ago. And he's never tried to get in touch." These are the things she tells herself when she lies in bed at night. Or when she's walking home after dark, heart beating too fast, sensing him lurking, ready to grab her and whisper threats into her ear. But soon, she won't have the reassurance of knowing it's just an overactive mind.

Bear feels stupid for being melodramatic, but what happened when he was a baby feels so divorced from the life he's known that sometimes he finds it hard to believe at all. Recently though, he's found himself working through imaginary scenarios. His father's face at the window when he goes to close the curtains at night, even though their flat is on the second floor of a Victorian mansion block. A neighbor leaving the front door open, their father hiding beneath the communal staircase. The telephone wire cut . . . Sometimes he picks up the receiver, just to check. He knows they'll be told when there's a release date, but still.

Lately he's found himself wishing his mother had met someone. Someone thickset with a mean side that only shows if his new family is threatened. He's wondered about Aaron who comes to patch up the aging plumbing in their flat every few months, never charging his mum the proper call-out fee and sitting down with Bear to play a game of *Mario Kart* before he leaves. He's not noticed a spark between them, and he might be married for all Bear knows, but he's certain Aaron could handle himself if he needed to.

It's not that Bear thinks *he* couldn't handle himself too, just that he's never been put to the test. At school, if he sees someone being given a hard time, he steps in, and he's not sure why, but the bully always stands down without putting up a challenge. He wondered once if it was his dad; if they back off because they think Bear might have that same loose-cannon gene. Whatever it is, he's not sure his presence would have this effect on someone capable of murder.

He worries, too, about who he'll be if their father sought them out now. He's shaped their lives through his absence. What if his presence changes who Bear is, his sense of himself knocked off balance as easily as a scoop of ice cream from a cone.

"D'you think he'll have changed much?" Bear asks.

Maia shrugs. "So much of who he was came from being respected, from people looking up to him. I'm not sure what he'll be left with when he's not a doctor. If he's not living in some big, perfect house. It's like everything that made him *him* will have been stripped away."

"I went to see it one day on my bike," Bear says. "I couldn't picture us living there."

It makes Maia feel odd to think of Bear cycling across town to stand in front of that house—they'd moved to the flat near Mehri and Fern's just after the trial, before his first birthday. She thinks of his life as being relatively untouched by their father, but now she can see him, toes braced against the pavement to steady his mountain bike, looking up at the windows, filling in the gaps of what he knows with things that may or may not be worse than the truth. She wonders who lives there now and if they feel it. If they sense the violence of what happened there. Not just with Vihaan, but all the things before. "Yeah, the flat has always been more *us*," she says. "You shouldn't go there. To the old house, I mean."

"I'm not trying to dig stuff up. I just . . ." He trails off.

"Yeah, I know," Maia says, and squeezes his foot.

CORA IS GOING on a date. She sits in front of the small tabletop mirror in her room and twists the barrel of a lipstick to reveal an unspoiled dusky rose. She smooths its chiseled tip carefully across her lips and then stares at herself. At the beauty counter, surrounded by other women, it had seemed normal—fun, almost—but now it just strikes her as odd to be choosing a particular part of herself to highlight in this way. A neon arrow: *Here, this is where you should look.* She realizes her lips have come to feel as unsensual as an elbow or a knee and it startles her to think they might be expected to reawaken, to become something more.

"You don't have to kiss him," Mehri had said. "It's just a date. You go, you chat, you eat dinner together. It doesn't have to be anything more unless you want it to be."

His name is Felix. He has an open smile and curly hair that flops back into his eyes like a coil in a spring rebounding whenever he pushes it away. At forty-eight, he's only a year older than her and it reminds her how young she is, because he doesn't seem old at all. He wears a shirt of soft brushed cotton unbuttoned at the collar, and she finds herself aware of the small triangle of skin this reveals—fresh and creamy white. Warm, she imagines. Then the bob of his Adam's apple. The light dusting of stubble on his chin.

He's a vet and tells her about the animals and their owners as though they are characters from a book he finds particularly endearing. "It's odd, you know. My contact with people is through this singular prism, but it's amazing how deeply I'll end up feeling I know them. I see how they deal with stress and grief, how they cope when their pet becomes incontinent and starts leaving gifts on the sofa." His eyes crinkle at the edges. "Most of the time I'll never know what they do for a living, but I'll hear the way they talk to their cat as they lift it out of the carrier. There's . . . I don't know . . . a vulnerability in that. That they let me in." She can picture him there, with his reassuring smile. The animals' fear. The faint smell of disinfectant.

He refills her glass from the bottle of wine they've ordered, asks interesting questions. He is easy to talk to. She likes him. He is the type of person she could be attracted to. He is nice to her. Kind. And this is the sticking point. She's used to people being nice to her—her children, Mehri and Fern, Roland, the other gardeners at work—but those, she thinks, are interactions that don't have the same consequence. As Felix talks, she feels herself weighing each gesture, each sentence, as that of a potential partner, someone who she might let into her life. And as they talk, she realizes everything that tilts the balance in his favor upsets some other internal measure. She feels as though she has entered a funfair house of mirrors, where whatever is there in front of her may not be what it seems.

LATER, ON THE PHONE TO MEHRI, she tries to explain. "No man can win. If he's nice, it just feels like he's trying to charm me. When he asked questions, do you know what I thought?"

"That he was on a reconnaissance mission to find your weak spots."

"Yes. Saving them up to use against me later. I don't want a man who's horrible to me, but how can I trust a man who's nice?"

"Because most men aren't like Gordon."

"I know that logically, but it doesn't change the way I *feel*. Even though I know you—Roland—wouldn't have set me up with just anyone, but—"

"Listen, Roland knows this guy's ex. Felix is still friends with her. That's not the dating history of an abuser, is it?"

"Why didn't you tell me that before?"

"I didn't know. It was only while I was sitting here waiting for you to call that Roland said."

"You were worried about me?"

Mehri sighs. "No. Or maybe a bit. But only in the way I was when Fern went on a first date."

"I remember that. You fell asleep on the sofa after a bottle of wine and didn't know if she'd come in safely until the next day."

"She's still alive," Mehri laughs. "No harm done. He was a nice boy. Jake, or Joseph. Something beginning with J. But listen, Cora, I love having you all to myself, but it's not right. You deserve to be loved. And by someone good."

"You love me."

"Yes, but I'm not going to take off your clothes and ravish you. You need that bit too."

"I'm not sure I want that bit," Cora says.

"Of course you're not. You've locked that side of yourself away to focus on the children. But look, Bear's fourteen—he's off seeing Bees—you never know, by next year he might be spending the whole summer down in Brighton with her."

"You're acting like I don't have a life. This is too much for one night," Cora says. "I've been on a date and now you're—"

"I'm sorry, you're right," Mehri says, and they both laugh, and the conversation moves on to Mrs. Wilbur, Mehri's neighbor.

The next morning is Sunday. Cora wants to enjoy her day off and the quiet of the flat before Bear arrives home, but she knows she won't be able to switch off until she's dealt with Felix. And so she sits in bed at 7:30 a.m. and composes a text she hopes is friendly, but also makes it clear last night was a one-off. Her phone pings a couple of hours later.

> Hi Cora,
> Thank you for letting me know where I stand. I had a lovely
> night anyway.
> All the best, Felix.

And in his perfectly punctuated politeness, he is again both some-one who seems well mannered and kind, and someone she cannot trust. She glances at her watch. It's a few hours until Bear is due. She could look through the seed catalog she's brought home from work, put on some Tchaikovsky and stretch her muscles. These are all things she would normally delight in. But today, she's impatient to be serving lunch and putting on the washing machine with Bear's clothes from the weekend. She wants to settle back into just being *Mum* again.

Julian

It's a long time since Sílbhe last visited Cian's studio. As she walks around the side of the house, it is exactly as she remembers, but she is suddenly self-conscious, aware of the intervening years and how visibly aged she has been by the loss of Cora. Even though she feels younger in many ways, cast back to a different stage of life by second parenthood.

He opens the door. Sílbhe had forgotten he would be older too. She finds his kindness and warmth etched more deeply on his face, bracketing either side of his mouth.

"I'm sorry to have left it so long," she tells him.

"No, no. Don't be daft," he says. "You've been busy. I understand. Come in, come in," and then he pauses, an edge of nerves showing through. "Or would you rather go over to the house? Where would you prefer?"

"No, here's grand," she says.

He makes them tea and they sit around his workbench, her rain-coat still on, the tungsten glow of a desk lamp dazzling her. He switches it off, leaving just the overhead lights. "Sorry, it's a bit much. The eyesight's not what it was." He smiles sheepishly. "What brings you here, anyway—or is it just social?" He tilts his head, smiles; an open door letting her know that would be welcome. She feels guilty it's not.

"Well, social. But I wasn't sure if you might be able to help me with something."

"Oh, sure, go on," Cian says.

"It's my grandson, Julian."

"He's doing all right?"

"Yes, yes, he's good. He's like you—likes to use his hands. Art, woodwork, metalwork. That kind of thing." He waits for her to say more. "But he's—I don't know, he's not like the other boys. He gets along. He's not bullied especially. But he's different." She pauses, be-cause it feels too much to explain how his past has affected him; to admit that her impression is that he experiences life in grayscale, rather than allowing himself to become immersed in all its colors. That there's a flatness about him. Instead, she says, "Maybe it's spending so much time around his gran, but he's better with adults."

"Understandable," Cian says.

"I tried to enroll him on a course. At the Adult Ed. He wants to do silversmithing. But he's fourteen; they say the insurance won't cover him."

"So, you want me to teach him here?"

"I wouldn't have asked, but when I saw that you were the course tutor, I thought—"

Cian can see she's embarrassed, knows she's uncomfortable to be asking something of him after all this time. It can't have been easy, turning her life upside down like that. For two children she'd barely had any contact with.

He nods. That's all she needs to know he'll do it. And he doesn't want her to have to say thank you, to feel indebted, so he changes the subject. "And Maia? That's her name, isn't it? How old is she now? She must be twenty-one, maybe?"

"Twenty-three," Sílbhe says. "I used to worry she'd leave, go back to England, but not so much now. She's a homebody, not really interested in socializing or boys. She helps out with the little ones at her old ballet class once a week. Just pin money, really," she admits. "Her real job's at Doyle's down in the town."

"The sandwich bar?"

"That's it. She's a bright girl—all As in school—she could have done more. But it changes your perspective. I just want them to be happy. Or content, at least."

"Are you?"

"Am I?"

"Content?" he says.

"Me?" She laughs, surprised by the frankness of his question. "I don't know that I've stopped to think about it." They sit in silence as the water spills down the guttering outside. "I feel," she says finally, "as though I have a purpose. And I guess there's a contentment in that. Of knowing who I am, what I'm meant to be doing on this earth. What about you, Cian Brennan?"

"Oh, I'm right enough," he says, looking around his workshop. And he is. When he's working. When the hours are absorbed in shaping metal. But he's also lonely. He feels like time is passing him by. Like he's missed something. He thinks maybe they both sense this, but she doesn't press him further.

"Will I bring him here then?"

"An evening, or on the weekend. Whatever works best."

"A Tuesday?" she asks.

He nods. "I'll look forward to it."

"And about payment—"

He raises his hand. "It'll be good craic. No need for that."

She'd known he would say this and is already thinking through how she might compensate him. Wine, whiskey, a book voucher. She knew these things about him once, the things he might like, and hopes he still does.

From the first time his grandmother drops him off at the studio and he crunches across the gravel and sees the workshop through the window, Julian has a sense of being set alight. His mind whirs with possibility that lies well beyond his current skills.

When Cian teaches at the Adult Ed, he starts with a set project. Something that introduces the basics and brings an easily won feeling of achievement. But a few weeks in, he recognizes Julian's frustration and says, "Okay, draw whatever it is you want to make. List out the details, and we'll have you learning on the job instead."

All week at school, Julian fills the margins of his exercise book with sketches. He finds it hard to narrow things down. He wants to make everything. But, eventually, he settles on two free-hanging sweet chestnut leaves. The larger in silver, the smaller nested above it in gold. At first, he draws in all the detail—the veins and venules on display like a diagram in his biology textbook. But later, he imagines this piece sitting against someone's skin, and strips it back, retaining only the long, thin outline of the leaf and its central vein. He knows instinctively this is closer to the jewelry he wants to make. Lying in bed, he realizes he doesn't want the precious metals to be highly polished like the brooches and necklaces his grandmother's friends wear. Instead, he wants them matte, with a slight texture to them, like the surface of watercolor paper. He turns on the bedside light and adds this to his notes and sketches, and when he lies down again, his whole body seems to thrum, as though he is *too* alive, too charged, too vibrant, for sleep. That old wavery feeling inside given a new form; instead of worry and loneliness, sometimes—now—it's also excitement.

When he describes the piece, Cian listens and then studies Julian's plans and says, "It's contemporary, for sure, mixing metals how you have. I like it." The boy has a clear vision for what he wants, and Cian remembers having that same certainty when he started out. He feels a flicker of the old anticipation as he goes over to the shelf and pulls down some materials.

Over the next few weeks, they heat and cool, bend and turn, solder and hammer, weld and sand. In an English lesson, Julian's teacher shares a Sylvia Plath poem—"Morning Song"—and the opening line circles his head like the catchy lyric of a pop song. He can almost feel his insides ticking along like the fat gold watch when he thinks of being in the studio, with the tools in his hands, making something out of nothing; Cian suggesting he change the angle or switch to a file with a finer cut, seeing the difference it makes; a task that moments earlier had felt full of friction, suddenly tameable. He feels dizzy with it. This—silversmithing—this is love, he thinks. It has set him going.

Julian's sessions with Cian start to overrun. He goes over to the main house and rings his grandmother to ask if he can stay later.

"Back in time for dinner, though," she says.

"Okay. Cian offered to drop me home. You won't have to come out."

"Have you said thank you?"

He doesn't answer and instead says, "Will I ask him to stay for supper?"

"Oh . . . okay then," she says, embarrassed she hadn't thought of it, already mentally sorting through the vegetable drawer in the fridge, reworking what she'd planned to make when it was just the three of them.

That was how it was, that first time. A casual invitation that paved the way toward merging their lives, for there being one extra person around the table on Tuesdays, and then the odd Saturday. Later Sunday lunch and Christmas dinner, because why not? There was enough to spare, and he'd only be sitting at home alone.

For Cian, Sílbhe and her grandchildren are like a slug of whiskey making his insides burn with the sharp pleasure of human contact. Of being invited in from the cold. And for Sílbhe, she feels the regret of not having done this earlier, of having wasted time, because she can see how good his presence is for the children. Having another adult to rely on. Initially, Maia was wary, but she's warmed to him. And both begin to ask things of him—a lift into town, help putting the chain back onto a bicycle—sensing they can, and that he'll say yes.

One evening, Cian picks Maia up from work in a snowfall. It's years since he's seen the white so heavy. "I wasn't sure if the buses would still be running," he says as he pops the passenger door for her, "and I was in town anyway." She doesn't need to know he set his work to one side, shutting up the studio early once he'd heard the forecast on the radio.

The heater blows warm air around the car and fat flakes dance above the windscreen, before flattening themselves against the glass. Maia feels warmth, right to the core of her. "Thanks," she says. "This is great."

Later, as the car whines up the hill and he sits forward in the driver's seat, face up at the windscreen focusing on the bits of road he glimpses in the moment after the wipers have passed across, she tells him about work. About the regulars who come in and order the same sandwich every day. "Mrs. McCarthy from the hardware store. You know her?"

"Know of," Cian says.

"She went to pay this morning and said, 'Oh, look now, it's one of yours,' as she handed over a coin in sterling."

"Oh?" His eyes are still on the road, but she knows he's listening, guessing she has more to say.

"We get them every now and then. Rita doesn't mind exchanging them when the rate's in our favor, though maybe that'll change once we switch over to euros."

Cian turns the blower down a notch and it's quieter, the rush of air filling the space between them less intense. "I'll turn it back up if it starts to fog over," he tells her. And then, "You've mixed feelings?"

She doesn't say anything, only feels her eyes prickle unexpectedly.

He glances across. Sílbhe's told him the regulars call her the English Girl, and he wonders if she still hankers for home.

"Yeah. I'm just being silly, though."

He reaches over, touches her arm. "Small things like these, they're a connection, aren't they."

"I still miss her." Her voice splinters as she says the words. She wipes at her face with the scratchy wool of her winter coat.

"I only met your mam down in the town a time or two, when she was still just a wee small thing. But you know, Maia, if you ever get to wanting to talk about her—how you remember her, like—then I'd want to hear. Although staying quiet . . . she's just as much in your heart that way too, of course."

Maia smiles at Cian's tender awkwardness and at being given this opportunity to remember, to say the good bits out loud. "She was beautiful. And even though she never danced after—after she had us, she had this grace. You could just tell."

Cian only nods his head, so she goes on. "And she loved books. He didn't let her have her own, but she liked reading to me, my books. Every night before he came home. *Anne of Green Gables. Little Women. To Kill a Mockingbird.* She was still reading to me—to us—right up until the end. Whatever I chose from the school library. She never judged, never said, *Not this one,* or, *You shouldn't be reading that.* I can still remember it. That feeling of being read to, of being wrapped up in her voice, those words, whatever place the story had taken us to. It sounds stupid, but it was like a magic carpet."

"Getting away from it all for a time?"

"Yeah, as if we'd actually gone somewhere together. I mean, away from that house, from him." She stares at the flakes splodging against her window, at the gentle etching of Cian's reflection caught in the glass. "She was a good mum. She wanted the best for us. That's why she stayed." She wipes at her face again. "I hate that it's all—I was only going to tell you the good stuff. But it's all tied up with him. I never knew her without him. Or only for those weeks in the refuge."

"How was she then?"

"I can hardly remember. There were so many other families—women and children—crammed in. Some of them we had something in common with. Beyond *that*, I mean. But others we'd just try to work around. They weren't necessarily who we'd have chosen to share a kitchen with. And people weren't always at their best. Everyone'd been through a lot. Mum had someone to talk to about stuff while we were there—a case worker or something—but with us she was just Mum. I think she must have been scared, though."

"For sure," Cian says, shifting gear to slow for an oncoming car.

"I'd never really been scared. For myself, I mean, before that. But I was once we'd gone there. They came sometimes. The men. I don't know how they found out where their wives were, but they came and banged on the door and shouted. Not him, others. But I felt like he might, at any moment. Or that he might snatch me off the street on my way back from school."

"Was it just the once? That you stayed there?"

"Yeah. But then she got a letter. From the court or something. And she knew he'd probably get custody. So we went home and part of me was relieved."

Cian nods. "Understandable."

Maia focuses on the windscreen. On the snow and the white edge-less landscape beyond. "I was fourteen when it happened; Julian's age now."

"You don't have to tell me, you know," he says. "But you can. If it helps."

"How much do you know?" she asks.

"Not a lot. It wasn't reported in Ireland. And the internet wasn't about in the same way. Your grandmother told me a bit, but I didn't want to, well, you know, pry. But I hear her being interviewed on the radio now and again. Believe it or not, I have *Woman's Hour* on every morning in my studio."

He lets out a small chuckle and Maia laughs too. "I should've guessed."

He smiles. "I think a lot of men listen in, you know."

"What do you hear? What does she say, I mean? Grandma Sí-lbhe."

"She said the most dangerous time is just before a woman leaves, or just after. That that's the time when the—the risk to life is great-est," he says, not knowing how to tread around it, how to find the right words. "She said that's why women stay, because leaving a man like that is even more dangerous."

"He was always awful to her," she says. "But not like—I hadn't known what he might be capable of, until that night. We were in the next room. He'd put something in front of the door, so I couldn't get in. I couldn't get to her. I couldn't help her. I put my hands over Ju-lian's ears. But that meant I couldn't cover my own. So I heard."

Cian shakes his head.

"The sounds. Even now, I can hear them. They replay in my mind like a tape on loop. I don't know how he'd found out we were leaving again."

"He was a doctor?"

"Yeah," she says. And she knows the implication. That there were endless ways he might have found out. That his practice—his colleagues—may have even had links with the refuge, with caring for the women there. It's something she's often thought about. Her mother's situation was even more impossible because of what he did. Who he was. "Bastard," she adds, the word catching in her throat.

Cian has never heard Maia swear and his eyebrows raise involuntarily. He hopes she didn't see. "No word is too bad for that man," he says. "You can say whatever you want about him. I'll understand. Or try to."

A FEW WEEKS LATER, when Cian has left for the evening, Maia is clearing away the dinner plates and finds one of his cream Brennan boxes on her place setting. When she opens it, she lifts the satin cover and finds a thin wafer of silver, the face of a pound coin impressed upon it. She sinks down into her chair and stares at this beautiful thing resting in the flat of her palm. It is queueing in the school canteen; Mrs. Radley handing over babysitting money—hers, if only for a while. It is England, which is Mum and home. And now, it is Cian taking care—bending over his workbench to make something just for her. She looks at its intricate face imprinted with a rose, a leek, a thistle, clover. She's never studied the coin like this before. But there's a comfort in seeing it captured in the delicacy of this thing Cian has made for her.

Later, sitting on Julian's bed, she says, "Did you know he was making it?"

She holds it out for him to inspect, its chain falling between her fingers. He doesn't take it but concedes, "Yeah, it's nice what he's done. Just pressing it into clay silver like this. Stops it looking like a medallion, you know?" He doesn't say that he wouldn't want this. That he can't understand why she would either. He hates England.

"I'm so touched he made it for me." She runs a thumb across it, tracing the swell and relief of the markings. They sit, each with their own thoughts, until Maia says, "What do you think the deal is? Between him and Gran?"

Julian shrugs. "I don't know. Nothing, I don't suppose. He's just here, isn't he."

"I think they make each other happy," Maia says.

Julian bends the wire of a paperclip, flexing it as far as it will go without the brittle metal snapping. "I guess. Aren't they too old, though?"

"What? To be happy? To be in love?" She pokes him in the ribs. "She's sixty-seven, she should have a life apart from us, you know."

He brushes her away. They don't have that easy draw toward fun she imagines regular siblings might have. There's a seriousness in how they are together, and her moment of mock playfulness—of pretending to be someone else—leaves her feeling stupid.

She yawns self-consciously, then stands to leave, and Julian can tell he's hurt her. "Sorry," he says.

"It's okay," she replies, not turning back. "Night."

"Love you," he says, when she's at the door.

"Yeah, you too," she says, but Julian can almost hear the sadness in her footsteps as she retreats down the hall.

Maia's words about Cian and Sílbhe stay with him. And as he works away in Cian's studio, thoughts drift in and out of his mind like water along the channels around a sandcastle. The hours rush by like minutes. He wonders about what they were like when they were younger, before his grandmother married. He wonders how it would change things to have Cian become a more central part of their lives. And realizes he's already integral to their day to day, and he's okay with that.

A couple of weeks later, before he knows he's about to speak, he finds himself saying, "Will you be marrying her? My grandma?" He regrets how possessive the *my* sounds, and adds, "Sílbhe, I mean." He knows the flush of Cian's cheeks without looking up.

"Have I done something to upset you? Overstepped?" Cian asks.

Julian shakes his head. "I just mean that it would be fine with me. If you did. With Maia too."

"Oh," says Cian. "Well, thank you very much. That's good of you to mention it." And then a few moments later, "But I think your grandma might have something to say about that."

"Aye, you'd need to ask her," Julian says, a smile hovering around his lips as he squeezes a band of metal between pliers.

Gordon

Maia follows the registrar from the room. His pager is going, and he frowns at it before checking his watch and striding off down the corridor. "Mr. Davies, can I have a word?" Maia says, trying to keep pace with him.

"It'll have to wait. I'm late for a surgery and I have precisely three minutes to eat my lunch before I scrub in." He looks at her then, as if wondering for the first time who she is and what she's doing there.

"It's about your last patient, though. I don't think it can wait." He sighs as she trails him along the corridor toward the canteen. It's only the fourth week into her placement on Obs and Gynae and Mr. Davies is already known for making the residents cry. "When you were asking if anything could have happened to have brought it on, I noticed her partner squeezing her hand."

"You're interrupting my few minutes of peace to tell me she has a supportive other half, Miss—"

"*Dr.* Atkin," she corrects, "I'm a house officer. But, no, I think he was encouraging her not to say anything. There's dried blood in her nostrils; she has watery eyes, dilated pupils; and she was irritable when you considered keeping her in."

Mr. Davies stops and turns to her. "And your point?" he says, checking his bleeper again.

"Placental abruption can be caused by substance abuse."

"I'm well aware."

"I think that might be an issue here."

"Okay. I don't have time for this. But if you think that's what's going on, get the lab to check her urine and delay her discharge."

"And if it is?"

"Let Sister know, and she'll make the relevant call." Maia nods, and as they walk away in opposite directions down the corridor, he calls out, "Good obs, Dr. Atkin." And she feels as though she's received praise directly from God.

THE ROOF GARDEN is really just a wooden bench, a plastic chair, and a plant pot of soggy cigarette butts, the surrounding hospital blocks obscuring any view over London, but Maia gravitates there whenever she's on a break. A bank of lockers obstructs the external door, so she and some of the other medics have taken to climbing through the staffroom window, although it's not until she's out, when turning back would be awkward, that she can see if anyone is already there. Today it's Kate, another house officer.

"Are you okay with some company?"

"Yeah, although I'll be gone in a minute."

"Oh, I can go back in," Maia says. "I don't need to interrupt your time."

"No, no," Kate smiles, waving Maia forward. "I mean, I really do have to go back in a moment, but until then I'd love the company."

She holds out a packet of Marlboro Lights, which Maia declines. Kate's appearance seems at odds with the cigarettes; her face is like a Pre-Raphaelite painting—rosebud lips, cheeks flushed pink, hair falling in heavy auburn waves.

"I just helped deliver baby Portobella," Kate says, smiling as she exhales a stream of smoke, and Maia sits down beside her. "A naming first for the hospital, possibly the world."

"Really? I bet she'll be a fun gal," Maia says.

"Yeah," Kate laughs. "She's actually cute as a button."

"I see what you did there."

"Oh, that was accidental, but I'm sure she's in for a lifetime of it."

It's only then Maia realizes that in the few sentences they've exchanged, she's misrepresented herself; she rarely makes jokes. But something about Kate makes her offer up a bouncier version of herself.

"I'm Kate, by the way."

"Maia. I think we were both at St. Thomas's on our last rotation, but our paths never really crossed."

"Really? I'm sure I would have remembered you," Kate says, arching an eyebrow.

Maia is surprised by the unguarded flirtation. Sometimes it's hard to read signals from other women, but in this exchange, there's a rare certainty. Maia smiles. "I think my best line was, 'You go, I can take the next one.'"

"Getting into the lifts?"

"Yeah."

"Well, thanks, belatedly," Kate says. She stands, winding her hair back into a bun, smiling down at Maia. "Would you fancy a drink tonight? I finish at seven."

"I'm not out until eight."

"I can wait."

"Great," Maia says, and then cringes at the idea Kate might think she's rhymed with her reply deliberately.

Kate turns back and grins, and Maia notices the way her nose wrinkles as she does.

Maia sits on the bench in the sunshine and wonders why she's acted like a fool in the few minutes she's spent with this woman, and if Kate will still like her when she realizes Maia is not all light-hearted banter and puns.

She wonders, too, if Kate will instantly guess the reason if Maia suggests somewhere other than the pub around the corner, and per-haps decide she doesn't want to be involved with someone who isn't out yet. Sometimes she thinks it would have been easier not to have followed her father into medicine. If she'd chosen to exist in an en-tirely different world.

BACH'S CELLO SUITE NO. *3* is in the CD player and when it comes to an end, Gordon takes a hand from the steering wheel and points to the glove box. "Before I forget, there's something in there for you."

Cora rests her fingers on the catch and pauses until he nods that she should go ahead and open it. Inside, there's a CD, its cover obscured by a Post-it. *For Cora, with love x,* written in Gordon's neat script. She lifts back the note. It's Grieg's *Peer Gynt* suites. She holds the case to her chest and sighs.

Gordon smiles. "Put it on. It's the fourth track," he says. "In the Hall of the Mountain King." It's a selfless gift; he loathes the mincing theater of this piece. Early in their relationship, he referred to it as the Disneyfication of classical music. Orchestral junk food. *Jesus Christ, Cora! Even its own composer hated it. It was meant to be satire!*

To Cora, though, it's the "Sugar Plum Fairy" with backbone and a little more edge. She sinks into her seat to listen, shuts her eyes, and sees the velvet burrow of the auditorium, feels the burning white of a stage spotlight. Her limbs tingle with imagined movement. Gordon takes a hand from the wheel again and rests it on hers.

When the piece finishes, he clicks off the stereo and they drive the last few miles through the Cotswolds countryside in silence, Gordon only taking his hand from hers occasionally to change gear. She blinks behind closed lids—a clamshell on tears that have appeared from nowhere; on the sadness that comes after the last note and not knowing when she will hear this again. And the longing for this scene to be as it seems. Just a man and a woman, in a normal marriage, doing normal things, so simple they might almost be taken for granted.

At the hotel, they leave their luggage and Gordon takes Cora's hand as they go to join the other couples already having drinks just off the lobby.

The wives welcome Cora in and affectionately protest not seeing her more often as they embrace. She knows they socialize without the husbands in the months between these annual gatherings. And that over the years, it has become accepted that, for whatever reason—her comparative youth, introversion, ballet (which everyone still seems to assume makes up some part of her life)—Cora will not be there. They don't seem to hold this against her. Instead, they treat her like a rare butterfly, accepting these moments when she is amongst them and appears, however briefly, to dazzle. Gordon once told her a butterfly's average lifespan is twenty-nine days. She wonders, when she adds up these moments where she exists out in the world, if her lifespan will be any longer. And which would be better? To have those days boiled down into one intense burst of color, or to have the pin removed from the thorax every now and then, dusty wings fluttering back to life, a little more time eked out before being locked away again?

Someone has ordered afternoon tea, and as Cora bites into a scone layered with thick clotted cream and strawberry jam, its sweetness causes her to close her eyes for just a second. When she opens them, Gordon catches her eye from where he's sitting further down the table with the other husbands, and raises his glass to her. She feels wrong-footed, as though the last step on the stairs has arrived before she expected, but she smiles, and for a moment, before they return to their conversations, it is just the two of them.

The women are discussing a book they've read, and Dorie tells Cora she finished her copy on the journey, that she'll drop it in with her later. The conversation moves on, but Cora's thoughts snag on whether the rules will change here, if she and Gordon might sit up in bed, side by side, reading companionably before sleep. Perhaps she could finish the book before they go home. She looks back at Gordon, who is now engaged in conversation with the men. He is laughing; he looks happy, relaxed.

In the afternoon, they set out on foot, first down quiet country lanes and then across fields toward Broadway Tower. Gordon drops back and walks with the women, and Cora can tell they're enjoying him seeking out their company and asking questions about their lives. He is only adding to their already-high opinion of him. A few years earlier, in barely hushed voices, gathered around an end-of-the-evening table, the other women had declared him to be the ideal husband: attentive, accomplished, impeccably dressed, athletic, a good father. Someone who has a way of making whoever he speaks to feel special. The sort of face you instinctively trust. Kind eyes, an open smile, good-looking, but not dangerously so. Cora had listened, blinking. Because, yes, all that is true.

"Basically, we're all in love with your husband, Cora," Dorie had said.

Another laughed, "And our husbands are probably all in love with *you*." But Cora knows that is just a kindness; she is a blank, a void.

The field above them is defined by peaks and troughs running parallel, cascading down its length every six feet or so. "Now what do you think caused that?" Dorie says to no one in particular, and Gordon tells them how the land would have once been divided into strips to be worked by different families, and how ridges and furrows formed through repeated use of non-reversible plows. Cora lets herself lag behind, imagining this space full of people, a seventeenth-century allotment. She notices how the sun catches the rise and fall of the grass, making the crest of each ridge shine brighter like waves of hair and the sheen of one hundred brushes before bed. But then Gordon is shouting. He is running toward her and, for a moment, she doesn't know what he's going to do when he reaches her. He is charging her, and she stands frozen, waiting for impact. But it doesn't come. Instead, he is scooping her up—"Come on, slowcoach!"—and he is carrying her, spinning her, whooping, as he sprints to catch up with the others and her arms are around his neck and she is laughing with relief as a blur of buttercups and undulating fields streaks past her eyes. She sees it from above, from the front. Through other people's eyes. Through the click of a shutter. There, honey on toast.

They climb Broadway Tower. Inside the old stone folly, the rooms are small, and Cora makes sure to stay near Gordon or one of the women; to not put herself in a position where she could end up alone with one of the other men. She looks at the view across the hills, down over the small town of Broadway, which nestles at the bottom. And she wishes she could stay up here forever.

They are warm-limbed and glowy-cheeked by the time they get back to the hotel and fall onto easy chairs to recover, before returning to their rooms to change for dinner.

CORA PUTS ON makeup in the bathroom mirror and Gordon stands beside her to shave, and for a while they talk to one another's reflections. "I saw you enjoying that scone earlier," he says, and she smiles, remembering the moment he'd caught her eye. But then he adds: "Might be an idea to rein yourself in at dinner," as he looks her up and down in the dress he's picked out for her to wear.

She takes a tissue from the glass box above the sink and turns away to dab at her face, trying to avoid smudging her mascara.

"Come on, Cora. It's not an unreasonable thing to say with your family history." A second invisible knife. Her father's fatal heart attack when she was seventeen, and the guilt he knows she still feels.

After his death, she'd stayed on in England for a few days, not wanting to give up a hard-won role in a new ballet. A decision she quickly regretted. At night she'd lain awake trying to picture her father bent over his vegetable patch dibbing seeds into the soil with an earthy finger. She could conjure his shape, but the image evaporated as she failed to summon the clothes he wore. When she'd gone home for his funeral, she'd opened a cupboard one night and asked, "Is there Ovaltine?" Her mother had apologized. "Oh, no, sorry, Daddy hasn't drunk that in years." And she realized her father's evening routine had changed and she hadn't been there to notice. Her memory of him outdated long before his death.

Gordon stands behind her, wraps his arms around her waist, and, for a moment, she thinks perhaps he's just been tactless, but then his palms settle one just above her abdomen, the other just below, in an instantly familiar pose. It is how pregnant women intuitively place their hands against their swollen bellies. He pats the space between. *"Bonne Maman,"* he says, kissing her neck. And he smiles at her in the mirror, raises an eyebrow, delighted that even the brand of jam seems to be colluding with him.

Someone is knocking. He slides his hands away, pats her bottom, closes the bathroom door behind him.

It's Dorie, with the book she'd mentioned earlier. Gordon is thanking her, making polite chit-chat, telling her Cora is in the shower, as she stands, side-on to the mirror, studying the way the dress skims her stomach.

AT THE RESTAURANT, they order enough dishes to share around the table and, while they wait for the food to come, Alice tells them about an Enneagram course she's been on that maps people into nine different personality types. Cora is interested, but the men set in straight away, eager to knock it down before they know anything about it. *People can't just be boiled down into nine neat types. Is it actually any more scientific than star signs? What could you possibly do with that information anyway?*

But then Gordon says he's been reading up on something similar that divides humans into sixteen personality types. "So, a few more, but both models sound like they have their roots in Jung's work. To be honest, I was skeptical initially, but some of us took the Myers–Briggs test at the practice and it was surprisingly accurate in pinpointing our work styles," he says, rotating the stem of his wine glass between thumb and forefinger. "It's helpful when it comes to, you know, understanding how a colleague might see something—it makes conflict less personal."

The conversation wanders off into recruitment profiling and Jeremy tells a long story about a headhunter, as Cora sinks back into herself, wishing their talk would turn back to personality types.

When the food arrives, they help themselves and pass things back and forth up the table. She's careful to put only a little onto her plate, Gordon's words still buzzing in her ears, but then he is saying, "Come on, Cora, you eat like a sparrow." She looks up, confused, as he begins ladling on extras, making a show of piling her plate high.

"And let me help you to some of this dhal too," he says, sinking the serving spoon deep into the curried lentils.

"Stop," she says in frustration, putting a hand on his wrist.

It is the lightest touch. The tips of her fingers barely making contact with his skin. But his reaction suggests she used force, his arm careening into a glass of wine and causing one of the other men to dive forward to stop it from tumbling.

Gordon stares at her, his facial expression reflecting her own surprise. And, for a moment, the dinner table falls silent, their friends frozen, all eyes on Cora. Her cheeks flush and she looks down, embarrassed and furious. There is no point trying to explain. It would only make her look worse.

It is Gordon who breaks the silence, feigning rescue. "Well, who doesn't know their own strength sometimes? It wasn't intentional, was it, darling?"

Agreement, strained laughter. Then everyone remembers a polite interest in their own plate and absorbs themselves in the task of gathering food onto fork tines. Finally, the relief of being able to exclaim over the flavors, which eases the way for someone to throw out a conversation starter, some stilted, irrelevant thing the others can grasp onto and spin out until they find a way back to the natural gait of the evening. But, mentally, they are already in their own hotel rooms, earrings on the little shelf beneath the bathroom mirror, watch placed carefully on the bedside table, saying, "Well, that was weird," somehow now more ready to turn to one another in the crisp cotton sheets and the comfort of their own imperfect relationships.

Usually when their parents go away, Maia stays at the house. But Gordon is nearly fifteen—old enough to take care of himself for a few days. He's done his homework, eaten one of the ready meals straight from its microwaved container, munched down a family-sized bag of crisps, and, later, he's going to "a gathering." He's not sure exactly what that entails, if it will be just a few people, or a proper party with alcohol and girls. But he knows Lily is going. She's the reason he's been invited. He sits next to her in maths and lets her copy his answers. "Thanks, Atkin," she says. And there's something about the way she says his surname—slow and deliberate—that feels like she's airing a bedsheet and letting its billowing softness settle over him. Her intonation—At-kin—like *at peace*. He's not used to people treating him like he might be someone gentle, someone worth getting to know, but he likes it. He wants to return the favor, to say her surname—Atkins—in the same way, but somehow the *s* changes things. And anyway, he prefers *Lily*.

On Thursday, someone in the row behind had said "Oi!" in mock whisper, causing them both to turn around.

"Not you, gimp," Alfie had said to Gordon.

"Don't be mean," Lily had said, turning to see what Alfie wanted.

"I'm having a little gathering at le weekend, Lily. Wanna come?"

"Maybe," Gordon had heard her say.

"Is that a yes or a no?"

"Is Gordon invited too?" He'd heard Alfie sigh, heard one of his friends sniggering into his arm.

"I s'pose. If he wants," Alfie had said.

"Do you want?" Lily had asked, turning back to their desk.

"Oh. Er, okay then."

There are still two hours until he meets Lily. He paces from room to room with no purpose. It's rare for his mum to be out, for her not to be quietly busying herself elsewhere in the house. He's not sure why that should be so oppressive, but somehow it is, and he celebrates her absence by scuffing a giant rainbow-like arc across the recently vacuumed carpet. After a while, he goes through to the kitchen, opens the pantry door, and looks at the top shelf where his dad keeps the spirits, which are only brought out on the rare occasions they have people over for dinner. Gordon scans the labels, unsure of what to pick, until his eyes catch on his own name. *Gordon's Gin.* He places his hand on the dark-green glass and takes the bottle from the shelf, feeling an odd delight, a connection. "Come to Daddy," he says as he unscrews the cap, instantly feeling stupid and relieved no one is around to hear. He lifts it to his nose and takes a sniff. It smells like the fir trees at the bottom of the garden. He brings it to his lips and drinks.

It's unpleasantly medicinal and if it didn't have his name on, he'd put it back and try something else. But since it does, he tries again, then shakes his head, letting his cheeks go slack so they make a *wb, wb, wb* sound as he tries to rid himself of the taste. After a few more swigs, it starts to seem more palatable, and with his head nicely fuzzy, he's less anxious about the night ahead. He holds the green glass up to the light. There is still plenty left, so he puts it on the hall table by the front door, deciding he'll take it with him to drink with Lily on the way to the gathering.

He meets Lily on the corner of her street at eight o'clock. She looks different out of uniform. Older, but also sweeter. She has on a flowery skirt and Doc Martens, and her black hair is in two plaits. They should look childish, Gordon thinks, but on her, they just look sort of cute.

"Nice hair," he says.

"Thanks."

"Look," he says, opening his coat to reveal the bottle tucked into an inside pocket and lifting it so she can read the label, "my very own drink." She laughs and he's not sure whether she's laughing at him or with him. But when he says, "D'you want some?" she nods and moves closer. She dips her head and gently tilts the bottle inside his jacket. She giggles and he notices her hair smells of apples. He breathes her in and feels like he might lose his mind. Especially when they start to walk and she catches his hand in hers.

When they arrive at Alfie's house, a boy from his history class answers the door. "Aye, aye!" he shouts to no one in particular. "It's Lily and the gimp!"

A cheer goes up from somewhere inside and as they walk down the hallway, Lily says, "He's just jealous," and squeezes his hand. Gordon lifts his inside pocket to his mouth and takes another swig all the same. He doesn't know where the cap is, but it'll be okay, as long as he doesn't do any cartwheels.

In the living room, there isn't enough space for everyone, so Gordon sits on the arm of a sofa and Lily rests against his leg. And somehow it's like a door opening. As the other boys talk, they occasionally make eye contact, and he knows the conversation is intended to include him too. "What d'you say, Gord?" one of them asks later. "Three smokes for help on my history essay."

It takes a moment for Gordon to understand what he means, and he finds himself saying, "Yeah, sounds fair," even though he doesn't smoke.

Later, he and Lily go outside. As they move away from the lights of the house, it's hard to tell where the garden ends. Enormous bushes punctuate the lawn like great looming boulders. Gordon trips in the dark and Lily asks if he's okay. He feels warm and woozy from the alcohol and being so close to her. When they reach a tree well away from the house, he pulls her to him, puts his arms around her neck, and kisses her.

Her lips are softer and more cushiony than he'd expected, and he likes it when her tongue ventures a small way into his mouth. He does the same back, and it takes a while to feel like he's doing it right, but somehow, with Lily, that feels okay. They stand, tongues exploring, one of them occasionally changing the angle of their head, which makes the kissing feel suddenly different, as if, even though it's one long kiss, they've reached a new part. Sometimes their teeth clash and he can feel her smiling, which makes him smile too. Sometimes their lips touch only lightly and other times it feels like they're stuck together with treacle, almost like they're trying to eat one another. They kiss soft and then hard. And when he backs her up against the tree and presses his erection against her, he moans into her mouth, even though he hadn't meant to. They kiss and he grinds and the voices from the house seem far away, while the one in his head is loud and euphoric: *You're doing it! You're actually doing it!*

He puts his hand on her thigh, beneath her floral skirt, and at first, she doesn't stop him. She is still kissing him. He moves his hand, edging toward her underwear, and she squirms away slightly and says something into his mouth. He's not sure what, though, and all he can think of is how he wants to put his fingers inside her, to know what she feels like. In one fluid movement that's somehow quicker and easier than he'd anticipated, he pulls aside her knickers and his fingers find their way to her fleshy warmth. She tries to push him away, tries to break off their kissing, but he just wants a moment longer and so he presses his lips onto hers more forcefully, pushing her head back against the tree trunk, keeping her mouth covered with his own, even as she says muffled words into it. He'd never realized how strong he is before. Even as she tries to move away, he's somehow able to hold her there. He wishes she'd stay still. Wishes she'd just carry on with the kissing, like she'd been doing a few moments earlier. But she is struggling, trying to get him to stop, and eventually his booze-soaked brain catches up and he realizes he should let her go. His fingers catch on knicker elastic as she breaks free.

"What the—"

"I'm sorry. I just thought—Don't be mad," he says.

They stand looking at one another in the darkness. He thinks she might be crying, but he's not sure. He reaches out to comfort her, and thinks, just for a moment, that it might be okay. That they'll walk back inside together, hand in hand. But instead, she says, "Don't ever come near me again, Gordon Atkin," and runs away across the grass.

Her words don't feel like a soft, billowing sheet anymore, and he feels a flash of anger. He stands for a moment, not knowing what to do. Then he brings his hand to his face, subtle, as though he might be brushing something away, and sniffs at his fingers. He inhales. He's always wanted to know what girls smell like down there. And now he does: sort of rich and musky. She can't take that away from him, at least.

Inside, there is no sign of Lily, but the boys let him into their conversation easily and he stands, nodding and laughing.

"Where's she gone?" one of them asks after a while.

"Who?"

"Lily."

"Oh, I dunno," Gordon says.

"I thought you two were together. Earlier?"

"Nah," Gordon says. "She's a bit of a slag to be honest."

"I wouldn't turn 'er down."

"You ought to," Gordon says, "she stinks down there."

"Urrgggh!" they all chorus, bending double with laughter. He can see a mixture of shock and delight on their faces and one of them gets him in a headlock, ruffling his hair with his fist. "You're all right, you are, Gord." And just like that, he is one of them.

Seven Years Later

2008

Bear

In the brief intermission between dissertation hand-in and graduation, Bear goes home to paint the rooms of the second-floor flat where he's grown up. A spontaneous visit, after Cora mentions taking a week off work to redecorate. "I'll come back," he'd offered.

"Oh, wow! I'd love that," she'd said, the smile coming through in her voice.

The windows are open and the freshness of outdoors mingles with the scent of wet paint, making the room shimmer with newness. With their eyes on the back and forth of their rollers, the conversation is easy and the silences the same. But still sometimes Cora has to bat away the thoughts that momentarily warp the room with a rising horizon of saltwater. *Remember this.* Yes, he's been away at university all this time, but he's still relied on her meager financial assistance, still come for the holidays around visiting Maia in Brighton. Their home has remained the anchor in these transition years toward adulthood. But soon, his career will take him away for good. First to an excavation at Khirbet Safra in Jordan, and then, who knows?

She wants these things for him. But still, a part of her craves folding him back into herself, having his small, dimpled hand in hers again. In Maia's. She suspects that, to be a good parent, she must pack away the mothering part of herself into a box and gently close the lid on it. She had not realized this is what would be required of her, had not seen it coming. And yet she will do so willingly. *Would you lay down your life for your child?* the world silently asks. Yes, she's done this. But she hadn't known there would be a second reckoning, where this would eventually mean laying down the arms of motherhood: caution, foreseeing, checking, reminding, nurturing, openly caring. Because a switch has been tripped, and rather than keeping the child safe, if left in sight, her love might implode. Might overwhelm him. So, she must seek to diminish her own presence in Bear's mind, make space for others to move into the foreground. What will be left of her then? she wonders, and immediately chastises herself for the thought.

She tries to imagine how Lily might feel. But she doesn't ask Bear, doesn't want to pull levers of guilt that don't even belong to her.

"Are you ever scared?" Bear asks.

Cora is surprised by the question and keeps painting, comforted that in this moment they're each focused on their respective patches of wall. "You mean of him?"

"Yeah," Bear says.

"No, I don't think so. Not anymore. I google him every now and then. Just to keep tabs on where he is."

"Me too. But I haven't found anything."

It squeezes at Cora's heart to think of him doing this; she likes to imagine Bear's life is untouched by Gordon. "You wouldn't have known his parents' address. But he's on the electoral register there. In London. He has been for a few years. Divine justice, perhaps," she adds, and then regrets it.

"How d'you mean?" Bear knows bits and pieces from Maia, but he wants to hear it in his mother's words.

"Just that he's not likely to be having much fun there. I think you were four or five when we finally stopped seeing them, but if you'd got to know his father, well—it probably explains a bit about what he was like."

"In what way?"

Cora pauses and then decides it's probably safe to reveal these details; it's not right to expect Bear to exist in total ignorance. Not now he's an adult. "His father, he was this amazing surgeon. A brain surgeon. He's retired now, but he did all this groundbreaking work. And Gordon was meant to follow him into that. But when he was on his surgical rotation, they realized he had an essential tremor."

Bear stops painting and turns to her. "A what?"

"Uncontrollable shaking. In his hands," Cora says. "It's not uncommon in surgeons and usually they can treat it with medication. Beta blockers or something. But that didn't work for him and so he went into general practice. And his dad couldn't deal with that."

"What was the problem? He was still a doctor."

"There's a hierarchy in medicine, and to a brain surgeon—one like Gordon's father, at least—a GP is almost like a glorified waiting-room attendant. They can refer patients on, order tests, prescribe, but it's not the same as having someone's brain under your knife and restoring the power of speech. His dad genuinely believed he was God. And that his son was a failure. When they'd visit, he'd say, *Ah, it's Dr. Gordon,* which was a dig, because as a surgeon he was a Mr. And he'd put out his hand and then say, *Sorry, I forgot. No need to shake your hand after all.*"

"What?"

"Meaning it was already shaking."

"Seriously? Couldn't he do something if he was this big-shot surgeon, though?" Bear's roller is dripping paint onto his socks, but he doesn't notice, and Cora chooses not to say anything.

"That was the weird thing. When we first met, he said it was an essential tremor, which is neurological. And that was how it was viewed by the medics. But it seemed more of a psychological thing to me, because it didn't exist outside of an operating theater. I watched him thread a needle once and his hand was solid."

Bear winces. Bees once told him their father used to patch up the damage he'd done rather than taking their mother to a hospital. But he doesn't feel able to mention this, even opaquely. He's already surprised his mum has spoken as freely as she has. "D'you wonder if he'd have been different? If his dad had been, I mean," Bear says.

"Yes. It's probably hard to imagine, but in some areas of his life, I really think he tried to do good. His patients thought a lot of him. And he was pretty forward-thinking in the way he ran the practice."

"It's kind of reassuring. To know it was his dad, and not some genetic thing."

Cora sees the flicker of uncertainty pass across his face and says, "Oh, Bear, you could never be like him."

"I know," he says, himself again. "But you can't help wondering. I'll be standing in a queue feeling impatient with the person on the checkout—how they can never seem to find the barcode—and I'll start thinking, *Is this it? Is this that bit of him?*"

Cora laughs. "Everyone feels impatient in queues. Really, Bear, you couldn't be more different."

They go back to their painting. The light is fading, and the color is darkening on the walls as it dries.

"Can I ask you something?" Bear says. He tries to keep his voice casual, as though he's not been steering their conversation to this point all along. "What happened? That day. What was the thing that made him lose it?" He's asked Maia several times and she's always said she's not sure. But then she doesn't sit and wonder with him, which makes Bear think it's because she already knows.

Cora's shoulders tense and her mind momentarily floods, wondering which way to jump. She engrosses herself in the wall and is relieved not to be looking at Bear when she says, "It could have been anything—there was always something making him angry. Just small things, like the television being left on standby or dinner not being ready on time."

Inside, she wavers, unsure if this is the right approach now, although she and Maia have always agreed this is a burden Bear should never have to carry. And it's not something she wants to reveal on impulse.

"So there was nothing more specific?" Bear asks.

Cora's neck prickles under his gaze. *He knows,* she thinks. *He knows, and I'm still not going to tell him.* "Not that I can remember," she says.

Bear doesn't say anything. He doesn't want to press her; this has never felt like his wound to reopen. But he thinks back to a day a few months earlier when he was applying for funding. How something had made him pause when he'd caught sight of the date his birth certificate had been issued: October 16. He'd looked at the black ink of the registrar's pen, the relevance of that particular date coming into focus. It was the same as Vihaan's death. The same date they'd visited his grave each year for as long as Bear could remember. He'd folded the certificate away into his desk drawer, but the coincidence rolled around his head like a marble. And then, a few weeks later, he'd been riding his bike home from campus and had come to a stop at a red light and, as his foot touched down to the road to steady himself, he'd had the thought. Yes, his name was Maia's choice, but why would a man like that have agreed to break with tradition and call his son Bear?

FOR THREE GLORIOUS weeks it's the summer of odd hours, waking at 2 a.m. and going to bed in the late afternoon as Bear and his flatmates keep time with the Beijing Olympics. It's a full-time job and they barely leave the house or make proper meals. Bear can't recall who bought the pack of bamboo skewers, but he already knows that when he looks back on this time, it will partly be defined by the foods they threaded onto them above the low coffee table. Small squares of takeaway pizza cut with blunt scissors, pressed alternately against pickled onions; the salt-on-salt of folded salami slices interspersed with olives; a boiled egg sandwiched between spinach leaves.

"Why does it all taste so much better on a stick?" they marvel, eyes glued to the screen.

When Lily has handed in her dissertation and finished her stint volunteering at the Fringe festival, she takes the train down from Edinburgh to spend the rest of the summer with Bear, where days flutter from the calendar as though caught by a gust of wind—twenty-fifth, twenty-sixth, twenty-seventh, twenty-eighth, twenty-ninth, thirtieth—and gone. On the final night—his lease up, his belongings stacked in boxes by the wall ready for Bees to collect in a hire car the next day—they lie in bed. The window is half open and outside Bear can still occasionally hear groups of students walking past in a scuffle of half-caught sentences and the beery rip of a too-loud voice. It is the kind of night where even at 2 a.m. warm air wraps around bare shoulders. The kind of night where the sense of ending and possibility is as heady as the jasmine that sprawls beneath the window ledge.

"Are you awake?" Bear asks.

"Yeah. Are you?"

"Yeah," he says, each sensing the other smiling in the darkness. "What will we do?"

"About what?"

"You know."

"I didn't think we'd make it this far, but we have. Do we really need a plan?" Lily asks.

"It feels unfair not to. I mean for you, at least."

"Because I'm the one who's staying? Or because you want a clean break?"

"The first."

"Just go and do your digging then. I'll be fine."

He smiles again and squeezes her hand beneath the sheets. He likes the way she teases him, makes his painstaking archaeology work sound like a dog burrowing into sand at the beach.

"But it will never be any different. There might be a few weeks between digs when I'll be back. But mostly—"

"You think—"

"I mean, I could get some cultural resource management work over here—stopping a build if we find something of interest, with some antsy developer breathing down my neck. But it's not what I want."

"Can I speak?"

"Sorry."

"I don't know what *I'll* be doing yet. I might be back home, or in Edinburgh if the Fringe job comes off. But I'm also thinking of applying to work abroad."

"You are?"

"Yes." She doesn't tell him that although she wants these things, she is partly driven by a wish to show him she has a life of her own, that she's not trying to pin him down. It isn't the right reason for pursuing something, but the result is that her life is opening up, becoming bigger by trying to fill the shoes of this independent woman she knows he will love. Does love. Has loved, since they were fourteen and were put next to one another in maths. Atkin and Atkins. *We're like our own pharmaceutical company*, he'd said.

When they left for different universities, they'd made no promises, but in that first Christmas break, they found one another in the pub on the first night home and slotted straight back together. They never asked what the other got up to in term time. If there was anyone else. But for Lily, at least, there had been no one. Just a lone experimental kiss with a girl on her course—Celeste's lips had surprised her by being so much softer than Bear's; she thought about those lips a lot. But she didn't think of Celeste. Sometimes boys walked her home after a rehearsal or bought her drinks in the subsidized bar, holding her gaze a moment too long. And by way of reply she would look away.

And Bear. Bear went out briefly with a history undergraduate, paid to throw shapes on a podium high above the other clubbers, like a messiah leading them in drugged dance as sweat trickled down their torsos and plastic cups of water were downed and then crushed beneath their feet. He'd liked her lean body, that she was so ready to be looked at.

But when she stayed over, she would say, "Pass the remote, babe," putting her hand out for a controller that was just as easily within her reach as his. And somehow, as he leaned forward to hand it to her, he was aware this was not something Lily would do. And that he didn't want this other incarnation of a girl. The pattern repeated several times, a wallpaper to those years. There was the chemistry student who laughed too loudly and whose hair smelt of isoamyl acetate instead of apples. And the girl on the Silchester dig in Reading, whose eyes sparkled when she talked about the midden layer of earth, the concentrated darkness speckled with archaeological treasure, but whose frame felt like a mismatched jigsaw piece when she first pressed it against Bear's at night. *Hang on,* he'd said, gently maneuvering himself on top of her, confused when that, too, felt wrong.

In the summer between their second and third year, he met Lily at the station when she arrived home from Edinburgh and the feel of her hand in his, the way she kissed him and, later, the way her body dovetailed perfectly with his, the exact kind of nothing and everything they talked about when they were together . . . it all felt right and inevitable. He didn't mention this to Lily, not wanting to extract some urgent commitment from her. But he stopped turning to other girls and expecting them to be her.

"So you're happy to leave things how they are?" he says.

"Yes. Are you?"

"Yeah," he says, and each feels the other smiling in the darkness.

HOME FROM THE AIRPORT, Cora, Maia, Sílbhe, Mehri, Fern, and Lily stand crowded around the doorway looking at the still-life of Bear's room. Already, a dust seems to have settled over his things. They lean against the doorframe, against each other, quietly surveying. It is a clash of boyhood and adulthood, never quite updated to reflect the latest version of himself at twenty-one. Finally, Mehri says, "Look at us. All pining over that boy. God, it's been glorious, hasn't it?" And everyone knows exactly what she means.

They eat pizza and watch *When Harry Met Sally* . . . It's not as good as anyone remembers and they talk over it and wonder what time of day it will be when Bear lands in Jordan.

At midnight, Lily walks back to her parents' house, a ginger tom mewling for attention as she nears home, dashing between gardens, always reappearing in a driveway just ahead of her. "Night, puss," she says, giving him one last stroke before letting herself in. She goes upstairs and sits on the edge of her childhood bed. She feels a profound emptiness. And in the bluish light of her moonlit room, the realization that Bear may never truly be hers seems cast in stark relief. He's not the only man in the world, she tells herself. Someone else will want to share a flat, a cat, a car, a house, children, a dog, a life together. But then, even a little bit of Bear seems better than none.

The next day, Lily is offered a paid position planning the following year's Edinburgh Fringe. She turns it down. She needs to leave too. Not just their hometown, but her university city as well. It's just too painful to be left behind. And so she applies for a role assisting a professor of Romantic literature in Rome, and far sooner than she'd expected, she is there.

She and Bear keep in touch by time-lagged texts and emails that ping at odd hours. Lily does not tell him about her neighbor, Davide, who resets the ancient fuse box in the corner of her living room when the lights go out, and who presses her against the wall and runs his hands up her thighs beneath her skirt, whispering her name— *Giglio*—in Italian. She doesn't feel guilty and nor does she feel it signifies an ending with Bear; it's all she can do to cling on to some self-respect, to cope with the fact of knowing Bear may never be ready to settle down with her. When Bear writes, she tries not to notice the girls' names that crop up increasingly often. If there is a threat, she tells herself, it's more likely to go unnamed. And so, she focuses on the things he does mention and tries to get a sense of his day, of what he will be doing at any given moment. She knows he eats watermelon for breakfast because they are cheap and plentiful. That he rises at 4 a.m. because it's too hot to work on site in the afternoons. That they cover everything over each night with huge tarpaulins, but still creatures get in and carry the earth from this decade into excavated areas 10,000 years old. She and Bear give the creatures nicknames and joke about his unwinnable battle, and she tells him about the Italian slang she is learning and about her clumsy foreignness. "It is just so mortifying to be English!" she writes. He feels it too. At the weekend, away from the dig site, he wanders around Madaba, soaking up the sounds and smells, and the Arabic, which floats across the city streets with its vowels that catch softly at the back of the throat.

After a few days without communication—when Lily stops work to refresh her email every few hours, and then every few minutes—Bear resurfaces and lets her know he's had amoebic dysentery. He emails a photo captioned, *Back to work, finally.* She studies it. He is holding a hand trowel, looking almost impish. His face is partly in the shade of his sun hat, but from what she can see, he is gaunt, and his T-shirt appears suspended from his shoulders as though on a clothes hanger. *Let's stop this*, she thinks. *Let's go back to England and do safe, normal things.* But her work is going well, and she knows she could never suggest he abandon his dreams.

MAIA AND CHARLOTTE have not been together long. Maybe four or five months, and they are still in that heady phase where they manipulate plans to squeeze in more time together and where everyday things feel exciting simply because they are in each other's company.

"Come along tomorrow," Charlotte says one Friday evening, threading her long fingers through Maia's. "We're restoring the most beautiful old water tower and the steels have just started to go in for this huge two-story curved glass extension."

Maia knows she wouldn't ask if it might appear unprofessional, but as she draws Charlotte's knuckle to her lips, she says, "Would it be odd?"

"Odd? No, the client is working in Amsterdam all week, so he's just grateful I'm willing to do another weekend visit. And this one's last minute because his builders have messed up." She shifts her position on the sofa. "But the main thing is we'll have the drive. Three hours there and back. We've never been in a car together."

Maia likes the idea of going on a journey with Charlotte. Of sharing that liminal space between A and B. The side streets around their flats in Brighton are too overcrowded for either to want to own a car, but Charlotte's architect firm has a few that the partners pool for site visits.

"Will there be snacks?" Maia asks.

"In the car?" Sometimes, like now, Maia finds herself saying things just to see Charlotte's sleek black hair quiver at her jaw before settling back into place, along with her composure.

"Yes," Maia says. "I'm imagining how good roasted edamame would be. All those little grains of salt getting stuck in the folds of leather around the gearstick."

"Oh, for goodness' sake," Charlotte laughs. And she leans over then, their lips meeting, her body pressing against Maia's, causing the cat to abandon its place between them.

THE FOLLOWING MORNING, when they are nearly at the end of the road, the seafront already sparkling into view, Maia regrets not packing her book. She asks Charlotte to wait while she dashes back.

She wonders later, if she'd remembered the first time—if she'd decided not to go back at all—whether she might have avoided crossing paths with him.

In a crowd, in a city, she is always looking for him. She sees the back of his head, his profile, his gait, in the form of every middle-aged man he might conceivably have morphed into during the decades since she last saw him. It makes her heart race, as though life—the world—is always on the verge of unleashing a grenade on her. But today she is not looking. She is lost in the easy lull of their conversation; in the way it feels, as the cars on the motorway slow to a halt, for Charlotte to place her arm across the passenger seat like a second seatbelt. This small action as instinctive as braking itself.

They sit. Five minutes, then ten, until finally a lorry in the lane beside them rumbles into action and pulls forward. "I hate that," Charlotte says. "That thing where it feels like you're suddenly going backward."

"I remember reading something about it. That it's an optical illusion to do with your brain using the things around you as spatial reference points. So our lane of traffic is staying still, but for a moment your brain . . ."

As she says this, Maia turns to look at the car beside her, and even as she carries on speaking, she is thinking, *Is it? It can't be.* She is so used to being proved wrong. But, as if he senses being watched, he turns and, for a moment, their eyes lock and they are staring at one another. Incomprehensibly. As though there might be a fault in the panes of glass that separate them.

Maia wants to look away. To duck. But just as much to keep him in her sight. "Lock the doors," she says to Charlotte.

"What?"

"Lock them! The doors!" she barks, feeling frantic, reaching to check if the button beside her is down.

He has turned his whole body toward her now. He is looking right at her, shifting in his seat, as though he might be about to get out. She jumps at the half-click of the mechanism and Charlotte's voice: "They were already locked. Why do we—" But then she is interrupting herself, "Oh, this looks promising," and they're moving forward, the car containing Maia's father seeming to roll backward. His face—its expression—already changing, as he realizes he's being left behind. And a second later, he and his car have disappeared from view.

As their lane of traffic gathers speed, Maia presses an imaginary pedal to the floor, willing them to go faster. "For God's sake, can't you just—"

"What would you like me to do? Ram the car in front?" Charlotte sounds more bemused than anything, as though dealing with a child. "Here," she says, leaning over to open the glove box. "I know you were just teasing me, but see how much I love you? Snacks."

Maia ignores the packet of edamame and turns to monitor the traffic. And when she doesn't see the silver of his car—at least she thinks it was silver. But was it? Her memory floods with possibilities. Perhaps it was blue, black even . . . It could be any color. It could be all the colors—the road courses with danger, every car now a threat. She sits low in her seat, flattening herself against the backrest as though attempting to compress her entire being into the leather, waiting for impact, waiting for him to chase them down. They're moving faster now, the car gaining on her heartbeat. Thirty miles per hour. Then forty. Blood hammering against her chest, making her want to vomit panic and fear all over the dashboard.

Charlotte puts a hand on her knee. "Are you okay?" And Maia brushes her off. Instinct. The metal chassis immediately transparent, because if he were to pull level, if he were to cruise alongside them, he would see. He would know. And he would be disgusted by her.

DURING THE SITE visit she sits in the car like a sullen teenager—book closed—reliving those few seconds over and over. She conjures her father's face, anxious she's distorting the image with each replaying. She was nine when she last saw him. He is grayer now—older—his features etched more deeply with lines. But anger, shame, regret . . . ? It's impossible to tell. And did he definitely recognize her, or might she have changed beyond recognition? But surely even he would always know his own child?

His expression morphs each time she pictures it. Sometimes he is benign, sometimes stern, almost maleficent. A word so close to magnificent, she thinks, sent off-course by maleness. But his expression is irrelevant. Far more important is the question of where he was going. And who might be waiting for him at the other end.

Charlotte and her client come back into view. It's not until later, on the drive home—when the day is already ruined—that Maia will tell her everything.

Julian

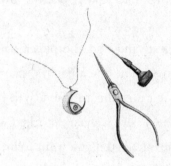

Each morning, as Julian walks down the corridor to his studio in the Old Chocolate Factory, he glances through the small internal windowpanes, absorbing fragments of each space. Some are so overwhelmed by a chaos of tools and mess that the artist inside looks almost dwarfed by it, as though their work threatens to consume them. Others are more orderly, with a discernible workflow: cutting table, industrial machines, bolts of fabric, pattern pieces strung from giant butchers' hooks.

The old factory hums with the sound of banging and drilling, with the whir of machinery, but Julian detects a quietness amid the din, and after a few weeks he realizes it is the relative lack of voices. Like him, people are mostly in their own heads, absorbed by whatever work is in their hands. There is an unspoken etiquette: music confined to headphones; cups of tea offered only if a door is left open;

not standing to watch one another as they work. Julian keeps his door closed but imagines himself as part of a hive.

Taking a space here hadn't been his idea but Sílbhe and Cian's. "Will you be looking at the garages they've converted down in the town?" his grandmother had asked, putting a newspaper in front of him.

He'd shaken his head and slid the paper back across the table without stopping to look. "I'm fine at Cian's, thanks."

But a few weeks later, driving to the city to hand-deliver orders to the different jewelers where they are stocked, Cian had said, "You know, Jules, I shan't be offended if you want to branch out, be around people your own age. We'll still see each other back at the house in the evenings, like." Julian didn't say anything, and Cian added, "Just a thought."

Even though Sílbhe had already laid the foundations, Cian's words were unexpected, and Julian felt them as a soft deflation inside his chest, like air being gently eased from a hot-water bottle. "Maybe I'll see what's about then," he'd said.

He knew his life had become more isolated since he left school three years ago, but he hadn't felt he was missing out on anything. His friendship with Connor and Liam had never revolved around common interests. Instead, they'd been forced together by what they didn't do. They didn't snap girls' bra straps or throw things at the teacher's back when she turned to write something on the board, and when they were no longer forced to participate in Gaelic games during their Leaving Cert year, all three defected. For Connor and Liam, it was because they disliked the cold and mud, and the way the teachers shouted them down even as some strapping yoke twice their size sent them flying. For Julian, it was more complicated. He was solid enough, and he liked the way his body felt springy and alert as he chased down a ball, but he found himself unable to put in the tackles, slowing or veering off at the moment he should have jostled against another boy's shoulders. The PE teacher bellowing from the sideline, "What are you like? Cop on and stop worrying over getting hurt!"

When Connor and Liam muttered their indignation in the changing room, Julian grumbled along. Because it seemed less shameful than the truth: that he was afraid of hurting someone else. When school ended, they'd kept in touch on Facebook, but Julian predicted they probably wouldn't meet again in real life and after a while he deleted his profile. He has business accounts on a few social media platforms, but he doesn't put much time into maintaining them. He has enough work from Cian's contacts and word of mouth. Cian tells him he should aim higher, that he should be approaching stockists in London. But the idea of sending his pieces across the Irish Sea gives him a sinking feeling. He hasn't been back to England since he was five years old. It's the land of his father; the land that failed to keep Julian, Maia, and their mother safe.

"Your Grandma Sílbhe, she worries. Wants to make sure if us oldies were to, you know, that you'd have people about." They'd both smiled at that; it's an ongoing joke that his grandmother will live forever. At seventy-four, she's the fittest she's ever been. She wakes at half-five each morning and leaves the warmth of the bed she shares with Cian, pulls on leggings that sag against her bird-like frame, and runs a six-mile loop around the surrounding fields, back to make breakfast before anyone else has even stirred. One day, as Julian was doing his accounts at the kitchen table, someone interviewed on the radio compared the act of running to a wish to escape something. "Will you listen to that," she'd scoffed. "I'm running *toward* my life—the three of you—not away from it."

Julian had smiled, not knowing quite what to say.

Sílbhe had continued, "When you start, they say focus on something in the distance, like a telegraph pole or a gate, and run toward it, and then when you get there, set yourself a new target and run toward that. I used to picture your next birthday, or one of you bringing someone home for the first time, and I'd run toward that."

"Please tell me you're not still waiting for that to happen!" Julian has almost given up believing a girl might take an interest in him.

Sílbhe had laughed too. "Any day now. But like I was saying, on a slow day, it's more of the same. Then on others, I'll look around and I'll get this—this elation, you know? Like, look at this magnificent sky and those trees and this grass. And if that isn't the most marvelous thing, I don't know what is. I think about your mammy too. About what she was like as a little girl. And what she went through later."

Then she'd busied herself with turning the bread under the grill.

Julian's own memories of his mother are blurry. Somehow, he remembers more of *him*, as though fear had impressed that presence on him more deeply. The memories of his mother feel untrustworthy, as though he might have constructed them around things Maia has told him. But when "Lucy in the Sky with Diamonds" comes on the radio, he feels sure he can remember his mum substituting the name with some variation of his own. Juley, perhaps. He has an image of grabbing at dust motes in front of some patio doors and her, kneeling just behind him, telling him to make a wish. Another time, he's sitting on her knee on a picnic blanket, and he can almost touch the warm cotton of her blouse. He remembers a kitchen—blue lino, cream cupboard doors—her shielding him behind her skirt, the soft texture of it, and the sound of shouting, before Maia took him by the hand and led him away. He doesn't know if that was the day it happened.

He knows his mother was beautiful. The evidence is in the photo frames dotted all around the house, but somehow that only seems to make her more unknowable, like some Hollywood actress who died tragically young. He tries to imagine wrinkles onto her smooth skin, flecks of gray into her hair, thinking that if he could picture the person he would have known now, it might make her more real. But it doesn't. He thinks it's probably harder for Maia, who knows what she's lost.

There's a girl at the studios. It was her artwork he noticed first. Huge wall hangings that remind him of the patchwork quilts his grandmother's friends make, but instead of fabric, the tessellating pieces are cut from battered yardsticks and the kind of old wooden rulers he remembers from school. The geometry of the shapes, how they interlock, the way disembodied inches and centimeters mark the surface, makes him want to stop and look for longer. But whenever he walks past, he's aware of a small blonde figure bent over the workbench, and only allows himself to slow briefly on the way to his own studio. After a few weeks, she begins to look up when she hears his footsteps. "Hey," she calls out.

"You all right?" he calls back, his words mistimed, skittering off into the dark nooks of the corridor as he continues walking.

He will hear this phrase later echoing around his head as he buffs an edge smooth or hammers a disc of silver to replicate the perfect melon-balled recess of a doming block. The words will not be drowned out by the scritch-and-bang of his tools but amplified and played on repeat until they cease to have meaning and become even more ridiculous to him than when they first left his mouth. He starts to dread these brief daily interactions.

But then, one day, when his arms are full with a delivery of new supplies he's just collected from reception, she appears at his door.

"Julian?"

He sets the packages on the workbench. He is thrown that she knows his name. She seems to pick up on this and says, "I recognized your boxes," nodding to the shelf where they're stacked, each one bearing his name in embossed lettering. "I have a piece——" He looks at her neck, then at her hand. She laughs. "It's not on me. Don't want to fangirl you—it'd be like playing Ronan Keating his own music. Not that I'm into Boyzone . . ." He doesn't say anything, so she adds, "I wear it a lot, though. Or did, until you got here. It's a necklace—a gold hoop with a silver bar across."

He knows the piece. "Oh, *Balance.* That's what it's called. Technically," he says, and feels pretentious for having mentioned its name, as though he takes his work too seriously. "You might not know that unless you bought it through the website, though." He is waffling and they both know this.

"I got it at Pears," she says. The jeweler's in Dublin was one of the first shops to stock his work. He nods, deciding to pull back from saying anything more because it can surely only make him seem even more awkward than he already does.

"So, Julian the jeweler," and he notices a dimple appear as she says this, then finds himself focusing on the smoothness of her cheek, waiting for it to reappear. "A few of us are going to the pub later. I—*we*—wondered if you fancied joining us."

"Oh. Ah." He runs through the reasons why he can't in his head. That he'll have to let Sílbhe know he'll be late for dinner. That the next episode in a series he's been watching is on tonight. But his reasons sound lame even to him, so he hears himself saying, "That'd be grand."

She smiles and the dimple reappears. "I'll knock for you. You all right to finish around five?" and as she goes to leave, she adds, "I'm Orla, by the way."

There are only four of them at the pub—few enough for one conversation, rather than splintering off into groups. He's glad of this, although he soon realizes it's not the kind of chat he's had to feign enthusiasm for with Connor and Liam: sport, cars, sports cars. Instead, the conversation feels familiar, as if a reflection of his own thoughts has grown wings and fluttered out into the world. Frap is telling them about a problem with a globe he's developing that can be spun in any direction on a double axis, so even the North and South Poles can be studied. Balancing the sphere of plaster so it always returns to rest in an upright position is proving trickier than he'd imagined and they discuss its weighting and what might be throwing it off. And then the conversation moves on, and Orla is telling them about a film set in Morocco, where a tiled floor in a mosque has sent her work on a whole new tangent. She finds a screenshot on her phone and they discuss how she'll deal with replicating the center, where the tips of a sixteen-pointed star converge. In the mosque they have grout between the pieces, which allows for imperfection, but Orla will want her slivers of wood to butt up against one another perfectly, meaning each must contain a precise 22.5-degree internal angle. There is an understanding between these people who work with their hands. They come from different disciplines, but they are all able to envisage the potential issues and apply knowledge from their own field to someone else's.

A few weeks earlier, Julian had come across a 3D-paper artist based in Ann Arbor, Michigan. Something in the geometry of his work had reminded him of Orla's and he finds himself showing it to her now. She pinches the screen to zoom in. "Wow," she says. "That's amazing." They scrutinize what the man makes and discuss whether he's laser-cutting the shapes.

Julian notices that whenever Orla becomes animated or wants to make a point, she momentarily touches her hand to his arm, his knee. It seems unselfconscious and he wonders if she does this to everyone. Frap and Seamus are across the table, not close enough to receive these casual touches, so it's hard to know for sure.

LATER, AFTER HE's watched the episode Cian thought to record for him, he goes up to Maia's room in the attic and asks her. "You think I'd know because I'm, what, female?" She laughs, but it is not an easy laugh. "Maybe if I'd touched more men's arms, I wouldn't be a thirty-year-old spinster still living with my grandmother."

They sit in silence for a while and Maia looks like she might cry. Julian isn't sure why he'd assumed she'd know. But her response unsettles him. Up to now, he's never really considered if she's happy with her life.

He's about to say something, but when he opens his mouth, Maia interrupts. "What's she like then, this girl? Apart from touchy-feely?"

He wants to say that she's bold. That she seems to realize he's trapped inside his own awkwardness and doesn't take that as a slight. She seems curiously fascinated by him, as though he might be one of the shapes in her artworks that needs puzzling into place. And although a part of him is uncomfortable with the attention, another part of him craves it. But he doesn't say this to Maia. Instead, he offers a non-committal, "Oh, just nice, you know."

JULIAN STARTS TO LEAVE his workroom door open more and finds he likes the interruptions, the setting down of tools to go to the refectory for a cup of tea. It's open to the public, but there's always someone from the studios in there too, and the combination of people he finds there changes each time. And he realizes he's comfortable with any of them. It's surprising, but also very . . . ordinary. If Orla is there, he finds himself drawn to her and tries to balance out his attention, forcing his eyes toward Frap or Gráinne. He observes Orla in snatched moments, waiting for her dimple to appear. He knows now she is tactile with everyone, not just him, and not just men. He is relieved. And disappointed.

IN EARLY AUGUST, rain falls heavy from the crack of dawn, lashing at the windows of the Old Chocolate Factory. Around lunchtime, Julian hears the sounds of people locking up their studios early. Seamus puts his head in before leaving. "Don't stay too long," he says.

"The drains are starting to overflow. The corner of Lower Geraldine and Mill is already underwater." Julian isn't worried. It's already rained so much this summer; they're used to seeing the end of their street collecting the run-off where the two roads meet at the bottom of a hill. Julian is immersed in his work—a new piece that looks like a small, hammered satellite dish in gold, a diamond mounted off-center in a polished silver setting that he's been refining all morning. As the afternoon slips away, he is vaguely aware that he rarely hears cars sloshing by in the road below, only the percussion of rain against windows. Besides that, there is an almost unnatural quiet. He works on, only taking a break when he feels his back cramping. Then, he goes to the window and sees the street below is a river, and when he cranes his neck to look right up Dooley Street, a driverless car appears to be floating across the junction. He's had his phone on silent and when he takes it from his pocket, he finds several messages from Sílbhe letting him know the river near home has burst its banks and the road will be impassable until the water level drops.

He will be fine here, he decides, as long as he has food. He goes down to the refectory and finds the building empty. The lights in the canteen are off. He's never seen it without customers before.

On the counter, cakes sit beneath glass domes. He leaves some coins on the side and maneuvers a wedge of carrot cake onto a plate, then sets it down on a table and sinks into the old church pew behind. With the first bite, he realizes how hungry he's become, and he is head down, forking up the crumbly sponge, when he hears something. He looks up to see Orla. Her jeans are saturated darker blue from the thighs down, and her Converse squeak with water against the cement floor. "Mother of God, it's wet out there," she says.

"You don't say," Julian smiles.

"My car died when some eejit in a four-wheel drive roared past and sent a tidal wave under it. So, I'm back."

He puts his fork down. "Will I help you move it out of the road?"

"No, I'll just hope it's still there tomorrow."

"How did you get in without flooding the place?"

"The door at the back. It's five steps up," she says. "Although the water's already up to the fourth."

She sits on a bench at the next table and starts to unlace her trainers. Julian realizes she is probably planning to take her jeans off too.

"I'll cover my eyes," he says, laughing gently.

"You've got a sister. It's just a pair of legs."

But where Maia's are soft and dimpled in places, Orla's are firm and smooth. He finds his attention drawn to them, covertly, between mouthfuls of carrot cake, which he is no longer hungry for, but continues to eat to distract himself from the undressing.

"Will I get an apron for you?" he asks, nodding toward the kitchen.

She pauses. "Like one of those hospital gowns, all demure from the front but turn around and . . . no thank you!"

Julian laughs.

Back upstairs, he puts her jeans and socks over the radiator in his studio and shakes out the scratchy gray blanket he keeps rolled up behind his desk to dampen the sound of hammering. He gives it to

Orla, who is sitting with her back against the old Victorian radiator, with those legs—those perfect legs—knees up, in front of her.

He stands by his workbench, and she says, "Will you make something for me? Can you do that? Make something in just a few hours?"

"What would you like me to make for you, Orla?"

"You decide. But tell me what you're doing. At each stage. So I'll know how it's been made."

He goes to the shallow shelves where he keeps the metals and then turns back, assessing the tone of her skin, although he knows it already. "I'll use mainly silver," he says, taking down a small sheet, "because it'll suit your coloring best."

"What coloring do you think I have?"

"Cool," he says, and he tells her to look at the veins on the inside of her arms. "People with warmer skin have greener veins, but yours will be purply-blue."

She studies the inside of her wrists and nods but doesn't look at him. He feels as though he's just run his finger along her skin, even though he's on the other side of the room. He wonders if she feels it too.

He talks to her as he works. Explains each stage, like she asked. "The blue tip is the hottest part of the flame," he tells her, as he adjusts it, "but we just want to gently warm the metal, so I'm using a more bushy, yellow flame."

"A fox-tail flame," she says, and he nods.

He tries to make his tone normal, workaday, but he can't help feeling as though his explanations are an odd form of seduction. As though there is an intimacy in her asking him to share these things with her. She is attentive, occasionally asking questions, but mostly she listens, and at some point, Orla and the blanket and the legs beneath leave the radiator and come to sit beside him on the wooden swivel chair that he'd brought over from Cian's when he first moved in.

"Annealing softens the metal," he tells her, his voice lower now she's closer, leaning in over his work. "Do you see the rainbow it makes?" He quenches the hot metal in cold water, drops it into the pickle solution to bring out its shine, files the edges smooth. His actions are repetitive, reassuring, predictable. Soften, bend, sculpt, hammer, smooth, rub, cool toward hardness again. Repeat.

It's grown dark outside by the time he has polished the piece to a gleam, smoothed its edges, attached crimps to the back to hold the chain in place. He hands the finished necklace to her, but rather than reaching for it, she moves her hair aside. He goes to stand behind her and lowers the chain down in front of her face, onto her neck. He sees the fine downy hair that continues beneath her hairline, the bony nodule at the nape of the neck exaggerated by her lowered head. He tries to fasten the necklace without touching her skin, but he is sausage-fingered and nearly drops one side of the chain. He hears the sound of his own breath as he focuses on catching the jump ring on the clasp's open arm. "There," he says when he finally does, the word coming out like a sigh of relief.

She spins the chair a slow half-turn to face him, one foot down on the wooden floor, one leg exposed from the blanket. She feels for the front of the necklace, runs her fingers across the hammered curve of it, then lets it fall gently back into place, just below the pit of her neck, exactly where he'd intended it to rest. "Thank you. It's lovely," she says, and the dimple appears.

He is not sure where the evening should go when she already has her trousers off and he's made her this piece of jewelry. But either way, he senses an expectation. From her. From himself. From the situation.

He excuses himself and walks down the corridor to the loos. He places a hand on either side of the basin and looks at his reflection in the mirror. He is not unattractive, he knows that. But somehow, he lacks the confidence he feels should go with this face. It's as though it belongs to someone other than him and he feels sure another man would wear it better. Holding their jaw strong where he carries it weakly. Maintaining eye contact where he lets it drop. He washes his hands, more for something to do than out of need. He feels the soft warmth of the water on his skin, the foamy slick of soap between his palms. It's easier to focus on these things than the girl who is sitting half dressed in his studio, waiting for him to return.

When he finally turns off the water and looks at himself again, his thoughts are clearer. He likes working here. He likes the new easiness he feels within this community of artists. He likes Orla. But to preserve it, he must shut down whatever it is that's been unfolding between them. There are things about himself—his family—that feel too hard to reveal.

When he enters his studio again, her back is to him. The blanket has been abandoned on the swivel chair and she is standing at the window. He lifts his eyes and sees her reflection watching him in the black of the windowpanes.

He goes to the radiator just to her left and takes her jeans from it. They are crispy and stiff, so he gently shakes them out, trying to encourage air and softness into them, and then he hands them to her. "They seem dry enough to put on now."

He registers her surprise and his insides contract with the realization he's hurt her. They both look away, but not before he sees her cheeks flush from white to red, so quick, it is as though someone has slapped her. He feels her embarrassment as she slides her feet into the cardboard legs of her jeans. He hears it in the curt zip of the fly. In her quick, barefooted exit from the room. In the friction of her saw down the hall, cutting through wood, and the long yawn of the night. And he is sorry. Sorry as he sits at his desk, motionless except for the tips of his fingers, which aimlessly push the discarded chips of silver and gold around on the desktop. But he feels sure it must be better this way.

WHEN DAWN COMES, Sílbhe stands at the window. The fields beyond the garden look lush, but she can see from the shallow pool on the flagstones that they will be waterlogged and she's likely to twist an ankle, or worse, if she heads out for her run. She lets the curtain fall closed and climbs back into bed. Cian stretches out an arm. "I like it when you stay home with me," he says, and she allows herself to be pulled into the warmth of his body, knowing Julian is not in the room next door to hear and that Maia is up in the loft they converted last year. She never wishes them away, but still, she is grateful for these fleeting moments when she and Cian find themselves alone. It has been six years, but their romance still feels new.

Later, Cian puts on his slippers and goes through to the kitchen.

He brings back a pot of tea, a plate of toast and honey. Sílbhe rests back against his chest as they eat, and they laugh at the quiet decadence of covering the duvet in crumbs and the luxury of having found a home in one another.

UPSTAIRS, IN THE ATTIC, Maia sits in bed with her laptop on her knees. She is seven years off her mother's age when she died. And it is only recently, after something Jules said, that she's felt an urgency to fill her life with the things her mother could not. She doesn't mean traveling the world or bungee jumping from planes, but the small everyday things her mother never got to experience. Maia is a favorite at Doyle's, but lately she's felt her life slipping away, realizing she's watched children of twelve or thirteen age and become mothers themselves, pushing a pram through the door with their mothers, now grandmothers, beside them. And while their lives have changed and evolved, shuffling roles between the generations, Maia's has stayed the same.

In early spring, Maia began getting off the bus a few stops early. Stepping down onto the gray tarmac and watching the retreating vehicle become a dot on the landscape before she started to walk. Craving putting one foot in front of the other and the space to think that offered. She found herself noticing the blackbird's courting dance, the glossy yellow flowers carpeting the steep banks beside the bridge, the wash of tiny blooms appearing in the fields to either side of the road; things her grandmother had always pointed out, but somehow Maia had never really seen. Yet their names came to her then. Cowslip. Dog violet. Star of Bethlehem. She'd bent down, the weight of her bag unsteadying her as she studied its white-green petals nestled amongst the lush grass.

That evening, hunting through a cupboard for cotton buds, she'd caught sight of the small bottle of Rescue Remedy she'd once carried in her school blazer. She unscrewed the lid, inhaled the rich scent of preserving alcohol. Her grandmother had given it to her soon after they'd arrived from England. "Just four drops whenever you're having a bit of a wobble and it'll calm your nerves," she'd said. And somehow, whenever she was away from Sílbhe's side, the gentle burn of those droplets hitting her tongue offered all the comfort of a St. Christopher. In the bathroom, she turned the bottle to read the short list of ingredients: Rock Rose, Clematis, Impatiens, Cherry Plum, Star of Bethlehem. *Star of Bethlehem.* The name giving rise to the odd sensation that comes when something rarely thought of appears, and then reappears, in quick succession. As though the universe is pulling at your sleeve, telling you it's significant.

She'd searched the internet, following links like bread crumbs through a forest. From Bach Flower Remedies, to homeopathy; from headlines claiming placebo, to articles explaining its theory; from local practitioners, to four-year training courses . . .

The following day, when the driver set her down by the side of the road, she walked until she came alongside a patch of grass dotted with Star of Bethlehem. She bent, brushed her palms across its petals, hoping for a sign. From the universe. From her mum. But there was nothing, just her own self-consciousness. She stood and gazed across the landscape. Vast in its openness; small in its familiarity. She didn't crave a big life . . . but she wondered if, within the confines of what felt safe—her grandmother, this terrain, Ireland—she might crack open the door on something new.

Now, upstairs in the attic, she checks her email and watches as unread messages cascade onto the screen. Most are sales emails she never signed up to, a few Facebook notifications, but in amongst them is the one she's been waiting for. The one she'd been told she could expect around the tenth. She hovers the cursor over it, and then clicks it open.

> Dear Maia,
>
> We're delighted to confirm that you've been successful in your late application to join this year's cohort at the Irish School of Homeopathy, where you'll begin your first year of study toward becoming a qualified homeopath . . .

When she's read the email and scrolled through the pages of attachments, she puts the laptop aside, gets out of bed, and stands in the dormer window. She scans the landscape, letting her eyes settle on the wavering line where blue-gray meets green. And even though floodwater stands in the fields all around her, for the first time, she feels as though she's ready to go somewhere.

Gordon

Gordon knows his father and grandfather sought satisfaction in the gristle and bone of the human body, but he's seen what happens if you can't beat, or at least draw level with, the top dog of the family, so he leaves medicine to Maia, and quietly sidesteps into the respectability of numbers. He ushers them into every part of his life, appreciating the logic and order of them. He finds comfort in the twist of a Rubik's Cube. In the grid of a sudoku puzzle with a timer set to two and a half minutes. The shuffle of letters and digits on the seesaw of algebra. The 1s and 0s of technology's underlying binary. The security of 256-bit advanced encryption standard. The precise language of computer code:

```
var c = new System.Security.Cryptography.SHA256Managed();
byte[] hash = c.ComputeHash(Encoding.UTF8.GetBytes(s));
```

When he's home for the holidays, he leaves lines of undecipherable code open on his desktop, hoping his father will see. White, yellow, and blue text against black, rendered in serious monospaced font. These are the tools of his trade: his scalpels, his forceps, his retractors. Sometimes he scrolls back and forth, letting the line numbers blur as his clean, honed code flashes by. That he understands what is impenetrable to others, has written every bracketed, semicoloned line of it, makes it beautiful. And the brain of the computer proves it as it works through his commands, produces the intended result, and says, *Yes, this makes sense. You are God.*

But when he tells his grandfather that his degree has landed him a place at one of the big banks programming algorithms that can make trading decisions in the blink of an eye, he looks as though the scent of something unpleasant has just passed beneath his nose. Gordon feels a flash of irritation, the prickle of his shirt suddenly too tight across his back. He signals the waiter and orders an expensive double measure of whiskey. He prefers gin but it doesn't carry the right weight with the men in his family. When it arrives, Gordon swirls it around the glass, then gulps it down in two swift burns to the throat. His grandfather balls up his napkin and tosses it onto the table. "It'll always be pearls before swine with you. I think we're done here," he says, signaling for the bill.

Gordon's father says nothing but raises his brows almost imperceptibly, probably relieved not to be in the firing line for once. As the three of them wait in stony silence, an image of a childhood toy enters Gordon's head. While Maia had been given a trio of traditional Russian dolls each wearing the same pretty smile, his set was hand-painted with the faces of monsters, each more unsettling than the last. Sometimes, he used to turn them to the wall before getting into bed at night. And all these years later, he's disconcerted to sense a similarity around their table now, something dark and unpleasant connecting eldest to youngest.

His days begin early, when trading opens. He watches the other men for signs of how to behave and quickly realizes there is no code. Anything goes. He can be the most unpalatable version of himself, and the next person will say or do something worse. It is a fraternity. And even though he has started low in the pecking order, he is drawn into the meaty arms of the city boys who clock off the moment the floor closes and head to the wine bars to soak their insides in champagne. His days are one long work-drink party and Gordon loves it. It feels like planting his face between the breasts of some voluptuous girl and leaving it there, letting her soft, warm flesh engulf him. He hadn't envisaged banking would feel this way, but somehow it does. It is excessive, wild, Babylonian.

TUESDAY IS FOR bleaching the coffee cups with lemon juice, vacuuming the curtains, sweeping the front doorstep, wiping down the kitchen cupboards, running a cotton bud along the lip of each door to catch any crumbs that might have fallen there. It is for laundering bed linen, dusting the leaves of the houseplants, and making lasagne. It is for looking at the empty calendar that hangs on the kitchen wall and scanning back across all the identikit Tuesdays that have gone before and all the ones to come. Like one of those mirrors that reveals the same thing over and over, but smaller, smaller, smaller. Because Cora shrinks with each week that passes, with each week that sits between her and whatever life she once had as a mother, a dancer, a schoolgirl, someone's daughter, heart beating out of her chest as she learned to ride a bike or felt the happiness of biting into flapjack warm from the oven before the syrup had a chance to harden.

Cora had always told herself that once the children had left, she'd go too. But then it still seemed a risk, when Gordon needed a base to come back to between university terms. She might never have seen him if she was miles away in some town he'd never heard of. But now he is truly gone, and his room is a shrine to an era she's unsure she could call happy or worthy of preserving. Yet how is she to know what constitutes a happy childhood? Every family must have their ups and downs.

She is fifty-four, and she feels the whole world is moving on without her. She's been given a life, but she has somehow failed to spend it. She hasn't worked outside their home since she was twenty-three. She has no friends to confide in, barely any relationship with her own mother. Her daughter rarely asks to speak to her when she phones and, if she does, it's something tagged onto the end of the call. *Must dash. Got to run. Can't stop. Gosh, is that the time?* She knows their contact will be drawn to a close before Maia has even said the words. And Cora does not cling or wheedle. Just tells the girl she loves her, to take care of herself, to remember to have fun. Because she's pleased she got out and has her own life up in London. She has no right to feel abandoned. This was never Maia's mess to clear up. But somehow all this has come to mean her husband is her only constant, the only person to make her feel she exists.

She doesn't even have the television for company now—the remote travels back and forth to work with her husband in his briefcase. The landline in the hall has been replaced by his mobile, but sometimes Cora still picks up the receiver and listens to the blank nothingness of the earpiece. Disconnected, it doesn't even offer the seashell echo of possibility. It is simply a lump of plastic held to her ear. One day, she washes a yogurt pot and holds it against the side of her head, letting herself be carried away by the feeling of other-worldliness she hears within. She remembers when she punched a hole in the bottom and connected it with string to another. And she and Maia would sit, one in the kitchen, one in the living room, letting the vibrations travel between them.

Some days, she lies on her back in the skewed rectangles of sunlight that fall across the living-room carpet from the patio doors, just for that moment when it shifts or darkens. Her favorite houseplant is the calathea Maia sent for Mother's Day. Not just because it's from her, but because its large leaves close into an upright column at night and then slowly fan out like open palms during the day. She loves the small sounds it emits as its leaves unfurl and brush against the wall.

But there are days, like today, when she feels furious with these things, which are not enough and only highlight her solitude. Then, she wants to take the leaves in her fist and tear them from their stems, to hurl the plant across the room and cover the spotless floor in soil and grind it into the pile of the carpet with her bare feet.

Instead, Cora takes a pan of hot, soapy water outside, props open the front door, and dampens a cloth to wipe down the white paintwork of the portico's fake pillars. The water cools quickly and her hands feel stiff and cold as she rinses the rag each time it colors with grime.

"Sorry, running a bit late this morning," the postman says, making her jump. When she turns, he is holding out the mail for her to take, satchel slung across his body like a grown schoolboy. She looks at him, and he moves the post an inch or two nearer, as if to let her know he doesn't have all day. She accepts it dumbly, surprised he doesn't realize this is illicit. Because lately the mail has been delivered straight to the newly installed box that sits on the outside wall above the planter, which only Gordon has a key for.

"Thank you," she says at last. The postman walks back up the drive and she watches as he works his way around the neighboring houses.

Inside, she sits on the sofa, the mail on her lap. She knows Gordon is in a meeting with a drug rep until midday. Sometimes he throws in these details to catch her out, appearing at the very time he said he'd be engaged. But this morning, his mobile rang, and she could hear the man's voice on the other end of the line as they agreed to set things back half an hour. And so, she sits with the weight of the letters. It's unlikely there will be anything of interest to her, but she wants what they represent: possibility, a connection with the outside world. She casts her eyes down and sorts through each piece in turn. She studies the postmark, the small print of the return address on the reverse. Lloyds Bank, BX1 1LT. Where is BX? Buxton, Brixton? She doesn't remember London boroughs having unique postcodes like that. Next, an A4 envelope. She feels its thickness, traces the edges of what's inside and decides it's a medical journal.

The third envelope is addressed to her—Mrs. Cora Atkin—printed in smart black type. How funny, she thinks, that people,

businesses, still write to her, believing she's a woman who will receive her own post, will open it, review its contents, and then act
upon them. She stands, goes outside, and posts the first two pieces of
mail into the locked box. And then she returns with the third, which
seems almost to vibrate on her lap. She feels if she were to stare at it
long enough, the text inside might become visible through the white
of the envelope. But when it does not, she takes it to the kitchen,
boils the kettle, and holds it over the steaming spout, heat pricking
at her fingers. The glue doesn't lift as easily as she'd hoped, requiring encouragement from the probing blade of a butter knife. But, finally, she's in. She glances at the clock: 11:35 a.m. With morning
surgery still in progress, she's sure Gordon won't pop home before
his meeting and so she draws the folded paper out.

Dear Mrs. Atkin,

*In relation to the estate of Mrs. Sílbhe Murphy, please
confirm receipt of the funds relating to the sale of the
deceased's property and any remaining proceeds after
fees and outstanding debts have been cleared.*

Yours sincerely,
David Causley, Solicitor

Cora reads the words. Once, twice, three times. And then a
fourth. And a fifth. Unable to comprehend what she's seeing. Her
mother. An estate. Deceased. She can feel pounding in her ears. There

is no need for yogurt pots or bits of string, the brush of plant leaves against plaster. She can hear the pulse of her own blood, her own self. And she is alive with fury.

She goes into the hall, pulls a coat from its hook, and shrugs it on, pushing the letter down into her pocket. She doesn't have a key, but she closes the door behind her, not caring what Gordon will think or how she will get back in later if she changes her mind.

It's more than two decades since their daughters took swimming lessons together. But there is no one else to turn to. She is the only person who has ever put a hand on Cora's arm and told her they will be there if she needs them. Charles Street. She cannot remember the house number, only a blue front door and a stained-glass window depicting a lighthouse. She feels like she flies there, though it is a good twenty minutes before she turns into the road. She studies the houses, trying to see which one slots into place with her memory. And then there it is, the lighthouse. The door painted a light butter-cup yellow now. She knocks and it's opened by a younger woman, about thirty, Maia's age. "Fern?" Cora says.

The woman shakes her head and behind her the voice of a young child calls out, "Mummy, I can't reach." She begins to shut the door.

"Wait. Mehri and Fern. They used to live here. Do you know where they've gone?"

"Oh, Mehri," the woman says, recognition on her face. "Yes. I can't remember, only that they were staying local."

"Might you have it written down? Their new address?"

The child calls again and the woman says, "Sorry, we've been here five years now. I can barely remember what day it is, let alone someone's address from all that time ago."

Cora takes the woman in properly now. She has that look of dog-tiredness that seems to subsume some mothers, as though their children continue to leach vitamins and minerals from them long after they've finished breastfeeding, leaving a rice-pudding complexion, cheeks yearning for rosehip.

"Sorry to have bothered you," Cora says. And she means it, but as she walks away, she wants to cry, because she has no idea what to do next.

So she walks. She doesn't know where she's heading, only that she has a need to be moving, putting one foot in front of the other to stop her thoughts from overwhelming her. Her mother's face edges into her mind—her hands, her profile. But she cannot let herself go there and each time an image of Sílbhe appears, Cora blinks, squeezing her lids down hard like the jaws of a dustbin lorry, compressing, crushing, until it disappears. Instead, she thinks of Gordon. About what to do next. She has no key to get back into the house. And she realizes she has left the discarded envelope on the sofa. If she had kept *all* the mail out, she could just say the postman had handed it to her and she'd seen something addressed for her. He wouldn't like it, but perhaps it would pass. But the fact that half the mail has ended up in the mailbox and one piece has been opened will suggest she was trying to deceive him. "Damn," she mutters as she walks along a street she's never encountered before. "Damn, damn, damn."

It is this, rather than the fact he has omitted to tell her of her own mother's passing, that makes her feel she can't return home. But she has nowhere else to go. She doesn't know Maia's phone number. She has no money. The police don't even register as an option after their visit all those years ago. She can't go to the library where Gordon regularly borrows books and where, sometimes, on a Saturday morning, they return them together.

So, she goes to the only place she can think of where they have no links, where she hopes Gordon will be unknown. Where they might have some code of ethics around confidentiality. Where there might be people who care.

Inside the vet's, she tells the receptionist that her dog is unwell, that its eyes are rolling back in its head, and asks if she might speak to a vet for a moment.

"But you're not registered with us?"

"I've just moved to the area," she says quietly, even though she doesn't recognize the people sitting on the gray plastic chairs in the waiting room. She scans the faces, watches the door and the car park beyond.

The curly haired vet calls her forward between patients, his elbow resting on the ledge of the receptionist's desk, Adam's apple bobbing as he swallows.

"Could we, erm . . . could we go—" and Cora nods to the consultation room he's just come from.

"Oh, yes, of course," he says, perplexed. "We won't keep you waiting too long," he says to the elderly woman sitting with a cat basket at her feet.

They stand to either side of a rubber-topped metal table, where a creature would normally be coaxed from its carrier for treatment. What she needs to say seems dramatic, like something sensationalist from a film or a book. But she's here now and has no other choice.

"I need help," she says and feels her bottom lip begin to go. He reaches for a tissue box on the windowsill, practiced in dealing with his clients' emotions. She takes the tissue but doesn't use it. If she stops, she won't go on. "I have no money, no phone, no friends. And my husband is . . ."—there is the feeling of driving over a humpbacked bridge, with no road on the other side to catch her—"he's not kind." She sees the vet does not understand and tries again. "I mean, I think he is an abusive man. To me."

"Just a moment," he says. And he opens the door a few inches and says to the receptionist, "If you could fit my patients in with Carolyn, please. I'll be unavailable for a while."

She does not feel the time passing, but when she looks at her watch it marks out the hours and the things Gordon may be doing a few miles away. Calling home after his appointment with the rep. Afternoon surgery. A fifteen-minute break at 3 p.m. The vet leaves the room briefly to make phone calls and returns to update her. He brings her a blanket. He's apologetic—it's one they use for the animals—but he reassures her it's clean. She hadn't realized she was cold, but when he wraps the fabric around her shoulders, its weight and warmth feel like something she's been craving. "We all feel the cold more when we're in shock," he tells her.

Is she in shock? she wonders. Yes, perhaps she is.

"Are you more of a cat or a dog person?" the vet asks, while they wait to hear back from an organization he hopes might be able to help. And she realizes she doesn't know. That she has no idea of her likes and dislikes, of who the person in her own body might be. She is barely a person at all.

"My mother had a cat," she says, feeling her eyes begin to tear.

The receptionist buzzes and he leaves the room to take a call. When he returns, he is holding a small gray cat. "This is Smokey," he says. "She's been with us for a few days, but she's all ready to go back home once her owner has finished work this evening." He places the cat on Cora's lap and, almost reflexively, it starts purring. She lowers her hand to its thick coat and it's like sinking her fingers into velvet.

It is nearly 5 p.m. when a woman comes into the room, the vet behind her. At first Cora thinks it's Smokey's owner, come to reclaim her, but then she introduces herself. "Hello, Cora, I'm Della. I'm from the Bowen House Women's Refuge. You're safe now." And Cora slumps with relief, because she believes her, because she looks both soft and hard all at once, as though steel-capped boots and fearlessness hover around the edges of her warmth. It's this that gives her the courage to walk through the empty waiting room and out to Della's car.

It's only as they pull away and she sees the vet's face disappear from view that she realizes she hasn't thanked him, doesn't know his name, cannot remember when the cat was lifted from her knee. She looks down and sees her clothes are carpeted with its hairs. She touches her hand to them and remembers her school skirt, threaded with fur in exactly this way. How old would she have been? Fourteen, the last year she wore uniform, before coming to London to study ballet.

MAIA IS AT the end of a shift that has eaten into her evening, forcing her to text friends to first say she'll be late, and then not there at all. She sits on the bench in the center of the room, her locker open, trying to muster the energy to change out of scrubs, when her phone rings.

The number is withheld, and she almost doesn't pick up, until she remembers the plumber who said he'd call her or Kate with a time to fix the shower that leaks water onto the hall ceiling below, its stain blooming in size each morning.

But when she taps the green button to accept the call, it is her mother's voice she hears. "Maia?"

"Mum?"

Her parents no longer have a landline and, lately, when Maia's gone to call her father's mobile, the lead weight of the dial tone has sounded in her ear, and somehow, she hasn't been able to bring herself to jump through the hoop of asking to speak to her mother. It's him she has spoken to more recently. She'd rung during the workday to ask his advice about how to deal with one of the consultants, and he'd been so pleased to hear from her, so generous in sharing his knowledge, she'd almost let herself forget the monster he'd been when she'd lived at home. She can't remember the last time she spoke to her mother. But now, she's on the other end of the line—unbidden, unexpected—and her voice sounds shaky and unlike her own. "Are you okay, Mum? Dad's number didn't come up—I didn't know it was you."

"Yes, I'm okay. Can I—can I put you on the phone to—to Della? It'd be easier," her mum says, her voice catching on the shape of the final word as though each syllable is a mountain to climb and fall around.

"Yes, but who's Della?"

Maia hears the muffle of the phone being handed over and then a woman's voice. Solid, trustworthy, but with no soft edges. "Maia, this is Della. I'm calling from a women's refuge. Are you somewhere we can talk?"

Maia straightens. "I think so," she says, glancing up at the empty locker room.

"I understand from your mum that you're aware of the abuse she's been receiving at home." Maia swallows—it's like washing down a stone. Because, yes, at some level, she is aware; does not believe the abuse stopped the moment she left home. "We've been called in today because things have escalated. Your mum's out of immediate danger, but I do have some difficult news to share."

Maia swallows uncomfortably again, shields her eyes, even though the unlit room is steeped in gloom.

"We believe your grandmother died several months ago, and—"

"No, that's not right." Relief. Vindication. "I spoke to her last week—"

"Sorry, Maia, I mean on your mother's side. Your Grandma Sílbhe," Della says. Maia's heart flip-flops at the unexpected name. She sees the flame in it—í—and then, as she processes Della's words, feels it wavering, as though a gust of wind has rushed in. There is a long pause. A silence where Maia almost forgets the woman is on the other end of the line. "Are you still there, Maia?"

"Yes."

"I'm aware I'm not giving you much time to take all this in, but I'm about to go home for the night and I don't want to leave you in the dark if your father gets in touch."

"My father?"

"Yes. I'm afraid he's hidden this news from your mother, and we believe diverted any inheritance to get around the issue of her becoming financially independent in any way."

"Have you spoken to him? Do you actually know this?" Maia

asks, aware even as the words are leaving her mouth that she is sid-ing with him. And that this woman, Della, will be judging her for it.

"Maia, I'm going to let you absorb all this overnight. I'm guess-ing you'll have some questions tomorrow, so if you'd like, I can put in a call at some point during the day?"

"Oh. Yes. Thank you." She thinks about her schedule tomorrow, surprised to find she still has a life and commitments beyond this phone call. "Midday? That would give me time before my next shift. I'm a doctor," she adds, unsure what this woman already knows about her.

"I can try for that, but my days can be unpredictable. So if I don't call then, I'll be in touch as soon as I get the chance."

"Do you have a number I can call back on? If I miss you?" Maia asks, taking the phone from her cheek before seeing again that it's a withheld number.

"I think it's best if I phone you for now." And Maia understands the subtext. That Della isn't sure she's on side.

When the call has ended, Maia sits in the rubble of her crumbling reality. She feels the weight of not meeting the woman's expecta-tions. Or perhaps, worse, proving her expectations right. And as she absorbs the news about Sílbhe, her father, her mother, she becomes aware of her own role in all this too. She, Maia, is a helper. She is tireless in the care she offers her patients. Admired by colleagues for always taking the time to see the bigger picture. Respected for the way she will connect the dots to treat the whole person, rather than just the symptom they present with. And yet, in her own life, she has pretended what she knew wasn't real, because it felt too big and hard to deal with. At eighteen. And in all the years since.

The door opens and when Maia glances up, it's Kate's face she sees, her thick red hair still holding onto the kinks of having been tied back all day. "Are you okay?" Kate asks, her expression making it clear she can already see Maia is not.

And it's then that Maia receives another shock. One that whips around her body, infecting every cell with shame, even as Kate unwittingly wraps her arms around her and places a nicotine kiss on her cheek. Because laid out before her is the realization that she has not only hidden her relationship with Kate from her family. She has also hidden the facts of her family from Kate. She has edited away all the unsavory parts of herself, to leave a version that is nowhere near the truth.

Seven Years Later

2015

Bear

It's November. Bear and Lily are meant to be watching a band he's wanted to see. She's listened to a few of their tracks on her iPhone and it's more accessible than she'd imagined from the name. A sort of pop-metal. But when Bear hasn't quite finished his work consulting on some artifacts in Egypt, he messages to apologize, to say he won't be able to make it and has rescheduled his flight to visit her in Paris. For an afternoon, Lily reshelves library books with uncharacteristic brusqueness, seething at his last-minute changing of plans, at her empty weekend ahead, at the wasted money. That it wasn't even a band she'd wanted to see in the first place! But when her thoughts and a trolley of returns have been reordered, she stares up at the glass ceiling of the Bibliothèque nationale de France and allows herself—her disappointment—to be dwarfed by it. She closes her eyes, breathes, attempts something like serenity.

She arranges to leave the tickets on the front desk for a colleague's younger brother, but he seeks her out in person. And he is so delighted, so breathless in his hushed thanks—a skateboard under one arm, cheeks bitten red by the cold—she feels almost pleased she and Bear were unable to go.

In the evening, a friend messages and asks if she's eaten. It's nearly 9 p.m. and although she's absorbed by some translation work, her stomach is growling. As her laptop powers off, she swipes on lipstick, spritzes perfume at her throat, touches her wrists to it momentarily, then puts on her long winter coat, turns out the lights, and lets the door fall shut behind her, looping a scarf around her neck as she clatters down the stairs. A tortoiseshell cat mewls in the foyer to be let out, and they step into the street together, heading off in different directions. "À bientôt, minou."

Bear lies on the sofa in an apartment near the Nile rereading an abandoned paperback he'd found when he first arrived. He's not really interested. He just needs the words in front of him, something to take his mind from the evening boredom. The final days on a job that's overrun always seem the longest. He's looking forward to visiting the English bookshop on rue de Rivoli with Lily and making his own choices. Bear sighs, and Cameron, who will also be leaving in a few days, suggests seven-card rummy, already reaching for the deck of cards.

At 9:25 p.m., as Lily walks along rue Faidherbe, she sends Bear a text. "Meeting V for dinner, minus your beautiful equipment. Wish you were here. Lx." It is their name for La Belle Équipe, a restaurant they have eaten at a few times; Bear loves to make bad translations.

Cameron shuffles. Beneath his discarded novel, Bear's screen lights up.

Lily slips her phone back into her coat pocket and rests her hand against it, not wanting to miss the vibration of a reply coming in.

Bear looks at his cards. Three aces and a four-card straight. What are the chances?

Lily turns onto rue de Charonne. A breeze whips at her scarf, and she catches the end that's come loose and tosses it back over her shoulder.

Bear takes a swig from his beer and shows his hand.

Lily is nearly at the restaurant. Veronique sits at a table beneath the awning, her face lit by fairy lights and the glow of an outdoor heater.

"Lucky bastard," Cameron says, gathering up the cards.

A black SEAT Leon turns onto rue de Charonne.

Cameron shuffles. Beneath his book, Bear's phone silently lights up again.

Lily kisses Veronique hello, catching the familiar scent of her friend's perfume. Car doors open.

Cameron deals the cards again.

A man shouts. His words are in another tongue, but it's a phrase anyone would recognize, although its meaning has long been distorted by misuse. Veronique's eyes widen over Lily's shoulder.

It is too late to change anything.

WHEN BEAR RETURNS to his book and glances at his phone beneath, it shows both Lily's text and the BBC newsflash on the lock screen, one above the other, as though they were always intended to be linked.

Meeting V for dinner, minus your
beautiful equipment. Wish you
were here. Lx.

Breaking News
Multiple attacks in Paris.
At least 18 people killed.

THE NEXT TWO days are a hollow of unanswered texts, and a rush of noise. The bustle of Cairo gives way to a slick white departures hall, a blur of people, the endless refresh and refresh and refresh of the news cycle on Bear's phone, scanning the same photos for her face in the background, the fabric of her coat, as the official death toll rises. There is a sleepless night. A long wait for a flight as texts arrive in a stream of pings that are never the one he's hoping for. Then the perma-hum of the plane thrumming through him. The foot-tapping wait at passport control. The tumult of Paris, which throws obstacles in the path of his taxi as it makes a loop around the city. He registers his name and Lily's details with the hospital gatekeepers who have now dealt with so many desperate people, their sympathy has become routine.

And then, as they sit in traffic, a text from Lily's parents. Brief, staccato sentences, like a telegram, its words in short supply.

She's been found.
In ICU at Salpêtrière.

Alive.

She's been shot.

Bear redirects the taxi and then sits in the back, sobbing, the rest of the world finally tuned out. She is alive. That she's hurt barely registers. He wipes his face on the sleeve of his jacket, under the glancing eye of the driver in the rearview mirror.

IN THE DAYS that follow, Lily's parents orchestrate things from her bedside, insisting it will all be more manageable once she's back in England with doctors who speak *the language*, even though Lily is fluent. "What's he saying?" her mother asks, before the surgeon has finished speaking. In conversations only Lily can translate, they discuss whether the initial reconstruction of her hip was successful, the possibility of damage to cartilage, nerves. A potential hip replacement. While her parents repeat in haunted whispers, "Thank God it wasn't her spine," and talk about her returning to live with them, as though it's a foregone conclusion. They do not consult Bear. But neither does Lily. He's surprised but can't let it show on his face. Instead, when they have a brief moment alone, he says, "Tell me what I can do for you. How I can help."

He wants her to say, *Just be here. Just stay by my side.* But she says, "Pack up my flat?" and again he is hit by the odd feeling that things are not as he expected.

He collects empty boxes from Lily's local supermarket and returns to her apartment. He starts by packing up the books. Then her laptop, her papers. Her desk drawers. Here he slows, handling her possessions with reverence. There is something in the form of each item that tells him it was as carefully chosen as the stapler she picked out weeks earlier when he was by her side in a shop in the Marais. But there is also a frugality. She does not have or need much.

He takes her jumpers from the drawers and transfers them into an empty suitcase, noticing the ones that have nothing at the neck, as though Lily had found the label scratchy and snipped it out. In the wardrobe, where cardigans and blouses hang, some fabrics say to Bear, *this café, that day*, while others belong to a life he doesn't recognize. He folds the garments carefully, breathing in her smell, which seems woven into the fibers. *Lily.* When he moves on to the impersonality of jeans and trousers, he wonders at how these don't hold the same stories. Why is it only the top half of a person's clothing that speaks?

On the floor of the wardrobe, there are two large, low boxes. He lifts the lid on the first and has the discomforting sensation of catching his own reflection in a shop window when he's not expecting it. It is filled with envelopes addressed in his own handwriting, stickered with the stamps he bought in each new country. He has traveled lighter than Lily and realizes he doesn't have his side in the call and response of their correspondence. He doesn't recall actively throwing her letters away. But perhaps he left them in the drawer of a temporary desk or abandoned them amongst a pile of papers. He's stunned by his own certainty that there would always be more of her words, that he could treat them so carelessly. As though there were an inexhaustible supply. He's come so close to being left with nothing; with only his own thoughts to read back.

He opens the other box, the word *Us* on its lid. Them. Him and Lily. It is messier, like the midden layer of earth, rich with artifacts of the everyday, the things that tell a story. Some are easy to understand. Ticket stubs to a museum. Boarding passes. A wristband from a festival. But there are others that leave him guessing: a small gray-and-white candy-striped paper bag with a feather inside. He holds it, scrolls through his mind trying to match up details, but nothing comes. He studies the items and mentally catalogs them.

Heart-shaped granite pebble with white calcite vein. Origin unknown. Ask Lily.

Folded cream napkin, marked with a coffee ring. Logo: Irini's Café. A Google search reveals the café is in Santorini, where they spent a week together in September 2010—Lily was in the middle of cataloging a book collection for some Italian guy's estate sale; and Bear had been between jobs, after finishing up what he'd come to think of as "the flying cockroach dig." He remembers baklava and morning coffee at the same place each day.

A blue/gray butterfly wing. Partially disintegrated. Preserved inside an unused tissue. Chalkhill blue? Maybe he'd found it at Totternhoe Knolls and given it to Lily on his return. That would have been late 2003, when they were sixteen.

He works his way through the box, puzzling over the gaps in his knowledge. Studying each item for clues, his memory jogged by a logo or an area code, coming up against blanks at others. It is past 2 a.m. when he carefully repacks the box. He feels as though he has just time-traveled through their years together. Their years apart. He climbs into Lily's bed and turns onto his side, facing the wall. His mind fills with fractured images of faceless men getting into a car, riding through the city as Lily dressed, as she walked toward them. As he'd played cards. His head swirls with regrets, analyzing how their fates had shifted unseen, as though on tectonic plates. Not once, but twice. First avoiding the concert that had been targeted in the attacks—teetering, about to cross a fault line onto another plane, until pressure, release. They continued on. Only for Lily to meet another fault.

He wonders where they'd be now, if he'd come when he was meant to? Would going to the concert have been better or worse? Her colleague's younger brother walked away unscarred, physically, at least. Would it have changed things if he'd seen Lily's text sooner, caused her to pause on the street for a moment to read his reply? Almost certainly. A few seconds could have made all the difference. He sees gloved fingers on a trigger, the white of bone, an X-ray on a backlit screen, her face, the roadblock of her parents, whose presence seems to say to Bear, *You have not been enough.* Their expectation that he will not step up.

He thinks of Lily's boxes of keepsakes and realizes these are the riches. What the hell has he been doing, he wonders, sifting through the earth on another continent, looking for the fragmented remains of someone else's life from a thousand, or ten thousand, years ago? Looking for broken pieces of china, a chip of clay, as though they were precious. As though they had more importance than the foundations of his own life with Lily, which she has nurtured all this time.

The next morning, Bear sits on the edge of the bed and studies the slice of bathroom visible through the half-open door. It's the only room he's yet to pack up. He sees her bath towel folded on the rail.

Her bottles of perfume and lotions sitting neatly on the shelves. And becomes aware, again, of the spaces where he's been absent. What would their lives be like, he wonders, if his shaving cream and nail clippers weren't tucked away in a wash-bag but mingled in amongst her things?

FROM WHERE LILY LIES, she can see the catheter bag dangling from the side of the bed is almost full. It bulges with straw-colored liquid that seems divorced from her own body. She studies the thin tubes entering the plastic pouch and wonders what will happen if someone doesn't come and empty it soon. Will the liquid flow back toward her kidneys? The alarm is just out of reach. She considers banging on the bedside table or shouting for someone. But she doesn't want to be *that* patient. To wake the person snoring lightly in the next room. So she waits, and as dawn light spreads across the walls, her fears bloom. She doesn't want to be alone. To hear the surgeon's words replay: *Vous avez failli mourir sur la table; you nearly died on the table.* She just wants her mum. And she wants to go home.

BEAR AND LILY sit side by side on a bench, overlooking the lake where he'd once worked as a boat boy between university terms, her wheelchair on the path nearby.

After the murkiness of last November, Lily has detected in her parents—in Bear—a desire to move on, to cast off what happened like a winter coat that's grown too heavy. But she's not sure she's ready when she still struggles to make sense of everything. When she can get around her parents' house, but her wound aches and she still feels a crushing whole-body tiredness if she tries to walk too far.

"I read another one of those articles yesterday," Lily says. "About how grateful someone is to be alive. How they don't even mind that they've had their leg blown off."

"Why read them if they make you feel bad?"

"Because I'm hoping one of them might feel like me," Lily says, looking across the lake to where a mother and child are feeding the ducks, swans moving in on them, gliding at speed through the water. "I'd always thought humans were essentially good. I knew there were bad ones out there, but they somehow hadn't seemed as real. Until this. Now I just feel so . . . so *victimized*. That this man watched me smiling, watched me hugging Veronique. But he still wanted to kill me."

"These people—terrorists—they're not even thinking like that. It could've been anyone. Yes, what they do is fueled by hate, but it's not personal."

"It *is* personal."

"I know the consequences are personal. But the act itself wasn't. It'll eat away at you to think like that."

She turns to him. "Do you have to do this?"

"What?"

"Rationalize it. I know all that, but it doesn't change how I feel."

A few of the swans are on the bank now, opening their wings, causing the child to cower behind his pushchair. The mother throws bread into the water to lure them away. Bear and Lily watch the drama unfold in silence, not near enough to hear what's said, only to witness the action: the mother coaxing the toddler back into his pram, and their slow retreat toward the exit at the far side of the park.

"Sorry. Maia's always saying that's something men do too. I can see it's annoying, though."

"It's something *you* do; I don't care what the others are doing," Lily says.

"Yes. Sorry, something *I* do."

"Bloody annoying," Lily mutters. And they sit simmering in her irritation, until eventually she asks, "When are you going back?"

"To where?"

Lily emits a sharp little sound and, although they're not alike, it reminds him of her mother. Bear imagines her parents have lost patience with him, that they've been telling Lily the relationship is impossible. That he's not committed. He hopes she would defend him but worries she might feel the same way.

He'd been going to wait to mention it, but it feels urgent now. "I've got an interview at a museum."

"Which one?" Lily asks. "Penn? Peabody? Giza's still under construction, isn't it?"

"No, I mean here. In England."

"Oh." Silence. And then, "How long would it be for?"

"It's a permanent position."

"I see." Lily watches as the mother pushing the pram comes back into view, reversing their route, patrolling the strip of land the swans scared them from minutes earlier. She's bending down now, the child leaning out of his straps to inspect whatever it is the woman has retrieved from the ground.

As the silence extends, Bear knows she doesn't believe he might accept something permanent. She's not even giving it a second thought. Instead, she is watching a truck slowly making its way around the lake, stopping beside each bin while the park warden empties it. Since the attacks, Bear has noticed her clocking everything going on around her, only half focused on him and their conversations.

"You know, when I was younger, Bees used to do this thing. She'd get me in a trap under her legs—a bear trap—and I'd have to try to break free. And when I did, she taught me to put my hands up, to say that I was Bear, that I was free and wild." He raises his palms, his fingers becoming claws, drawing Lily's attention from the truck for a moment. "It was just one of those silly things, but I don't know, maybe I've always believed it, that I was meant to be out there adventuring. A wild thing." Bear looks at Lily, but from the side, her face is hard to read. "But since Paris, I've kept thinking I might have got it wrong. That maybe freedom is just about choosing the life you want. Even if that life's in one place, doing the food shop together. Arguing over who forgot to buy loo roll."

Lily gives a little nod, and Bear doesn't know how his words have landed. But then she says, "Nice work, Atkin," just like she used to when they were fourteen and sitting beside one another in maths, although her tone has an edge now. "But maybe you could realize this stuff without me having to nearly die."

He reaches for her hand and gives it a squeeze. "I thought we were both happy. That we were both doing what we wanted?" It's a question, but he knows this is only half true.

She laughs then, a thin sort of laugh. "I think I can only admit to it now, when I'm no longer willing to play, but I feel like I've been

trying to mold myself into the woman you'd love since we were teen-
agers. Never asking for too much, never pinning you down. Showing
you how independent and worldly I could be. Your equal." He goes to
interrupt, but she raises a hand. "But I'm tired of it now. I'm just so
tired. And I've no idea if you mean these things; if you'll really take
work in the UK, if you're capable of staying for good. So, I'll be honest. Yes, I want you to have a job that will bring you home to me
each night. And this might come as a surprise but, yes, I also want
children. And not in some fuzzy, distant way, but soon. In the next
few years. And, no, I don't want to bring up a child alone. And, no, I
don't want to have to spend the rest of my life apologizing for that,
or being made to feel like some ogre who's trapped a butterfly in a
net, or having Maia judge me for asking her precious little brother to
put someone else before himself—"

She stops abruptly. As though shocked by her own words—by the
mention of Maia—when, moments earlier, it had seemed she was
only just getting started.

They sit in silence. For a minute, then two. Until eventually, Bear
laughs. It's a laugh that makes the bench's backrest shake. Lily
glances at him, uncertain. And then he says, "God, I've been insuf-
ferable, haven't I?"

He gets up and squats on the ground in front of her, rests his
palms against her thighs. He presses his forehead to her knees and
for a moment—to him, to her—it feels he's unwittingly adopted a
pose resembling prayer. Repenting, asking forgiveness. For a time,
he's wordless.

"Thank you," he says into her skirt. "For waiting. For putting up
with me." He looks up. "Do you know the things I love about you,

202 | FLORENCE KNAPP

Lily? Really love?" She shakes her head. "Because, yeah, it's true, I do love that you speak so many languages, that you know your way around European cities, that you're my equal. Not even my equal; you're better than me. But I also love the way you sleep curled up like a dormouse," he says, mimicking her pose. "I love that when you send me letters, you sign off with your first and last name and I've never known why you do that, but I haven't asked in case it makes you stop. I love that you add lemon to everything you cook. I love that in winter you keep those weird heated handwarmers in your handbag to give to homeless people. I love that I can pick you out in a crowd, not just by your hair or face, but by the way you move. I love that cats follow you home and that you think that happens to everyone—and it does, but not every day. Not every time they leave the house." She is smiling, but he's not finished. "I love that when I introduce you to someone, you know exactly what to say to make them feel good, even though you've never met before. And even though it's not great for my ego, I love that they'll come away liking you better than me. I love how your clothes are kind of drapey—I don't know how to explain it, but the way your wrists look where they meet your cuffs, it's sexy, and I love your ankles in summer when you're wearing jeans, and the long bone that runs along the top of your foot." She's laughing now. "I'm serious. I know I'm not saying any of this properly, but I think it's something to do with grace. I love how graceful you are. And I love how much grace you've given me. But I'm sorry you've had to. And I'm sorry I've been so grace*less*. That I've acted like some kind of idiot Indiana Jones all these years."

Lily leans forward, kisses Bear's forehead. "I love knowing those things." She takes a breath. "But I don't know if it's enough. I need to know what it means, if anything. For us. Our future. If we have one together."

He stands, massages the life back into his knees for a moment, and then takes his wallet from his pocket. He peers inside, riffling through its contents until he finds what he's looking for.

"I joined a gym," he says, holding out a card as he sits down beside her. Lily takes it, studies the small digital reproduction of his face. He is smiling and wearing one of Cora's old, oversized T-shirts. "Do you see the line beneath my name?" She stares at the words *Annual Membership*, and then looks up at him. "I took it out a few months ago. Before I applied for the position at the museum. Because I knew even then I was going to stay."

"Why didn't you say, though? Why didn't you tell me you'd joined a gym for a whole year?"

"I don't know. Because I'm weird. Because I needed to test out how it felt without messing you around? Because people always join gyms and quit after a month? But I'm telling you now, because there hasn't been a single day when I've felt tied down by it. By what it represents."

She reaches across the bench and takes his hand. Eventually, she says, "I can't imagine you in a gym. What do you do there?"

"Mainly weights. The other guys are all built like fridges, but they're nice. They even offer to spot me now."

"Go on," Lily says, letting him explain this new terminology.

"Basically, someone just stands there ready to step in if you can't manage it—it means you can lift more without the risk of injuring yourself. But it makes the whole thing more social because obviously you end up chatting."

"Can you notice a difference yet?"

Bear has caught his reflection in the changing-room mirror and his biceps seem more defined. His chest now two small mounds rather than the flat canvas it's always been. "Probably not," Bear says. "It's still early days."

"Why are you doing it?" Lily has turned to look at him now, no longer giving her whole attention to the warden's van or the boy doing keepy-uppies with a football down by the lake.

"I'm not really sure."

"Is it so you can fend off would-be attackers?" Her eyes are laughing, although not unkindly, and he feels like maybe a little piece of the wall she's built up around herself is crumbling away.

He ponders if there's any truth in what she's said, if that *is* why he's doing it. Because he's never been someone who's gone to the gym before. It's oddly out of character. Almost embarrassingly so; he hasn't even told Maia. Bear shuffles along the bench toward Lily and nudges her, presses a sideways kiss into her hair. "That stuff you mentioned earlier. None of it scares me, you know? I think I want those things too."

"Oh. Well, that's good," Lily says, and she leans into him, and nestles her head into the biscuit-scented warmth between his shoulder and chin, as they look out across the lake.

BEAR HAS ALWAYS found it odd when people settle down not far from where they grew up, as though they've lacked the imagination to go elsewhere. But after seven years abroad, the idea of being near

Bees and her wife, Charlotte, in Brighton, and having Cora, Mehri, and Roland only an hour up the road . . . it just feels right.

Lily is slumped on the sofa, dusty from unpacking boxes. "Look at that," Bear says, gazing at the mishmash of rooftops lit red-gold in the evening sun, paving the view toward the seafront.

"I think I'll like being at the top of this hill," Lily says, coming over to rest her elbows on the windowsill next to his. "They'll arrive from that direction." She looks down the street, thinking of the train station where her parents and Cora might come in, of Charlotte and Bees' house.

"Like a castle. We'll be able to see them coming."

"I don't think there's an enemy," Lily says, laughing. "I like your sister." It was a clumsy attempt at reassurance; they'd both wanted to move to Brighton, but still, this is Maia's hometown. He notices Lily said *like*. Not love, though. Also, that she'd spotted what he was trying to do. He leans further out of the window, craning to see into the next street. "Are you expecting me to watch for you coming home from work each night like that?"

"If only," he says, bending back and twisting his lips to plant a lazy kiss on her cheek, although, in reality, he hopes Lily will have her nose in a book. Before the attacks, she'd read voraciously, her mind a vast archive of authors and titles, ready to be called on during quizzes or whenever a friend wanted a recommendation. But she finds it more difficult to recall things now, complaining that her thinking feels jerky. That sometimes, when she's asked to look something up on the library's computer system, it takes a few seconds for the inquirer's words to reach her fingertips. Her doctors say this is normal after a traumatic event, but she's thrown by it. "Do you need to go to bed now?" Bear asks, thinking the move might have exhausted her.

"Yes, Bear, I need to go to bed with you—desperately—right now!" she says, rolling her eyes.

"Thought so," he smiles, happy to be misunderstood.

BEAR HAS BEEN at the museum for six months. He doesn't know why he ever felt this kind of work would be restrictive; he speaks to experts from all over the world, and travels when he's considering acquiring a particular piece for the permanent collection. But the thing that's surprised him most is the children. Sitting in on a workshop one afternoon was like opening a door to a secret room. He watched as they searched for fragments of broken china planted by the staff in a mudbox, listened to their odd conversations: *This stuff is actually as old as a dinosaur; Yeah, they stamped on all the plates and broke them.* When Bear noticed a child reluctant to join in, he knelt beside her and demonstrated how to use her tool to scour the earth without damaging the hidden artifacts. A few minutes later, when she and another girl placed fragments bearing the same blue-and-white print side by side, their classmates gasped, as though two halves of a real-life puppy had been reunited. As they returned to sifting, Bear saw a boy who'd previously been attacking the earth with a trowel now using its edge to gently peel it back, layer by layer, keen not to miss anything. He recalls his own delight in this. Of being a boy with a big, wild energy and finding stillness when he discovered a way to concentrate it. When he funneled it into careful, painstaking work. He wondered who he'd be if he hadn't spent all those hours scrubbling around in the dirt as his mother worked close by.

Later, he'd asked his boss if he could lead a children's session each week. Richard had smiled as though he was talking to one of its attendees and explained, "We actually follow a specific structure for schools, all carefully planned out months in advance to provide a rounded offering." Bear had sat on the train that evening annoyed, unsure if working within the bureaucracy of a large organization was right for him after all. But then he thought about his previous nomadic existence, and somehow that no longer felt right either. He wanted—needed—to be with Lily. And his family.

They went back and forth, with Bear putting forward ideas and Richard saying no, causing Bear to formalize them first in writing, and later, a PowerPoint presentation. Until one day Richard had sat down on the edge of Bear's desk and said, "Houston, we have a compromise. I've moved hell and high water to get it, so this really is my final offer. How about you run a weekly session for home-schoolers? It can be more"—Richard rolled his hand as if to suggest something wafting and indefinable—"informal. You can base the content on your own whims and whichever children turn up. It can exist completely outside our schools program. A drop-in, if you will."

At the end of Bear's most recent class, a quiet child with curly hair—a regular now—had waited around, his mother watching on anxiously from the back of the room. When Bear had finished answering questions and waving people off, the boy had approached. "Thanks, Bear," he'd said, and then, breaking into a grin, he'd added, "I really *dig* your lessons." Bear could tell the boy had been saving up the joke all week.

They'd high-fived and Bear had suggested they officially end the next session with a few minutes for archaeology jokes. He was already planning to wear an old T-shirt Cora had bought him that said "MY LIFE IS IN RUINS" on the front.

LILY AND CHARLOTTE are making lunch, waiting for Bear, Maia, and Cora to return. "It's a funny sort of day, isn't it?" Charlotte is saying. "Most of the time, I feel like it's just all of us in it together, but then each year the anniversary comes along, and I'm reminded that they're bonded by this awful thing. And it's something they'll always carry with them."

Lily pats lettuce leaves dry between layers of kitchen roll. She is thinking about Bear. About what he'd said to her on the eve of his birthday a few weeks earlier. "You know, Charlotte, Bear said something the other day. And I'm not sure it's something I could ask Cora and Bees . . . but I thought maybe you might—" Charlotte stops picking at sweetcorn from the colander in the sink and turns to listen, the frame of her black hair resettling at her chin. "Bear thinks—he wonders if there's some kind of link between him being called Bear and Vihaan's death. He just—he can't quite imagine his father having agreed to a name like his. He noticed a few years ago that the date his birth certificate was issued is the same as the anniversary."

Charlotte is fingering the sweetcorn kernels like worry beads now, and when their eyes meet, Lily realizes that, with her silence, Charlotte is asking her if she really wants to know. To consider what she would do with the information. Lily thinks about Bear. Of what he'd gain if his hunch became fact. If his own name—his essence—

became inextricably linked with a man's death. And Lily thinks how it might feel if she decided not to share whatever she found out with Bear and was left holding the knowledge by herself. "Sorry, forget I ever said anything," she says. "Maybe it's best not to know either way."

"Mm, I would think so."

"Thank you," Lily says, hearing the implication in Charlotte's response but grateful to still be able to claim ignorance.

IN THE EVENING, once the children have returned to their own lives, Cora sits with Mehri in her back garden, the two of them wrapped in a wool blanket against the autumn chill.

"This day always seems to make such a fool out of me," Cora says. "Another year for Vihaan unlived because of the choices I made."

"Well, yes," Mehri says. "Would you like me to pass you that broom? I'm sure it will help with your self-flagellation." She takes a sip of wine. "Seriously, though, how long till we get to the year when you accept this isn't your fault? It's *his* fault—that monster who tricked you into marrying him. Admitting that doesn't mean you're any less sad that Vihaan died."

Cora feels the truth in her words, but it's not so easy to move on from. She's not sure she even wants to. Being in Vihaan's debt forces her to try to live a better life. "Fern rang last night," Cora says, ready to change the subject, at least. "Mainly to say she'd be thinking of me, but we ended up chatting for a while."

"Anything to report?"

"Nothing she hasn't probably told you herself already."

"Ha, as if I'd know what's going on in her life—I'm only her mother." Mehri laughs, more proud than resentful. "That girl flits around like a dragonfly. She's more committed to her work than any man."

"She did say that she's stopped seeing the microbiologist," Cora says. They never meet Fern's partners and are more likely to know them by their job titles or hobbies than their names.

"What is it this time—more organisms than orgasms?"

Even though Fern isn't there to hear, Cora feels guilty—she's not sure they should even be *thinking* about Fern's sex life, let alone discussing it, although she knows Mehri would say this in front of Fern, and that she'd reply openly. Mehri has always treated parenting like she's cooking a big warming pan of something: a pinch of that, a pinch of this, she's sure it will turn out fine in the end. Cora's own approach has always felt more like baking a cake: carefully measuring out ingredients and trying not to ruin everything. She admires Mehri's way.

"She didn't mention that specifically," Cora says, "just that she was getting a *bad vibe*. They went out for dinner a few nights ago and he tried to order for her." A snort of laughter escapes Mehri on the bench beside her. "I know, it doesn't show a brilliant understanding of Fern, but he's sounded pretty promising until now. I did wonder if it was an overreaction. If she's sensitive to these things because of what happened."

"Seriously, we're back here already? Cora, you're my dearest friend, so I mean this kindly, but you are not responsible for the goings-on of the entire world. Yes, people's lives bump and collide and we send one another spinning off in different directions. But that's life. It's not unique to you. We each make our own choices."

"You think I'm self-absorbed?"

"A little," Mehri says, and Cora doesn't need to look to know her eyes will be gleaming with laughter. "But I'm bossy and eat and drink too much; you and Roland still love me. We all have faults, azizam," Mehri says, patting her hand. *Darling. Dear.* Cora always feels so loved when Mehri bestows these terms on her.

Somewhere in the neighboring streets, a few early fireworks are being let off, and the two women raise their heads as the sky fills with trickles of color.

ONE WEEKEND WHEN Bear has returned to Cora's to fix a dripping kitchen tap, his head in the cupboard beneath the sink, he says, "I've asked Cian if he can make something for me." Cora is surprised. She's in touch with Cian from time to time, but it's a few years since her mother died, and they've never been quite sure what role he played in Sílbhe's life. They'd always referred to Cian as "Grandma's gentleman friend" between themselves, but Sílbhe had never elaborated, only mentioning his name frequently enough for her family to know they were something to one another. *Oh, Cian and I are going to the opera,* or, *No, Cian was able to drive me.*

At her funeral, the man's eyes were red from the start, and he'd sobbed into a pressed handkerchief as though she'd been everything to him. Beforehand, the undertaker had shared his request that she might be buried with two pieces of jewelry. When Cora had opened the first box, she had found her mother's wedding ring. She was unsure when she'd stopped wearing it, perhaps when her knuckles became gnarly with arthritis. But a fine necklace chain had been added, which looked new. The second held a bracelet so small it could only ever have been intended for her mother's birdlike wrist. It was engraved with the inscription: YOU GO WITH MY HEART. LOVE ALWAYS, CX

"Do we have your permission?" the undertaker had asked. And Cora had nodded, feeling the trespass of being consulted, the trespass of looking at these things Cian had carefully prepared.

"When did you last speak to him?" Cora asks, passing Bear the wrench he's reaching for.

"We usually write. After Grandma died, I just carried on emailing from wherever I was. And I guess I've not stopped just because I'm back. I like him. And it's been helpful, you know, after Paris and everything."

"Does he write back?"

"Yeah. I'm not just sending missives into a void." Bear laughs from inside the cupboard.

Cora feels that odd momentary wonder that occasionally hits her to find that Bees and Bear are grown-up, independent people maintaining family relationships with no encouragement from her. She doesn't know why, at thirty-eight and twenty-nine, this surprises her, but it does. And she feels bad that she has not been more dutiful in maintaining a relationship with Cian herself.

"What are you going to ask him to make for you?"

"Oh, I don't know, some kind of anklet. Maybe a medallion," he says, laughing.

"Oh," Cora says, suddenly clicking. "You mean a ring! For goodness' sake, Bear, get out of that cupboard and tell me."

He tightens the compression fitting and then shuffles out. "You know, it wasn't until I was packing up her apartment that I realized everything Lily owns has this perfect form. You know, like she's really thought about it." Cora smiles. "So I thought I'd want it to be something really ergonomically satisfying, you know?" And then he catches himself and Cora can tell he's actually nervous about this. Uncharacteristically awkward in his desire to get it right. "God, it sounds like I'm talking about getting her a new garlic press, doesn't it?"

"No, I know what you mean. The kind of thing she'd want to twizzle around on her finger just because it feels nice to touch."

"Yeah," he says. "That's kind of what I told Cian on the phone last week. And I think he got it. I asked him to make it from gold and platinum."

"Oh, that's contemporary for sure, mixing metals. I like it," Cian had said with a soft chuckle. "When will you be needing it?" Bear had told him there was no rush—it's just something he wants to set in motion. "Well, my boy, it'll be a real honor to do this."

And even though it's just a turn of phrase, for a moment he'd felt unexpectedly touched, winded almost, to be referred to that way. *My boy*. When he hears Cian speak, Bear feels an odd nostalgia for something he's never had.

Julian

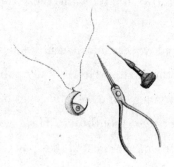

Julian sweeps around the supermarket on Fitzgibbon Street, dotting from the crisps and biscuits aisle to the ice-cream freezers, a jar of gherkins already in his hand. Just as Orla's cravings seem to exist at some primitive level, Julian's urge to satisfy them seems coded deep in his core. And like a contestant on a game show, he hears a ticking clock as he hunts down the items he needs. At the tills, he pauses momentarily, taking in the newspaper headlines TER-RORIST ATTACKS KILL OVER 100—FRANCE DECLARES STATE OF EMER-GENCY; MASSACRE IN PARIS.

When he gets in, Orla says, "You're back!" as though he's an explorer returning from an expedition. She told him once that when she asked him to go to the shop, she worried he might step into oncoming traffic and their future would be snatched from them because of her yen for mint choc-chip. It makes him smile to realize hunger gets the better of these worries. *Jules or ginger snaps? Jules or ginger snaps? Ginger snaps.* She seems to have an underlying faith that everything will be okay. But when he hears about something like the Paris attacks, it only confirms his view that everything *can* be taken away in an instant. His own life tells him these things happen to real people.

They sit in the window seat, her feet in his lap, as she spoons ice cream straight from the carton. He runs his palm against the pale stubble on her unshaven legs; she rolls her eyes but doesn't move.

"So," Orla asks between mouthfuls. "Have you given any more thought to names?" Orla has suggested they pay tribute to his mother: Cora for a girl; Cormac if it's a boy. He likes the idea of including her, she who has been denied the opportunity not only to be a mother, but now a grandmother too. Perhaps it would be a way of edging away darkness with new hope. But Julian remembers her as *Mum.* A soft word, which belonged only to him and Maia. Cora was one of *his* words. He remembers how it felt to hear her name said in a particular way. *Cora!* like a red flag. *Cora!* like a warning bell. Even now, the memory causes his shoulders to stiffen, his stomach to drop. He wonders if he could reclaim it for her, for the next generation. Liberate it. Yet—and it feels disloyal to admit it, as though the blame might lie with her—he bridles at the idea of forging a link between their baby and someone who died so tragically. *Tragically. Tragedy. Tragic.* Words that belong to news stories. And to his family, although he doesn't want them.

He's never wanted any of it. While his grandmother seeks out the opportunity to talk about what happened, to raise awareness, he's never wanted to dwell on it or display it as part of who he is. He hated having to confess his past to Orla; just the thought of it had caused him to raise his guard on the night of the flood all those years ago.

It was Cian who'd nudged him toward putting things right. "I don't hear you saying so much about that girl lately. Orla, was she called?" And when Julian had nodded, Cian had said, "I still miss the years I didn't have with your grandma, you know." Julian had looked up, seen Cian's eyes glistening, and his words had stayed with him in the weeks after, circling around his head while he worked.

At first, he'd considered writing to her, setting it out in a letter where he could choose the right words. But he hadn't wanted to commit the facts of his parents to paper.

And so one evening when they both stayed late, he waited for her bandsaw to fall silent and then knocked on the glass of her open door. She looked up and, on seeing him, a flicker of uncertainty crossed her face.

"Do you have time for a word?" he asked, and when she nodded, he crossed the room and leaned against the rolled top of the radiator. "I wanted to apologize about that night of the flood, like." She said there was no need, started sweeping offcuts into the corner with an efficient *must-press-on* air. "I wanted to explain something. Will you be putting down the broom a moment, Orla?"

"I'm—"

He interrupted where usually he would have held back. Now he was there, he just wanted to get it over with. "When I was five, my mam was killed." She stopped sweeping at that. Stood in the middle of the room, not knowing what to say. "It's not something I usually tell people about. I guess, when I say usually, I mean at all. But that night, I felt like I couldn't get into something without, you know, opening up. And I wasn't sure I was ready. I didn't want to lose what we had. Your friendship."

She raised her eyes at that. Not unkindly, but as if to say, *Well, that didn't go so well.* And he said, "Yeah," acknowledging what had gone unspoken. For a moment, it broke the tension and they laughed. "But I want to tell you now. If you'll listen."

She sat down on a stool, and he noticed the way she rested her hands in her lap, palms up. A gesture—although perhaps he was reading too much into it—that seemed to suggest a lack of judgment.

"My father," he said. And the word stuck in his throat like a gumball. He wasn't used to using terms that implied possession, not for this man unworthy of a name. "He was—Well, he abused my mam. Like *domestic* abuse, I suppose you'd say. And then one day, he killed her."

"Good God." Hands no longer open but pressed to her face. Julian stood, unsure what response might be growing in the space between them; the seconds bloated into minutes, hours, days in his mind. But finally, Orla looked up and asked, "Are you all right?" Hand moving to her mouth in the next moment. "Of course you're not all right. Sorry, I'm an eejit." And then, "I don't know what to say. But that's awful. You poor thing."

Julian wanted to sweep the conversation into the corner with the sawdust. He waved away her apology, tried to make light of what could not be made light. "But d'you see, I couldn't have got into anything without telling you first?"

"Because you're still dealing with it?" she asked, uncertain.

"No. Because it's only fair. I didn't want to be, like, tricking you into something. You know, get into a relationship—or whatever it might have been—and then be like, *Yeah, that guy you're seeing, well, he has half the genes of someone capable of murder.*"

"Oh," she said.

He felt that word—*murder*—hanging in the silence, dirty and contaminating. "D'you see now? Why it was difficult for me? That night."

Orla made circles in the dust with the tip of her shoe. And when she looked up again, she asked, "You really believe that? About the genes?"

"Well, I don't think I show any signs. You know, I have a pretty even temper and stuff, but—"

"Don't," she said. "I already know." She stared past him out of the window for a moment or two before speaking. "So, I've been out with a few fellas. But I've never thought to tell them that my da had an affair with his secretary."

"It's different," he said.

"I'm not so sure. I reckon the cheating gene is one most potential partners might like to know about."

"The cheating gene won't kill anyone."

"Neither would you, Jules. The sort of person who's capable of it, he doesn't confess his entire family history before even kissing a girl."

He smiled then, or at least let the grimace fade from his face. "So, you wouldn't have felt misled, like? You wouldn't have been horrified?"

"Only by what you've lived through. That something like that could have affected someone I know and care about."

"So would you—"

She interrupted. "That's what I was going to say earlier. I didn't think you were interested. I've been seeing someone."

"Oh," he said, the relief he'd felt moments earlier curling at the edges.

And so, they'd moved into an odd sort of friendship. Easy in trust and fondness, awkward in the attraction that sat between them, palpable but unmentioned.

But something in their conversation that night, about who he was and what he was made of, shifted things, and it felt like a door had opened, through which Julian could see potential relationships and his life growing bigger. Even if not with Orla.

For two years, they stayed in that no-man's land of working down the hall from one another. Comrades, colleagues, friends. Orla's relationship hadn't lasted long, but still they danced around one another. Until an evening intended to be just a quick drink was still unfolding as the pub landlord closed the doors on them. He remembers the sound of their shoes on wet pavement, their conversation echoing as they walked aimlessly along shuttered streets, the feel of his arm brushing hers, two bags of chips, and the salty tang of her kiss.

Later, Orla would say she always knew they'd end up together. But she'd sensed Julian needed time to become more himself.

"As though I were a tadpole gathering courage to metamorphose into a frog, while you were sat at the edge of a pond waiting to kiss me?" Julian laughed. "Seriously, Orla."

"No, you seriously, with your *maybe your jeans are dry now.*"

He laughs whenever she brings it up. He feels like a different person now. That wavery feeling quieter, stiller. Not gone completely, but if it were a piece of paper held beside a fan, the fan has been turned right down, leaving it wafting only gently in its breeze.

But some things remain no-go areas. Like England. Where he

doesn't have any wholesale stockists, despite mounting interest. Sometimes he will receive a commission from a customer in London or Bath or some other unfamiliar city. He's working on one now, an engagement ring sought by a man from Oxford named David, after he'd spotted Julian's work while he and his girlfriend were on holiday in Ireland. As they discussed the design in a long-running exchange of emails, details of his and his partner's life emerged. That his girlfriend has dark hair and pale skin, that she teaches secondary-school English. That, like Julian, she recently watched the retrospective about Philippe Petit crossing the void on a highwire between what were once the Twin Towers. That her name is Lily.

Last weekend they saw a honey buzzard, rare in England; David wonders if they're more common in Ireland. Julian asks Cian, who tells him they're most likely later in the year, blown off-course by strong winds. Julian has told David a bit about where he works at the Old Chocolate Factory; he's mentioned that he's about to become a father. He imagines the two couples would have enough in common to enjoy a drink together in person, and he's happy the ring he's made will be a part of David and Lily's lives. But still, when he thinks of shipping boxes wholesale across the Irish Sea, each one filled with something he's crafted, it feels too much.

Orla has suggested it several times, especially now the baby is coming. The money would help. But Julian doesn't want his jewelry—the boxes bearing his name—on display there, as though it's a place he feels no animosity toward, a place he's at peace with. When it wasn't just his father who killed his mother, but her adopted country too—where people who might have saved her during all those years of abuse looked the other way.

Like his grandmother, he blames God too. Because surely if there is a God, he also let his mother down. He doesn't want their child baptized into that when the time comes. Orla says it's just a rite of passage required for entry into 90 percent of the local schools. That it doesn't have to mean anything more to him. But there's something about it that feels hypocritical.

As Orla sets the empty ice-cream carton on the floor, Julian asks, "Why d'you still go to church?"

"Tradition," she says.

"Even though you moan about it every Sunday?"

"Only while I'm still in bed. That doesn't mean I don't get something out of it once I'm there. It's not even really the religion bit. It just warms you, the familiar faces, feeling a part of something. And the incense too. It smells like home. Safe, you know? And you sit there in the quiet, listening, and you get to thinking about something you've been wrestling with. And I don't know if it's those big high ceilings that just spirit it away—the blessed space—but when I leave, I always feel lighter. Ready to go into the week."

"But what about confession? Why would you want to tell someone your sins?"

"So I can be forgiven," she says, as though it's the most obvious thing in the world. "The alternative's hanging onto them. Having them grow inside you and making your face look like sour milk."

"Is that how I look?" he asks, souring his expression.

"You don't need to go making faces. Even smiling you could curdle fresh cream." Orla laughs, nudging his stomach with her toes.

She's sitting in the window seat that looks out onto their small road. Her blonde hair is lit up from behind by the sunshine. Her hand is resting on her belly. "There you are, looking like the Madonna. What bad things do you do that need confessing?" Julian asks. He can't think of a single thing she does that merits being called a sin.

"Stuff."

"What stuff?"

"I don't know. Maybe like not always thinking good thoughts. So, when Gráinne's work was exhibited over in London last year, instead of being pleased for her, I had all this horrible jealousy banging around in my head. About how her work isn't even that good and how that big yellow piece the critics loved looked like something a toddler might have done. And how sometimes I think she's better at applying meanings to her work retrospectively to make it seem deep, rather than just doing good work in the first place." Orla's cheeks flush like peach skin. "Yeah, maybe I'm still carrying some of that." She laughs, and her halo aura only seems to grow bigger and more lovely to Julian.

"But I agree with all that," he says. "Is it really sinful just to think it? You gave her a hug and bought a round to celebrate. It's not like you went into her studio and slashed her canvases."

"Oh, but I probably wanted to! But, yeah, that's part of trying to be a good Catholic. To notice when your thoughts aren't healthy. To do penance and try better next time. But from a selfish point of view, like, it also just stops it eating away at you too much."

Orla's version of religion always makes sense to Julian. But then he thinks of the Fathers, the abused choir boys, the unmarried mothers forced to give up their babies. The men who beat their wives and then head to the confession box for absolution. And he wants no part of it.

MAIA CROSSES THE BRIDGE, and at the main road, turns south toward town, which has a canopy of dark cloud hanging over it. She switches off the radio and uses the rest of the drive to think through the day's patients.

She checks her watch and makes a run for it across the street to Doyle's as fat splotches of rain begin to fall. When the bell above the door rings, Maureen looks up and smiles. "If only I'd still got you behind the counter. We've had the world and his wife wanting a cooked breakfast this morning, I tell you. And Lizzy's called in sick. Again. That girl, she'll be the death of me, she will."

"Well, at least I can get my own coffee," Maia says, going into the kitchen.

"Oh, be off with you there. Getting your uniform all dirty," she says, shooing Maia away. Maia's never thought of the wardrobe of navy and white she wears on workdays as a uniform, but she supposes it is in a way.

She heads back across the road, trying not to slop the hot drink down her front, and turns on the lights and heating in her practice rooms.

Her first patient of the day is a middle-aged woman. She came first with persistent headaches around the time of her divorce, returning a year later with symptoms of menopause. Maia asks questions to help narrow her choice of remedy. *Do you prefer hot or cold drinks? Spicy or sour flavors?* Sometimes, these supporting details fail to reveal a clear picture and Maia knows she'll spend hours consulting her battered copy of Murphy's *Materia Medica*. But other times, some small aside feels like being handed a corner jigsaw piece, the other symptoms coalescing around it. "I think I know what we'll try this time," Maia says, heading to her medicine chest. There is something reassuring about opening a drawer and seeing all the carefully alphabetized caps labeled with their different potencies.

As Maia taps pilules into a bottle and prepares a label, the woman mentions seeing her ex-husband with an old friend. "How are you feeling about it?" Maia asks.

"I don't know," she admits. "Sometimes it feels easier not to think. It'd be like opening a dam."

Maia nods. She knows this feeling. She's been seeing a counselor for the last few years, but she, too, has been slow to lift the heaviest stones and look at the dark earth beneath, where her fears and worries flee the light like scurrying woodlice. She's talked about her early childhood, said just enough about that awful day to acknowledge its existence. But she hides the details even from herself.

Lately, she's been wrestling with other things too. The idea that Julian, nine years her junior, is moving on with his life at a pace that's outstripping her own: married, with a mortgage, and a baby on the way. People tell her to get down to the annual matchmaking festival in the tiny village of Lisdoonvarna, where couples have been brought together for over a century. They joke that she needs to lay her hands on Willie Daly's lucky book to break the spell and meet Mr. Right. And she smiles and laughs along because she wants to be good craic. But inside she feels an Englishness: what business is it of theirs and why does she have to be *fun* all the time?

But it's not just this—Julian lapping her, failing to find the right man. One evening, watching the television with Sílbhe and Cian, a piece on the referendum around legalizing same-sex marriage comes on. "Is it not just common sense that folk should be left alone to get on with their lives?" Cian says.

"It's down to the Church that it's even taken this long," Sílbhe says.

Maia is surprised to find herself comforted to hear their views confirmed out loud.

The television shows a montage of public opinion—at a bus stop, in the aisles of a supermarket. Most are in favor, apart from an older man in a flat cap who says gravely, "No, I don't think it's right."

Two women are interviewed on a beach. One blonde, one dark. They wear knitted hats. One has pierced ears, the other a small nose stud. They're not touching, but you can tell they're together. And they glow. They just glow. The presenter's question is lost on the wind, but their answer is clear. They say they're in love, that they just want the opportunity to spend their lives together like any straight couple.

Watching the rest of the news segment, Maia feels the same discomfort she does whenever a sex scene comes on TV if she's watching with Sílbhe and Cian. As though she mustn't move, mustn't betray any sign she's aware of what's happening on screen by reminding them of her existence. Even though she immediately aches to uncross her legs, to move a stray hair from her face, to breathe. She realizes she feels a personal investment in the referendum and reddens—although she's unsure why; they've already made their views clear. It wouldn't matter to them if she's gay.

So, it is not family pressure, guilt, or the Church that she takes to counseling. But something harder to deal with: her own judgment.

"I'd always thought it was because of what happened to my mum.

That that's why I'm not with anyone. But then, I was watching this couple being interviewed on television about the referendum. Two women. And I realized perhaps I wanted that. That it somehow felt right, you know? But then I felt ashamed too."

"Because you might be gay?"

"Because I might be an imposter. Jumping on a bandwagon."

"Can you say more?"

Maia glances at the clock, reassuring herself there's enough time left to go into this. "Everyone says being gay isn't a choice. That you're born that way. But I'm thirty-seven. And I'm only thinking about it now."

They revisit this idea over several sessions. And Maia feels she and her counselor are like two old ladies from her grandmother's quilt group, gathering around with magnifying glasses, peering at the stitches, inspecting from all angles. *Well, it looks like a quilt. It feels like a quilt. There's definitely a layer of wadding in there. But is it actually a quilt?*

"What if I only want a relationship with a woman because I'm scared of having one with a man? In case he turns out like *him*."

"Would that matter to you?"

"Yes. I'd be making life choices out of fear, avoidance."

The counselor pauses. "I'm trying to put myself in your shoes . . ." Maia looks down at her own trainers, imagines the therapist coming to join her in them. She remembers walking around the living room that way with her mother. Her feet planted atop her mum's, their legs moving as one. "What if those two things were to coexist?" the counselor says. "That you could be both gay *and* understandably fearful of a romantic relationship with a man?"

Maia blinks away the memory and considers the question. "So my gayness is, what, natural *and* manmade?" They both laugh at her choice of word. "I keep asking myself why now, though."

"And have you come to an answer?"

"Obviously it wouldn't have been an option in my father's house. But I've been with my grandmother for so many years now."

"But the things you can't admit to yourself at a formative age, do they suddenly become acceptable with a change of circumstance or because you've reached eighteen?"

Maia doesn't think about how she might meet someone, doesn't join a dating site, or consider telling her family. Instead, she just turns the possibility of being gay over in her mind like a smooth pebble in the palm of her hand, and occasionally she thinks of the couple on television. And when the right to same-sex marriage is enshrined in law on November 16, 2015, a bubble of hope inflates in her chest, as though some distant part of her future has been secured.

Gordon

Neither of them is home yet. Her son is meeting Maia after work; her husband is . . . where? He doesn't tell Cora when he won't be home. So this evening she makes dinner as usual and as six-thirty turns to seven, as the melted cheese topping on a feta and spinach bake starts to resolidify, she waits. Waits for his key in the lock, waits to see what his mood will be. Her mind pitter-patters around the idea that, this time, he might be dead. That perhaps, somewhere between work and home, he's been hit by a motorcyclist as he's stepped out to cross the road, and is now in a hospital, medics attempting to jump-start his heart. But then she shoos the thought away, as though he might return able to discern what she's been thinking.

At eight o'clock, she covers the untouched dish in foil and puts it in the fridge. Then, she makes herself some bread and butter and eats it standing, prepared to put it in the bin if needed.

Next year, he's due to retire. She tries to imagine what her life will be like then and tells herself perhaps things might change when he's no longer a doctor. After she'd agreed to come back last time, she'd believed it was on different terms, only later realizing it was not what she'd expected. At first, he'd been kind and gentle, praising her cooking, talking with her about his work and books and politics, taking her out for dinner. Bringing home a cashmere sweater, presenting her with jewelry. He'd even suggested they renew their vows. He'd got up early each morning—"No, stay there, it's okay"— and brought her tea and toast in bed. And she'd believed it all. She'd felt as though she was floating on a cloud.

She also felt tired. Gordon said it was probably the emotional upheaval, the relief of being home again after her latest episode. That was how he referred to her attempts to leave, as though they were brief dalliances with madness. But he'd kissed her forehead, made her dinner, and each evening she'd drifted off, her head against his chest, his arm around her, as he'd shared the day's news—how the prime minister had resigned; the previous one reinstated. *Who needs TV or radio when you have me?* he'd joked. And so they'd fallen into that routine, of him caring and her being cared for. And the weeks and months seemed to pass in a blur. A woozy time, where she questioned the resentments she'd once felt, wondering if she'd misinterpreted his actions; had she really not seen the sacrifice in him doing the food shop each week after a full day at the practice? Had she not stopped to appreciate the small treats he sought out for her, the bundle of asparagus that sometimes appeared, even though it was a favorite he despised?

"I love spring," she'd said, admiring the daffodils in a neighbor's garden as she opened the curtains one morning.

"Very early for February, though," he'd replied. And she'd felt sure it was April.

She wondered if he could be right; if her tiredness wasn't just relief at being home, at the shift in their relationship after all these years. But a few weeks later, it hadn't lifted, and her thoughts were increasingly foggy and confused. "Don't worry," he'd said as he folded her into his arms. "It may be some kind of post-viral fatigue. I'll arrange for an assessment."

"What kind of assessment?" she'd said.

"Just to make sure everything's as it should be, cognitively. No big deal: it's what I'd do for any of my patients. Pretty much standard procedure post sixty; I should probably check myself in for one." She'd been touched by this uncharacteristic moment of vulnerability. It was so unlike him to concede any kind of weakness in himself.

On the day of the assessment, she'd felt more energetic and wondered if it was really necessary. "Perhaps it's adrenaline," Gordon had said. But still, when she was asked to count backward from ten, she'd stumbled over the numbers, and when she'd named the current prime minister, said what month it was, she saw the assessor glance toward Gordon momentarily. "But I thought—" and Gordon had covered her hand with his. "It's okay, you're doing really well," he'd told her, and she'd felt sure something wasn't quite right, but was also oddly comforted by having him care for her.

She'd become used to Gordon helping around the house. Used to the feeling of being loved. It reminded her of the early days of their relationship and made her feel vindicated in staying with him all that time. But then, it seemed to shift back without warning. One evening, as she squirted washing-up liquid under the running water and asked, "Do you want to wash or dry?" she heard him sigh.

"You seem much better now. I'm sure you can get back to doing the cooking and cleaning."

"Oh, yes, right," she stumbled. And so they'd returned to their normal posts—her doing the dishes in the kitchen, as he watched the evening news in the living room.

Cora can't remember now what caused him to snap. Only how it ended. With bruised ribs, and her gathering her things to leave again; she hadn't come back for this. But then Gordon presented her with the document. *A Lasting Power of Attorney.* Proof of his legal control over her health and welfare, over her finances and property.

"Oh, Cora. Did you really think I'd let you go again after last time?" He touched a finger to her cheek, as though to console her. Then he returned to the sofa. "I thought you might make it harder for me . . . But, no, so desperate to be loved." He patted the seat beside him, inviting her to sit down. "Did you really believe they'd got John Major out of the cupboard to lead the country again, though?" he said, shaking his head at her stupidity.

It was still her plan, at that point, to find a way of contacting Maia. The police even. She just needed to bide her time until he'd left for work the next morning. But when she woke, he said a locum would be covering his morning surgery and told her they were going on an adventure. She knew he was playing with her, yet she was still thrown when they pulled into the car park of an old people's home.

But then, as he told the receptionist they had an appointment to be shown around, that they were interested in seeing the dementia floor with a view to housing a relative, she understood.

The dementia wing was three floors up—*extra protection for anyone prone to wandering*, they were told by Erica, the manager, as she ushered them through the double layer of security doors with a key fob. Erica was businesslike, but careful to greet each resident warmly by name in between answering Gordon's questions. *Yes, very happy to continue administering whatever medication the resident had already been prescribed; No, we've never had a resident escape the bounds of the building; Yes, we're used to dealing with paranoia—accusations against staff and relatives are common with dementia patients.* And as if to demonstrate her point, as they entered the day room, a lady seated in a vinyl-covered armchair wearing a plastic bib began to squawk, "No, no, no! I know what you want! Don't hurt me!" Her eyes as wild as her uncombed hair.

"That's Elsie," the manager told them, as though naming her might explain her distress.

They drove home in silence. And only when they'd pulled onto the drive and Gordon had turned off the ignition did he speak. "There, isn't it nice to be home?" The engine ticked as it cooled down. He didn't need to say anything else. She understood. It felt as though her spine, the gaps between vertebrae, were collapsing. As though she were sinking into the car's upholstery and might never get up from it.

It has changed things, though, having their son living at home with them again. Cora keeps waiting for things to go back to the way they were—them against her—but the younger man is different.

Cora sees there is a rawness about him, like fair skin beneath scorching sun, eyes blinking into too-bright light. She wants to draw him to her, to cuddle him, but that's never been the relationship they've had, and she doesn't know where to begin.

Rob opens the plastic tub of rabbit-skin glue, and the odor hits Gordon straight away. It doesn't smell bad when it's fresh, but when it's not, it's a reminder something has died. Rob cringes as he snaps the lid back on. "That's what I get for going on holiday. Do you fancy making some more up while you tell me how you've been getting on?"

"What proportions—eight to one?" Gordon asks, knowing the consistency Rob likes for sealing a canvas.

Rob nods as Gordon opens the cupboard. He is grateful to be able to do these simple tasks—it helps to have a purpose at Rob's studio when he needs to get out of his parents' house; to make their relationship feel more reciprocal than sponsor/sponsee. "So how did you get on last week?" Rob asks, switching on a paint-spattered electric radiator in the corner.

"Okay, I suppose," Gordon says.

"Oh? That doesn't sound too good. Did you drink?" Rob had been readying his small artist's studio above a pet shop for work, but now he's leaning back against the sideboard crammed with paints and mediums, watching. He does this, Rob. Has the ability to make it seem like they're just hanging out, then in the next moment leaves Gordon feeling as though all his attention is trained on him. Not in the way his dad does, more like someone watching their favorite football team taking a penalty: barely able to blink for wanting to see the net bulge. It's nice to have someone rooting for him, but it's weirdly intense too.

"No, no, it's nothing like that," Gordon says, and Rob visibly relaxes. "Just, you know, that thing of looking back at what an arse you've been to different people over the course of your life."

Rob gives a low laugh. "Yeah, I know that one."

Rob hasn't touched alcohol for more than a decade, but his eyes are permanently red-rimmed, as though his body has chosen to wear his regrets like a tattoo. He'd had a wife and child, once.

Gordon's own downfall makes him cringe. It was gaudy and cinematic, and not in a good way, just in a way that feels clichéd. Losing his composure at work; coming in on a Monday still stumbling drunk from the weekend. And where once he'd been one of the lads—*Gordy-boy!*—through the haze, he'd sensed himself becoming a pariah. The climax came just near Junction 8 on the M25, where he overturned a Porsche and his body had to be cut from its crumpled metal with hydraulics. He remembers someone talking to him, warning him of any loud noises, reassuring him he was going to be okay, and he recalls wanting to die rather than having to bear that person's unwarranted kindness.

There's been a surprising relief in losing everything, though. He always aspired to be someone, and now he's nothing, he finds that somehow feels like more.

"I was thinking about this girl. Lily," Gordon tells Rob as he levels off a measure of crystallized rabbit-skin granules. "I—we—were fourteen. I sat next to her in maths. She was—now I look back—one of the few people from school who was really kind to me. For no reason. Just because she felt like it. And I . . ."

He tells Rob about the night of the party when he'd pinned her against a tree, and later, how he'd turned on her and encouraged the other boys to do the same. "I didn't know what it would do to her. How it would pan out. But it was different after that. When boys passed her in the hallways—even the ones who weren't in our year—they'd sniff their fingers and make, I don't know, retching noises or something."

As Gordon opens a bottle of deionized water, he glances up to gauge Rob's reaction. Rob has one hand splayed across his chin, thumb brushing against two-day-old stubble. But he looks more thoughtful than judgmental, so Gordon continues, even though he's wishing he could just put all this away in a box somewhere.

"And the girls, they just sort of drifted away from her. She got this stammer, in class. And I didn't know what was happening at the time, but now, well, I think she'd started having panic attacks too. After that school year, she never came back. I thought she'd moved away or something, but then one of the girls—her mum must have known Lily's mum—found out she'd totally cracked up. I remember sitting there laughing with the others, making jokes about the local loony bin—Maudine, it was called; I think it's gone now—but I was shocked."

"And you think the two things were linked? What happened and her breakdown, I mean."

"Probably. She was just a normal girl before that. Well, not normal. Special. Bright. Really good at English and stuff. And just really kind, like I said."

Gordon is aware that so much of what he's said has come out wrongly. *Cracked up. Loony bin.* He wishes he was better at choosing the right words. There was a time—goading his mum to gain his father's approval; being *one of the boys* at work—when his words fitted in. Were expected, even. But now they don't feel like him, none of this feels like him, or at least not a part of himself he wants to keep.

A few weeks ago, when he'd arrived early for a meeting, Gordon had sat in some nearby gardens, beside a lichen-covered reproduction of *David*: nose sheared off, a limb hewn away. And ever since, he hasn't been able to shake the image of a shattered statue—not just a missing arm, but a literal pile of rubble; disembodied lips and fingers, a jumble of barely distinguishable body parts. Gordon has the overwhelming feeling that what he's doing here—at group, with Rob, in every part of his life—is attempting to use those fractured, misshapen pieces to build something new. And the realization dawning on him is that it's simply not possible to keep the cracks from showing.

Gordon returns his attention to Rob. "Anyway, I looked her up online the other night. Yeah, I know," he says, seeing Rob grimace as if to say, *That's never a good idea.* "She's married. Two kids. Works in law. At first, I was just pleased for her, that everything had turned out okay, you know? But then I went onto her firm's website." He winces at the memory, the moment of realization. "And she's this— this human rights lawyer, specializing in justice for women and girls. Rape, assault. And I just—I just thought, *I did that.* What I did changed the whole course of her life. And she's still carrying it with her." He sighs. "It's probably what motivates her, makes her good at her job. I mean, I'm not trying to take credit for it—more the opposite. That she's turned my . . ."—even though Rob is already nodding, Gordon pauses, trying to find the right word this time—"my darkness, into something good. She's won, in spite of me."

Gordon realizes Rob hasn't said a thing this whole time and suddenly worries he may have crossed a line; he's not sure he's meant to lay things like this on his sponsor. "Sorry, was that a bit much?"

Rob shakes his head and his eyes look even more red-rimmed than usual. "I just feel sad for you. And her. But you're right, she's made something good out of it." They stand in silence for a while and eventually Rob says, "But you didn't have a drink?"

"No, I just felt like shit."

"Nice," Rob says, with a look of gentle satisfaction.

"Can I not come with you?" Kate asks, tapping a cigarette into an ashtray on the bedside table. Maia busies herself with looking through her bag for something. "Maia?" Kate repeats, moving to sit up in bed.

"We've been through all this," Maia says. Kate wasn't even meant to be free today; it's only because Dr. Shah asked if she'd swap shifts that it's suddenly an issue.

"That was before the accident. Before you said he seemed like he was morphing into someone you actually liked."

"It's still too early." She pictures Gordon in the psych ward after his accident. He'd always had such a physical presence. Solid, well-built. But when she entered the room that first time, he was sitting in a hospital bed, all his focus on getting a slice of overcooked carrot onto his fork, and he'd looked so reduced. So vulnerable. They never touched—not then—but she'd put her hand to his wrist and sat beside him on the bed. Neither had spoken, but after a while, giant teardrops sploshed onto his plate. She'd traced the birthmark on his forearm, circling its edge with her fingertip. "It's like a heart," she said. "I'd never noticed that before." He'd pulled away then, not roughly, but so only his inner arm was visible. "It's deformed," he said, his voice raspy. She strained to catch his words as he added, "I must've been bad even before I was born." He'd sobbed then, so loudly the ward nurse looked up. Under her gaze, Maia felt compelled to lean in and comfort him, to let her shoulder grow wet with his pain.

"Too early for who? Him or you?" Kate is saying. "Because after what he's been through, I don't think finding out you're gay is going to be that big a deal to him."

"That's never been the big deal. The big deal is him telling our dad."

"Which I still don't get. You're thirty-eight, Maia."

"Thirty-seven."

"What? Stop deflecting. I could come along as a friend, your flat-mate. You don't even have to tell him."

"Don't do this."

"Do what?"

"This," Maia says, as she checks her hair in the mirror and picks off one of Kate's long red strands, which must have migrated from the brush. "Wheedling. It isn't you."

"No, it isn't. It really isn't. Except with you, because you give me no choice. I've spent seven years—seven years!—pretending to everyone at work that we're not in a relationship in case someone tells someone and that someone happens to know your dad, and then happens to actually mention it to him. Like, *Hey, Dr. A, I heard your daughter was gay!* because that's really the kind of thing people still bother to mention in 2015."

"And we've spent seven years having the same argument."

Kate takes a drag on her cigarette and when she speaks again, her voice is calmer. "All I'm asking is for you to let me meet your brother. Because I love you. And I want to know your people, even if they're not perfect." She sees Maia's jaw tense and adds, "I don't mean your dad. But Gordon. Your mum, if there's ever a safe time for that."

Maia sits on the edge of the bed, folding and refolding the fabric of her dress. Kate kneels beside her, brushes Maia's hair to one side, nuzzles the warm skin of her neck.

"How long would it take you to get ready?" Maia says quietly, while outside rain thrums against the window and a just-emptied wheelie bin clatters down the side alley.

"Not long."

"Okay then," Maia says, not really sure what she's agreeing to, but knowing Kate deserves more.

Kate has already started coiling her hair into a bun as she disappears into the bathroom, and while she clatters around getting changed, Maia sits in her coat, waiting. She feels physically tired by their argument, but when she thinks of walking to the tube station, she's glad she'll have Kate with her. She will deal with the rest—her brother, dinner—as it comes.

HIS SISTER INTRODUCES the woman only as Kate. And Gordon isn't sure why, but as they stand on the corner deciding what to do with the hour before dinner, Maia struggling to keep her umbrella from turning inside out, he realizes they're probably a couple. Maia's never mentioned a man, but then she hasn't talked about a woman either. With nine years between them, he's never really known much about her life. Only in the last few months has this begun to change. Now, he knows that she likes watching hospital dramas to try to diagnose the patient before the on-screen medics do; that she's never been overdrawn, although she has run up a £20 fine at the library and is too embarrassed to go in to pay it off; that she rides a bike to work each day, but can't run because her ankles are weak from the years of ballet when she was younger; that she has a cat called Poppy.

Maia looks from him to Kate in that recognizably nervy way of someone who has just introduced two people and is unsure what they might be thinking of one another. Gordon decides it's probably best to assume they're a couple and let them correct him if he's wrong, and as they walk down St. Martin's Lane toward the gallery they've decided to shelter in, he says to Kate, "How long have you two been together?"

"Seven years now, I think. That's right, isn't it, Maia?" Kate says, and Maia nods, her face flushing.

Gordon cringes. "Seven years. Sorry, I guess I've never asked."

"Oh, that's okay—my brother still hasn't met Maia. At least in person," Kate says. "He lives in Australia."

Gordon is grateful that Kate is trying to make everything seem normal. But for the second time today, he feels he's being confronted with the person he once was. First at school with Lily, and now, just a few months ago, before the accident. Someone who couldn't be trusted, even by his own sister.

Their voices, even their footsteps, echo in the gallery, and he wonders if it was the best place to have come. Although Rob often talks to Gordon about art, when Kate comments on the light or a subject's expression, he can't think of anything interesting to say in return, so instead only murmurs his agreement. Maia is quieter than usual, but a few times he catches some tiny intimacy pass between the two women—a look, the way they stand before a painting with their shoulders almost touching—and he feels crestfallen. As though he is on the outside, when he's only just started to feel on the inside with his sister. He shakes himself, knowing he has no right to feel jealous. "I like this one," he says, pointing to a Cézanne, determined to make an effort.

Kate doesn't seem to mind the simplicity of his statement and says, "Oh, me too. That's one of my absolute favorites."

"Yeah, lots of energy," Gordon says, and this time, Maia turns to look at him. Their eyes meet for just a second, but he picks up some indefinable thing, like thanks or approval. It seems to allow her to relax into her own body for the first time since they've met today.

They stop in front of a hideous image, a painting on loan from a gallery in Madrid. It shows a naked man, frenzied and wild-eyed, consuming a smaller figure, its bloodied, headless body clasped between his hands. Maia nods toward it and says quietly, "Does it make you think of Dad?"

Gordon studies the artwork—his eyes traveling across it, taking in each detail—then the label beside it. *Saturn Devouring His Son, Francisco Goya, c. 1820–23*. His stomach drops. It sandpapers a rawness he hadn't known was inside him, and it feels too much to carry on looking.

⌒⌒⌐⌐⌒⌒

I<small>N A PASTA</small> restaurant back near the tube station, the three of them chat easily as they twirl spaghetti onto forks. The mood only changes when there's a break in the rain and Kate excuses herself to go outside for a cigarette. As soon as she's left the table, Maia says, "I'm sorry, I shouldn't have said that earlier. In the gallery, about the painting and Dad. It was stupid."

Gordon seems surprised she's mentioned it and brushes off her apology. "Is that how you see it, though?" he says. "*Do* you think Dad consumed me?"

He sounds so vulnerable, so earnest, Maia wishes again she could take back her words. She glances out of the window at Kate's familiar profile leaning silhouetted against the wall. The tip of her cigarette glowing in the darkness, first up near her face, then resting down by her side, the dot of red light bouncing slightly as she taps away ash with her index finger. Maia doesn't need daylight to fill in the gaps; she knows Kate's short, clean nails and the way she closes her eyes momentarily just before she exhales. She turns back to Gordon, sensing his eyes on her, waiting for an answer. "I don't know if *consumed* is the right word. Manipulated, though. You were rewarded for being awful to Mum, before you'd had a chance to . . . I don't know, form your own conscience, I guess."

She pauses, not knowing if this is what he needs to hear. But he's still sitting there looking like an animal caught in a trap pleading for her to let him out, so she goes on. "So it screwed with you. He didn't care about you becoming your own person, he just wanted to mold you into something that could hurt Mum."

Gordon's head drops and they're both silent now. The waiter arrives and asks if everything is all right with their meal and they both nod and say it's delicious, even as the pasta congeals in their bowls. They make small talk, but it's as though the painting is still with them, and suddenly neither has the appetite for what's in front of them.

Maia sees Kate stubbing out her cigarette beneath the sole of her shoe outside, and in a rush of words, an attempt to salvage things, says, "You know, it's not just you. We've both let Mum down. You'd think at my age, in my profession, I'd have found a way to help her, to fix things. But it's different when it's family. I can't work out how he has such a hold over her." Kate is approaching the table now. "I don't understand why she stays; why she goes back. The only thing we can do is be there when she needs us."

Kate sits down. "Is everything okay?" she asks, her hair darkened in patches where rainwater must have dripped from the awning.

"Yeah. We were just chatting about Dad. Nothing quite like it to ruin the mood." Maia looks at Gordon rather than Kate as she speaks, hoping he'll understand they're in this together. Because whenever she thinks of her mother, her whole being pricks with guilt. For not being enough. For not being a daughter Cora will confide in. For not challenging her father as she's grown older, because the moment she's in his presence, she's nine years old again, hollow and scared, the wind blowing straight through her. Medicine is their only common ground. Their only safe topic. Which comes as a relief, but also a betrayal. So it's easier not to think too much. To exist in the calm between the moments of intense, mind-spinning panic, which arrive without warning and make her breath ragged until

Kate has talked her down. Until she finds a way to normalize her mum still being in that house. With no direct access to her own children, not even a door key to come and go as she pleases.

They skip dessert and Kate asks for the bill.

"Sorry," Gordon says, as Maia opens her wallet.

"I was the one who suggested dinner. It's fine." She knows there was a time when he would have nonchalantly tossed a credit card onto the table and that it must pain him not to be able to contribute now.

Outside, the three of them shelter in a doorway on the opposite side of the street. "I hope this hasn't been too much for you," Maia is saying, searching Gordon's face for clues, but whatever connection they've made has somehow fallen loose. He's avoiding eye contact, staring at the people through the windows of the restaurant they've just left.

He's probably dreading going home, she thinks. It depresses her to think of the three of them in that house. Still gathered joylessly around that table. Her mother has left four times now. The first and the second time, Maia had thought it was permanent. She has begun to count off these attempts, seeing their only purpose as bringing them one step closer to seven. Seven is the magic number. A talisman. It is the average number of times a woman will attempt to leave an abusive partner before she's finally successful. She'd said this one night before sleep and realized from Kate's pause, from the not-quite-silent intake of breath and her hand squeezing Maia's, that she was thinking, *But it's an average. There will be outliers. There will be some who never manage it or who run out of life trying.* And Maia knows how unscientific, how irrational, her thinking is when it comes to her family.

"Goodbye then," Gordon says.

But Maia isn't quite ready to part. She needs to extract some sort of assurance from him. "You won't . . . Gordon?" She uses his name to try to draw his attention back to her. "You won't, er, mention this to Dad, will you?"

"Mention what?" he says, and she can tell he's not really hearing her.

"About me and Kate, and—"

"She'd prefer it if you didn't tell your father she's gay," Kate says flatly.

"Oh, right. Yeah, not a word."

GORDON'S EYES ARE flickering back to the couple in the window, to the glass of wine in the woman's hand, its velvety liquid falling toward the lip of her glass as she tilts it to drink. Maia is saying something, and he knows he is thanking her and saying what a nice evening it's been and that they should do it more often, but in his mind, he is already halfway down the street.

Once they've parted at Leicester Square tube station, Gordon heads along the road. The pavement is busy with people, but he doesn't see them. His eyes are on the signs above the shops, thinking about the velvet-red of the woman's wine. He can already taste it on his tongue, catch the whisper of its scent as he imagines taking the cork from the bottle he'll buy.

Eventually, he finds a corner shop, sees the white strip-lighting inside. He travels between the aisles with the focus of a sniffer dog, moving around other shoppers as though they are inanimate obstacles. And then he finds what he is looking for. Rows of Merlot, Shiraz, Pinot Noir, Malbec. Gordon picks out a cheaper Cabernet Sauvignon and there is instant comfort in having the bottle in his hand, in its pristine label, its contents dark and promising. He wants to sink into it, to consume it and let it consume him.

But then, just as he is approaching the till, his eyes catch on it. There, on the shelf behind the checkout. *Gordon's.* Its familiar green glass. The cursive script that spells out his name. That says, *Yours.* And that now also says, *Lily.* And *lawyer,* and *assault,* and the way he'd felt today when he'd shared his memories of that night and its aftermath with Rob. And later, realizing his own sister hadn't trusted him. And he is thinking, *Oh, God,* and wanting to be far away from that bottle, from that name, from *his* name, from the red Sauvignon, and the mistake he was about to make. He shoves the wine back onto a nearby shelf, crushing it in amongst family-sized bags of crisps. And then he turns and sprints from the shop.

"Hey!" someone calls after him. And he holds up his empty hands to whoever might be out on the street watching him go, and runs.

Seven Years Later

2022

Bear

Pearl digs at the dry earth with a small trowel and when she feels there is a sufficiently large hole, she lays down the tool, and arranges a cross-hatching of twigs across the void, selecting just the right lengths to bridge the gap. She takes a small blue watering can over to the outdoor tap at the back of the house. Her mother's voice calls out from inside, asking if she needs help, and Pearl calls back, "S'okay. I've got it," as she grips the stiff metal lever and loosens it. She smiles. Proud that, like most things, she *has* got it. She takes the can back to the hole in the lawn and pours a light sprinkling of water across her work. She watches as the earth turns dark and the twigs are set in place a little better. Then she squats down, the hem of her dress trailing in mud. She takes three shiny leaves stripped from the laurel bush earlier and lays them over the twigs to darken the hollow beneath. A perfect den for woodlice and creepy-crawlies. She will look tomorrow and see if any have come. But in the meantime, she works her way across the lawn to check on the homes she's created on previous days, slowly peeling back one leaf at a time, careful not to shock the creatures with a sudden rush of light.

Lily watches Pearl through the window as she folds a basket of clean washing. She can see so much of Bear in her. In her independence, her love of rummaging about in the earth, her gentleness. During lockdown, while Lily worked on cataloging the library's ebooks, Bear took care of her schooling, skimming over the work her teachers set online in favor of practical things. On the hill outside their house, they'd lifted the paving bricks to forage beneath them for treasure. Practiced adding and subtracting with Roman money. Lily would overhear Pearl trying to pronounce the Latin names: *aureus, denarius, quinarius,* and laughing with Bear over an emperor who'd minted thirteen different coins bearing his own image during a single year's reign. "Shall we make coins with us on them?" Pearl asked. "Even more than Quietus!"

Later, when Bear's museum work moved online, he and Pearl had streamed their archaeological adventures to the home-schooling community and encouraged them to bury their own time capsules.

Lily had enjoyed those days. The three of them always within earshot of one another, cocooned. A protective web spun around their home. In the hour just before sunset, they would venture out. "Remember masks!" Pearl would say, hoping to stop at the café serving ice creams from an open window.

And in the quiet beauty of the world, they would coast down the center of carless roads on their bikes, the silky smooth of the tarmac rushing beneath their wheels, Pearl sitting on Lily's handlebars. "Faster, Mama, faster!" she would shout, as Bear whooped alongside them, seagulls squawking overhead. Halcyon days. Days that, around the edges of fear, glistened with strange newness and freedom.

It was a Thursday when it happened. An ordinary day, its agenda set by the nocturnal banging of the cold-water tank in the loft.

"I'll fix it today," Bear said into his pillow, as sunlight finally spilled through the thin veil of their curtains. Sitting up in bed, he mentally retraced the solutions he'd found on a plumbers' forum earlier in the week. Fitting baffle vanes inside the cistern, replacing the diaphragms or, his own choice, installing a larger ball float.

"We could get someone in," Lily had said.

"Why risk it? And I can take Pearl; she'll like pottering around up there."

Anxieties—the area of unboarded joists near the eaves, the gaping hole of the open loft hatch—flickered across Lily's mind and then faded. She'd stretched, content, because Pearl would be with Bear. Bees' wife, Charlotte, had once told Lily how, carrying a basket around the wide aisles of the posh supermarket in town, she'd felt insulated, as though nothing bad could happen while she was cradled by its spacious architecture, surrounded by its carefully ordered produce. "That's how I feel when I'm with Bear," Lily had said, the words forming before she'd had a chance to consider them.

Charlotte had laughed. "Lucky you. Don't tell Bees, but I'll need to keep going to Waitrose to get my fix."

Lily had been embarrassed. By how clichéd her view of Bear—a man—might seem. She'd added, "I think it's all those years abroad doing his digging. I guess you just end up being very capable when you spend so much time in the middle of nowhere." Although she realized it wasn't that at all. It was how he'd changed after Paris.

Charlotte had nodded, dark hair brushing at her jawline. "Yes, that's true—it *is* oddly reassuring having him close by. And you, of course, but you know what I mean."

Up in the loft, Bear and Pearl took the lid from the cold-water tank. "Have you got it?" Bear asked. Pearl stepped in to grip one of its sides and together they leaned it against the rafters, droplets of condensation soaking into dusty chipboard flooring.

"I can see into Mrs. Greene's garden from here," Pearl said, standing on tiptoe to look through the small cobwebbed window on the gable wall.

Bear lowered his hands into the water, positioning his spanner against a brass nut. "How are her runner beans looking?"

"Tall. Preeetty tall. Her wigwam is bigger than ours."

"What do you think? That taller canes encourage her beans to climb, or she's put them in because they outgrew the shorter ones?"

"I'm not sure," Pearl said, her face pressed close to the dusty glass. "But I'd sure like to know her secret."

Bear smiled to himself—he loved hearing Pearl adopting grown-up phrases.

As he worked, Pearl sorted through an old pile of books. "I don't remember any of these. Are you saving them for if there's another baby?" she asked as she turned thick fabric pages, pausing to peer into a circle reflecting her own image.

"Nope. Mainly so that when we're old, we can remember reading them to you," Bear said as he tightened the metal arm of the new ball float. "There. Want to help put the lid back on?"

She put the book aside and stood up. "Why does it need a lid?"

"To keep the mice out."

"Are there mice up here?" Pearl asked, peering into the eaves, as they slid the plastic cover back into place.

"No, it's more of a *just-in-case*," he said, brushing his face clear as he felt the light tickle of something touching his skin. "Shit!"

Pearl covers her mouth, giggling. "Fifty pence!"

"I think I've been stung." Even before the sentence is out, Bear feels the crease between nose and cheek start to swell.

Pearl blinks at him through the gloom. "Ouch, I can see where it got you. Does it hurt, Papa?"

He presses a finger to the tightening pad of skin. "Only a bit. But I'll be fine. I hope we haven't got a nest up here," he says, looking around. "Although I'm sure we'd have heard them. Maybe one just followed us up." He notices the strewn pile Pearl's left behind. "Now let's tidy up these books and choose some to take back down." They spend too long lingering over pages. Half an hour has passed when Pearl picks up *The Very Hungry Caterpillar* and declares that if she were wanting to turn into a butterfly, she would definitely start with ice cream. She asks Bear what he'd choose first, and when he tells her watermelon, he notices that his voice sounds hoarse. That his throat feels odd. He speeds through the last few pages, then neatens the pile of books.

"Come on, let's go down. Here, fireman's lift," he says thickly, as he hoists Pearl onto his shoulder and navigates the metal rungs one-handed. She giggles again, and he is reassured that she does not detect his urgency, does not notice how swiftly he deposits her on the carpet and slides the ladder back into position, how deftly he prods the loft hatch back into place with the hooked pole. But inside, his heart is racing, and he feels his face expanding, his tongue growing thicker, as he moves about the landing. He unplugs the iPad in his office, and motions Pearl into her room. There, he taps the icon for children's television, and Pearl is delighted to be presented with cartoons before evening. Before lunch, even.

He's lightheaded now, but just needs to hold himself together until he is far enough from Pearl. He stumbles down the stairs, gripping the banister. Where is Lily? In the garden? In the kitchen? He peers into the empty living room and calls her name. But his words get lost in throat and tongue, which—with each moment—expand like leavening dough. As he sinks down onto the sofa, he bangs a balled hand against the coffee table. Once, twice—

"Bear? Is that you?" And then Lily is there. In the doorway. White dress, dark hair, lips moving with words he can't decipher. She kneels beside the sofa, tries to get him to talk, to make sense of what she's seeing.

"Pearl! Pearl? Do you know what's wrong with Papa?" Bear grips Lily's wrist, jerks his head from side to side, but it's too late. Pearl is already on the stairs, her small face appearing between the wooden spindles, too scared to come any closer. "Oh, God, I didn't think," Lily says, glancing back at Bear. He loosens his grip on her arm. Blinks. As if to say, *It's okay; there's nothing to be done now.*

Lily softens her voice, turns back to Pearl. "Do you know what happened? You were with him in the loft."

"We read books," Pearl says, eyes wide.

"But nothing happened?" She takes in Bear's swollen face, touches a hand to it. "Nothing hurt him?"

Pearl's bottom lip quivers. She nods. "A wasp."

And Lily has seconds to perform a magic trick. Seconds to avert what is now inevitable. Though she has no magician's hat from which to draw some life-saving elixir. No magic wand to wave.

But then the seconds are gone. And only frantic, disbelieving minutes follow, minutes where hope is clung to like a punctured life raft. Where breath is blown into a throat drawn closed; where small, dimpled fingers conscientiously tap the digits 9-9-9 into her mother's phone; where bargains are made with an unfamiliar God; where paramedics glide toward them under a passage of blue lights, still believing there's someone to save.

HOURS—OR PERHAPS A lifetime—later, Lily and Pearl arrive back to a house steeped in darkness. Their key in the lock feels alien. And when they turn on the hall light, it dazzles them.

A terrible silence curls into every corner of every room and stays for days. Their voices get lost in it. Their words come out like sponges thrown against rock, bouncing off and then falling to the ground, no hope of cutting through. They move around the house like creatures lost in the woods. They cling to each other, not leaving one another's side. A glass of water, a trip to the loo, a forgotten handkerchief, something left in the next room; they move as one, not wanting to let the other out of sight.

They follow government guidelines and only meet family outdoors. A few days before the funeral, they sit on the promenade with Bees and Charlotte, looking out to sea. "Have one, Mama," Pearl says, holding out her paper bag of chips. The vinegar catches in

Lily's throat, making her cough, and a woman walking past pulls her mask higher on her nose pointedly. They look at her retreating back—broad and well padded, insulated by the belief that the virus is the only risk.

"She'd do better tutting at the uneven paving slabs," Charlotte says.

"Oh, God, don't. It's as if you're wishing it on her," Maia says. Lily laughs, a small, guilty sound. But one that spreads to the others, growing into a honking, howling, roaring thing, making their shoulders shake and their eyes water. Until—inevitably—the laughter tumbles over itself. And this part, at least, Pearl understands.

Back at home, they sit on the sofa and Pearl lowers her cheek to the seat cushion. "Is this where Papa died?" she asks, knowing it is, but needing Lily to say the words out loud. Again, and again. As though it can only be made believable in the retelling.

They do jigsaw puzzles, build LEGO towers, read stories, and with each piece placed, each block stacked, every page turned, Lily feels Bear's absence. One day they make scones and as they press the cutter down through the thick rolled pastry, Lily is astounded that Bear can be dead, and they are left here baking. That the world is continuing to turn. That she is continuing to function.

"Is Papa going to be dead forever?" Pearl asks.

"Yes," Lily says, the word falling like a stone through water.

Pearl sleeps in the big double bed and Lily, careful not to wake her, goes into the bathroom throughout the night to sob into her hands, streetlight falling through the window, illuminating their toothbrushes. Bear's is already stiffening with lack of use. She rinses it, wanting to bring it back to life. But it immediately feels like she's washed away the thing that made it worth keeping, and she places it in the bin. Fourteen to thirty-two. It is not, was not, enough. She wants to grow old with him. She wants to feel his arms around her. She wants to bury her face in the biscuit-scented warmth of his neck.

CORA HAS SPENT the past few days visiting the gardens where she used to work. The owners have let her have her old key. She has knelt beside the peonies, tears spilling onto the earth, watching the tight ball of their petals loosen a little each day, willing them to brim open at just the right moment. To throw back their heads and sing—to be at their most glorious—on the morning her son leaves this world. On the morning his lovely body is turned to dust.

Now, as she gets out of her car, the dawn chorus greets her. She lets herself into the gardens through the creaking gate, walks the gravel paths, crosses the orchard lawn, its grass wet with dew. And finds the peonies perfect. Generous. Whole-hearted. Like Bear. She lowers her face to them, buries her nose deep in their centers, lets their petals caress her cheeks. Her trousers soak through at the knees. When she feels she's spent enough time here—but when will she ever have spent enough time here?—she pulls back. She takes a favorite pair of snippers from her bag. She's used to hard pruning, to cutting things back, but she's never grown flowers for cutting. She dithers over the first bloom, craning to assess each specimen from all angles. Finally, she chooses one. The first, she thinks, will not be the best, but still a good one. She supports the base of its head between two fingers, and with the other hand, she positions the blades lower down the stem, and cuts.

THE FUNERAL IS socially distanced, mourners isolated in their bubbles, their numbers capped.

Cora has Mehri, but she cannot touch her granddaughter, cannot reach across the void to pull Lily into an embrace. And so they stand in the car park beforehand, sobs muffled by face masks. Offers of comfort falling short, landing somewhere in the two meters that divide them.

Through the windows of the hearse, Cora can see the spray of peonies, hydrangeas, and eucalyptus adorning Bear's coffin. The flowers are beautiful. They look exactly as she'd hoped. But the intimacy of the days she spent minding them . . . taking them to the florist and sitting on her doorstep this morning, talking quietly before the town woke . . . that softness, is gone.

Inside, they sit apart. The chapel, their words, their movements, live-streamed so that people Cora has never met—Bear's friends, his colleagues from the museum, contacts from all over the world—can sit at their computer screens and watch. Observing their grief. She hopes the image is too blurry to pick up how Bees' back shudders throughout the service; she hopes the sound quality is too poor to capture the low animal moan Pearl emits as the curtain draws around the coffin. In the middle of her reading, Cora looks up and sees the camera's intrusive eye. She muddles her words, but she doesn't care if they notice. In a fleeting rush of rage, she hopes it makes them uncomfortable, she hopes it makes them look away. Even though none of this is their fault.

"I feel like I have nothing," Maia tells Lily one night on the phone. "Like he was there, and now he's not, and I can't make sense of it. The lack of . . . of anything in between."

It's not logical or kind, but sometimes Lily feels as though she and Pearl may be left with even less of him if she acknowledges what anyone else meant to Bear, but still, she finds herself saying, "Did you know about the dream he used to have?"

"I don't think so—what dream?"

"About you. He'd had it ever since he left home."

"Oh," Maia says, and Lily can tell this is something she hasn't heard before.

Lily pictures Maia in her familiar living room, puffy-eyed, just wanting *something*. And surely, she can give her this? So she takes a breath. "In the dream, he was dying—"

"I'm sorry—I'm not sure I can do this right now. I thought it was going to be something nice."

"I know it sounds bad, but really, Bees, I think you'll want to hear. I think it might help."

Lily hears Maia catch her breath and knows she's crying again. When she doesn't say anything more, Lily goes on. "In the dream, it was always the same. He wasn't sure of the cause, but he knew he was dying, and he was terrified and alone. But then you were there. Pushing him on a swing or mouthing lines to him in a school play. All different things. But it would always end in the same way. In a race—like on sports day. He was winning but didn't want to be. And he'd have this dread. Of getting to the finish line, knowing there'd be this white ribbon across it, and that when it broke across his chest, that would be it. But then you'd appear in the crowd. He said he always felt so happy and relieved you'd come. He'd run backward to try to stay level with you, but then, no matter how hard he fought it, he'd be pulled toward the ribbon anyway. But he wasn't scared anymore. He only told me about it because I got fed up with him yanking the duvet around him. I'd always end up wide awake, but he'd go straight back to sleep with this contented look on his face. He said that was how it had always been for him: that you were always there, always making him feel safe and loved."

"Oh," Maia says, in a small and wavery voice. Lily sits listening to her breathe. "Thank you," she says eventually.

"I should have told you earlier," Lily says. "But maybe I'd wanted it to be me who could be the one to comfort him like that. I've kept wondering, though, if you were there with him—on the sidelines—when he actually died."

LILY DOESN'T KNOW why she keeps Bear's phone charged on his bedside table. Perhaps for the occasional texts or emails that arrive from someone who doesn't know and the brief moment that allows her to imagine, in another life, if things had gone differently, he might be here to read it with his own eyes, to tap out a reply with his own fingers. But one day it *rings*, an unexpected noise that makes Lily and Pearl look up from their jigsaw and pause. They race up the stairs, desperate to get to it before it stops. Pearl dives onto the bed as Lily taps the green button to answer.

There is a man on the other end. Can he speak to Bear?

A moment of silence, shock. An awkwardness in his recovery. Oh, he's so sorry. So sorry to hear that. He's calling about the electric car her husband ordered last year. She didn't know? The pandemic has affected production, but it's finally ready for delivery. Already paid for in full.

As the man talks, Lily pictures Bear poring over his bank account, squirreling away money for their first car. They've never really needed one living so near town and the station, but she's always wanted one. Wanted to drive through the countryside listening to music. To go on holiday without a taxi to take them the last leg of the journey. To visit her parents and Cora without train times running through her head. She pictures Bear online, researching. Pictures him in the showroom, her beautiful husband, doing something lovely for her in the middle of an ordinary day, before the world shut down. Where was she then? Perhaps walking along the seafront, or at the library. And she'd carried on, unaware. Of him, and this special thing. Unaware, too, of what it is to have that person in your life, that person who will plan surprises, who will try to fix wings to your back.

Pearl, who has been listening in, her temple resting against Lily's, says, "Ask what color it is, Mama!"

The man hears. "Black," he says. Just what Lily would have chosen herself.

AND NOW, 2022. They are two years on from Bear's death. And Pearl, this child they made together, is six. She says, "Tell me the story of . . ." and Lily will tell her some tale featuring her magnificent father. She will worry she's turning him into a mythical god, some creature too good to have ever really walked this earth. But she can't dial him down. Make him less brilliant than he was. "We were lucky, weren't we, Mama?" Pearl says, and Lily nods.

ONE DAY, WHEN Pearl is out with Maia, they meet an elderly couple with a puppy. It pounces on leaves as they skitter in the wind, falls over its own feet, chases its tail, can barely sustain its line of interest before it is delighted by the next thing. Maia asks if they can stroke it, and while the adults talk above her head, Pearl touches the dog's velvety ears as it nudges her leg, wanting to get closer than it already is. She catches snippets of what they're saying: how dogs don't need to live as long as humans, they're simply so good at finding the joy in life. As if we are put on this earth to extract a certain amount of happiness and can leave once the job is done.

"Is that like Papa, Bees?" Pearl asks as they walk away.

Maia's breath catches and her eyes prickle. "Sort of," she says, and she feels Pearl's fingers spidering their way across her palm into her own.

"I'm glad you're quite a serious sort of person," Pearl says, squeezing her hand. And Maia understands her meaning; that she wants—needs—the rest of her people to stay for longer.

"Don't worry, I'm not going anywhere."

Maia smiles, thinking of her little brother. Remembering how she's always been in the shadow of his exuberance, his ability to make things special, but how that's been her privilege. And now look at what he's left them. Beautiful, capable Pearl.

"TELL ME THE story of my name," Pearl says as she sits cross-legged on the draining board as they do the dishes together. And Lily tells her how it was. How Bear had said they should think about how their own names would fit with this new person who would complete them.

"Of course! Animal, vegetable, and mineral," he'd said, delighted. "Her name should be a mineral."

Lily had brought up a list on her phone. Jade, Ruby, Opal, Emerald, Crystal; reading out the names until . . . Pearl.

"Pearl," Bear had repeated, trying it out for himself.

"But it says a pearl's not actually a proper mineral." And Lily had read out the explanation: "Although the pearl itself is made up of a mineral, its organic origin excludes it from being an official one."

"It's not like a lily is officially a vegetable either, though. More like vegetable *matter*," he'd said, laughing.

Recently, Lily and Pearl have started playing the game together. First question: animal, vegetable, or mineral? Pearl tries to narrow down whatever it might be that Lily is thinking of, but when it's her turn to dispense clues, she always says, "Animal," to that first question. Lily thinks up questions to lead her on a winding route to the answer she already knows. "Is it . . . Papa?" she will eventually ask, and Pearl will smile, gratified.

The school days are long, and Pearl emerges exhausted. Away from the gates, she asks for a piggyback, and even after a shift at the library, Lily plows up the hill, Pearl's warm body draped across her back, empty lunchbox banging gently against her side. Her hip burns beneath their combined weight, but it makes Lily feel more alive, pulled back into her body from the stupor of grief.

THEY ARE PLANNING on getting a cat. "It's not instead of Papa," Pearl clarifies when she tells Cora about it. And Cora nods approvingly, realizing they are inviting a creature back into their lives to maintain the trinity of animal, vegetable, mineral. That there is a strength in deciding not to hobble on forever without that animal energy in their lives. Bear would be so proud.

IT WAS DURING the first lockdown, before Bear died, when pavements and windows were still covered in hand-drawn rainbows, and every Thursday at 8 p.m. front doors were opened to clap for the NHS workers who cared for the sick, that Maia heard from him. His letter arrived between bills and a pizza-delivery flyer.

She didn't recognize his writing. Either because it had taken on the slight tremor of age, or perhaps because she'd erased it from some once-held mental file. And so, she read the first line, not realizing who the handwritten pages had come from.

Dear Maia,

I hope this finds you well. You may not remember—it may not even have been you—but years ago, 2009 perhaps—I believe we spotted one another in a traffic jam. I was sure it was you and I think you recognized me too. I've thought of

you often since that time and I've wanted to write on many
occasions, but out of respect for the new life you've surely
built, I've been wary of intruding. Somehow, the pandemic
has changed things, though. In my late seventies, with death
lurking on every door handle, I have a greater sense of time
being finite. Of contact being now or never . . .

She folded the letter and pushed it back into its envelope as though the contents might leap off the page into her mind uninvited if she didn't put it away quickly enough. She carried it around in her bag for days, feeling its presence, an outline of her father straining at her shoulder as she decided what to do. She wondered how he'd found her address; it was years since she'd had any contact with her grandparents.

One afternoon, she packed away her patients' case files early, and picked her way down the pebbled beach to sit in the shelter of a wooden groin. She took out the pages again, aware this time that her fingers were touching paper that he, too, had held. She looked up at the sky, hoping the sharp sea air might cleanse her of this, but she only had a sense of salt hanging heavy and setting the feeling. Reluctantly, she looked down and began to read.

When she'd finished, she leaned against the sea defense. She wasn't sure how much time had passed when Charlotte crunched onto the beach and sat down beside her.

"It's a letter from my dad," Maia said, turning over the corner of the envelope. "It *was* him, that day in the traffic jam." Charlotte was sifting her long fingers across the pebbles then. "He's writing to make peace, apparently. To renew my faith in humanity. Our potential to change." Maia gave a little laugh.

"Has he? Changed, I mean," Charlotte asked.

"Possibly. After he left prison, he went to some charity for domestic abusers. And, later, ended up working for them. He probably would've been good at that; he was actually a good doctor, before everything, Mum's always said. A better doctor than husband, anyway."

Charlotte was looking out to sea, but Maia knew she had her full attention. She had a knack for sensing when to wait, rather than ask questions.

"I have a half-sister, apparently. He actually had a new relationship. A normal one, he claims. Not anymore. But just because they fell out of love, he says, rather than anything more sinister. It doesn't sound like the daughter has much contact with him, though. She's seventeen."

"Goodness. A sister. I'd never even thought of that," Charlotte said.

"Me neither." After a while, she added, "He apologized to me, in the letter. Also to Mum, and Bear. If I want to pass it on."

"Do you think you'll tell her?"

"I'm not sure what good it would do. Other than stir up a load of painful feelings."

They sat in silence and eventually Charlotte said, "Will you reply?"

"I don't know. I think I'm going to probably sit here for a while longer and see if the answer comes to me."

"Okay then," Charlotte said, pulling herself up. She smoothed down her culottes. "I'll be at home. Back for dinner?"

Maia looked up, squinting, the low evening sun in her eyes. "Yes, by seven," she said, and Charlotte squeezed her shoulder and walked back up the beach.

Maia watched as the sun began to set. As the waves crashed nearer and nearer, cresting one shelf of pebbles, then encroaching onto the next. When they landed just a few feet away, she took off her shoes, balanced them on a weathered post, and waded out into the Brighton sea, icy water biting at her skin. When it was thigh high, her dress sticking to her, she took the letter from its envelope and pressed it to the surface of the water, watching the ink flow from its pages, until only smeared, disintegrating paper was left in her hands. She would have liked it to take minutes, but it only required seconds. She balled up the remnants, and then turned, and picked her way back up the beach, pebbles digging into the soles of her feet. She tossed the salt-watered mass into a litter bin on the promenade, and it hit the metal with a soft thud. Then she sat on the sea wall, put on her shoes, and walked back to her own life with Charlotte, leaving the father she once had to his.

CORA HAS BEEN aged by the loss of Bear. By the lack of goodbye. By being separated from Pearl and Lily in her grief. But just like last time, when Vihaan was killed and Gordon imprisoned, it is Mehri who has stepped in to hold her up. Mehri with whom she laughs and cries through the darkness. Mehri who, as life begins to open back up again, gently leads her toward the light, like a creature emerging from hibernation. Blood running colder, slower, but still, with a sense of having survived.

One evening, when she arrives at Mehri's, they stand talking in the kitchen and Cora becomes aware of male voices, of there being someone else with Roland in the living room down the hall. "Who is it?" she mouths, and Mehri tells her it's a friend of Roland's—Felix—who's dropped by unexpectedly to lend him a stylus for his record player.

"You mean the guy I went on a date with?"

"A date?" Mehri says, as Cora shushes her. "Oh, yes. A date! Goodness, how long ago was that? Twenty years?" Mehri shakes her head in disbelief.

Cora knows their overlapping visits are a coincidence, but still, she feels awkward as she puts her head around the living-room door to say hello.

"Oh, Cora, isn't it?" Felix says. "It's great to see you again." His smile is instant and genuine, and nothing in his manner seems to suggest he harbors resentment—or, perhaps, any memory—that Cora hadn't wanted to take things further. He has a kind face, though Cora is surprised to find him so much older. But then she reminds herself that she is too; they're both nearing seventy.

"We're about to start on dinner. Will you stay and eat with us, Felix?" Mehri asks.

The four of them pull together a meal, the crackle of vinyl in the background, Mehri and Roland bustling around the kitchen, as Cora and Felix chop vegetables at the table.

Cora tells him about Pearl, about how she takes the train down to Brighton to bake with her each week. "Mostly bready stuff. She likes to poke her fingers in the dough, shape it into animals. Cats mainly. She's just got a kitten."

"My stock-in-trade once. I'm retired now."

"Oh, yes, of course." She'd forgotten he was a vet.

"I used to enjoy hearing what their owners had called them. I always liked the times they'd gone for something human-sounding. Like Derek. Or Clive."

"Well, Pearl's called hers Cat." She sees Felix smile. "It's not as unimaginative as it sounds," Cora adds, and she somehow finds herself telling him more. "We lost my son—Pearl's father—during lockdown. His name was Bear. I guess Cat is a nod to that. He was—" She stops chopping and glances at the ceiling, trying to think of the right words. "He was his name. Sort of soft, and cuddly, and kind. But also brave and strong."

Felix puts down his knife and covers Cora's hand with his own, while she rights herself. She's aware of Mehri and Roland in the background, still moving around the kitchen; for a moment, she'd forgotten they were there. Mehri, she knows, will have been surprised to hear her talking so freely. She's surprised herself.

"And is the cat like its name?" Felix asks.

"Oh, yes, just like it. It lives life on its own terms. But—and I don't know how it's done this—it's made their house feel like a home again. When I think, for a long time, it didn't."

For a while Felix doesn't say anything. Then he says, "Yes, I know that feeling. I lost my wife to cancer just before lockdown. Our house . . . it's been a difficult place to spend so much time alone over the last few years. A cat would have been nice. If only to hear the sound of it coming and going, using the litter tray."

It's strange to realize how much they've lived through since they last met. That they've both suffered such losses. Cora has noticed a rawness about him, sees that his nerves, like hers, are close to the surface.

As the evening wears on, they grow tunnel-visioned, eager for what the other has to say. They barely notice when Roland and Mehri drift off to make a fruit salad, to talk to Fern on the phone. Cora briefly wonders if they're being rude but knows their friends won't mind.

They are serious, then light-hearted. At one point, Cora finds herself demonstrating a particular ballet move to illustrate a story from her youth. "I can't tell you how many years it is since I've done that in front of someone," she says, as she goes to sit back down.

"That's true. We've been friends for thirty-five years, and I've never got so much as a plié out of you," Mehri says as she comes back into the room. She stands behind Cora's chair and bends to kiss her cheek. "We're off to bed, azizam."

"What time is it?"

"Oh, after midnight," Mehri says.

"I hadn't noticed it getting so late." Cora taps her phone screen and sees it's actually past one.

"The night is still young," Mehri says, as she puts her wine glass beside the sink. "Perhaps, if you're not quite finished here, you could wash up before you let yourselves out?" she adds, eyes sparkling. Then she turns to Felix, "It's been lovely barely talking to you. I can't tell you the last time I've seen Cora having so much fun. You must come again."

Mehri leaves them to the dishes, to each other. And later, Felix's offer to walk Cora home, and her acceptance of it, is unthinking; they are already absorbed in a conversation that will continue to slowly unspool across all the years they have left.

Julian

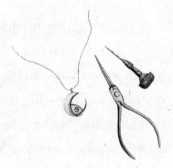

As Julian re-enters his studio, he swipes through the photos on his phone and messages Cian with an image showing a consignment of boxes, which only fifteen minutes earlier had been piled in front of him. Now, the bench along the wall is clear for the first time in months. It's only 11 a.m., but it feels like a moment that should be marked in some way. If he was a smoker, he'd sit out on the back steps near the fire escape and exhale the stress of the last few months in a cloud of nicotine and tar. He thinks of his jewelry boxes, bumping around the city in the back of the courier's van in a cocoon of bubble wrap, as they make their way to port, and then on to a place called, ironically, Liberty. A department store in London that Cian tells him is built from the timbers of old ships, with a mahogany staircase that creaks as you climb it and makes you feel the whole building might be listing on a wave. Cian says there are ghosts there too. Julian wonders if they'll meet some of his own. If he hasn't melded a few into the metal as he's crafted this shipment. He's not someone prone to magical thinking, but still, he worries his own thoughts, his memories, the stress of this time, might have somehow become fused within each piece. Although Maia says she doesn't think it works that way.

He's leaned on Maia a lot during the pandemic, since Orla left with the children. That first lockdown, when his stockists were closed, when unemployment suffered the highest monthly increase in the Republic's history, it was like free-falling through open sky, a crash-landing rising up to meet him. Nothing he could do to stop it. And while many seemed to be making sourdough and growing veg-etables, there was no support for the self-employed. Not at first any-way, and Julian and Orla's interactions quickly came to feel like sandpaper chafing up against itself.

"Why have you bought more coffee?"

"What?"

"It's a luxury, not an essential."

"It's essential to me."

"More than feeding your own children?"

The words could have been said by either one of them, depending on their mood, depending on who was more anxious in any given moment. And the woman he'd once romanticized, the way she'd looked as she turned to him just like that, the peachy glow of her skin in that last hour before sunset when everything was cast in gold . . . he no longer did. She was just Orla. Jeans slightly too tight, dark circles beneath her eyes, an annoying habit of clicking her tongue absent-mindedly until Julian felt the noise might bore a hole in his skull.

In the May of that first lockdown, the washing machine flooded the kitchen and Julian spent two days amid a growing pile of tools, trying to fix it, feeling he was always just one YouTube video away from a solution. "Let me come down and look at it for you," Cian said. "I'll be careful. I can wear a mask." But Julian refused, too worried about giving him the virus, of breaking the rules, and a neighbor or the gardaí finding out. And so, they'd taken to washing their clothes in the bath, wringing out each item, and leaving them to drip-dry from the old Sheila Maid rack above. The whole house felt damp, and the kitchen floor began to darken where the wooden boards failed to dry out. At night, slugs appeared, thick bodies stretched thin like pulled bubblegum to breach the slightest gap. Julian stuffed wire wool into the cracks beneath the skirting boards and around the water inlets, but it did nothing to slow the invasion, and when Orla came down in the night for a glass of water, she put her hand on one oozing across the kitchen tap. Everyone wakened, lights on, adults glaring at one another as they soothed the children back to bed.

"This house!" Orla said as she crawled back under the covers.

"Did you not think screaming like that might have been an overreaction?"

"I hadn't planned on it, eejit."

Julian lay with his hands flattened beneath the covers, a lid on his anger. Always too fearful of who he might become to do things any other way.

Another day, when the girls were arguing, Julian had asked, "Will you be dealing with that, Orla?" He was sitting at the kitchen table doing his accounts, while she cooked dinner.

"Will *I* be dealing with it?" Orla said, as the volume increased in the next room. Julian looked up from his paperwork and saw frustration, or perhaps even a flash of hatred, on her face. "Have you ever thought that *you* could be the one to go in there and read the riot act? I know that might mean not being Mr. Popular for once but, actually, they're your children too, Jules. Why should you always just get to do all the warm and fuzzy stuff?"

He sighed, raised his hands at her tirade as though in self-defense.

"Don't do that! Why do you always do that?!"

"I didn't do anything."

"You did! That face! That face that's meant to make me feel like I'm some sort of unhinged banshee. I might be furious, but what I'm saying is completely reasonable. You know, Jules, when you set a boundary for a child, it makes them feel safe. Did you get that? Safe. They'll look at you like you're some kind of gobshite in the moment, but really that's you being the good guy."

"Orla," Julian said, wincing at her language, at the possibility the girls might hear.

"Do you have to be so passive in your own life *all* the time? I'm trying to tell you something—to give you a chance—and you can't even hear it. You can only think about *how* I'm saying it."

One of the girls—Aoife, Julian thought—was crying by then, the words *Give it back!* audible over Orla's shouting. He went through to the living room where the two girls were snarled in a tug-of-war over some toy. "Okay, who wants a biscuit?"

But before they could answer, Orla was there, tearing another strip off him. "That's your solution? A biscuit! It's nearly dinner time but you'd rather give them a biscuit than man up and be the adult here? When are you going to grow up, Jules? When are you going to start putting us first?" She left the room, slamming the door behind her, and he'd felt so tired. Because no matter what an argument *appeared* to be about, it always came back to this. That he was unable to leave behind the past—his hostility toward England—to secure their future.

At night, Maia's words circled in his mind, something she once said about contempt being the most corrosive thing in a relationship, the indicator of a marriage on the rocks. He felt it. The crashing carnage of jagged words on damp air; hostile bodies that no longer turned toward one another. And he couldn't see what he needed to do to change it, even though Orla screamed it at him in pretty much every argument they had. Had done for all the years they'd been together, as though all her frustration had its roots in one single thing. But it was only when Cian spoke the words that he heard them.

There's something about that—when the quietest person, most reserved in their opinions, most reluctant to impose their thoughts on others, finally speaks; you hear. Oh. *Oh,* and you're suddenly face to face with the truth. "Julian, son. You will lose your family for good if you keep with this foolish pride. Sell to England. It's just a place. It's not your father."

His family had already gone by then, though. To Orla's parents. When Ireland started shutting down again in October, Orla had said for the sake of them both—for the children too—they couldn't go through another lockdown together. *I can't be living with you like this, Jules. Always plucking at you to try to make you into the person I want; I don't like who it's turning me into.* Although she hadn't taken everything, the house felt dismantled. Empty coat hooks in the hall, shelves with books and board games missing, the toothbrush holder with its unfilled spaces.

Without Aoife and Niamh, without Orla to get home for in the evenings, Julian started working longer hours. He spent more time at his computer, approaching stockists, trying to drum up business. Some days sending emails felt like dropping stones down a well; the only confirmation they'd landed anywhere at all, the occasional bounce-back: *This email user no longer exists.* He found unspoken tales of closures and redundancies everywhere he went. It should have made him feel less alone, but it didn't. He imagined these people having fallen into exciting new roles, ditching their old lives in favor of fledgling start-ups or positions at companies that could ride out the pandemic. Sometimes he imagined they'd found their way into making jewelry themselves and he had the sensation of lift doors closing, no room inside for him. He picked through old emails, searching for contacts who'd once approached him. It was a shameful feeling, seeing how many he'd let go unanswered. And now he must hold his hands out, begging.

Some nights he slept at the Old Chocolate Factory, only breaking from his work to say good night to Aoife and Niamh over Zoom. The calls were frustrating. It was hard to keep their attention through the screen and they would float away like dandelion seed heads, momentarily reappearing, cheeks glowing, pajamas on, smelling—he knew—of bubble bath and fabric softener, before drifting off again.

"Come and speak to Daddy, Niamh," and then some side conversation, negotiating a bedtime story. "No, no, come on, quick. Daddy's waiting." He could hear Orla trying to make it work, trying to draw them all together through the screen, but never quite managing it.

Some nights, their faces would crowd in, filling his laptop for those last seconds prior to being released from duty. Other times, it was just him and Orla there at the end. Both sad, but unsure how to fix things. "You look tired," she'd said. And he'd rubbed at his face, suddenly feeling it. "I'll be right. I could probably just do with getting my eyes checked."

Some nights, he would drive over to visit them. Orla's parents were uneasy with the idea of him coming inside, though Julian wondered if this wasn't a convenient cover, an excuse to excommunicate their feckless son-in-law from the family. And so they went to the park, breath cutting funnels through the early-evening darkness as they stamped their feet to keep warm while Niamh had one last go on the climbing frame. Walking back toward the gates, they'd swing the girls up in the air between them and Julian would find himself taking mental snapshots, as though a photographer were always standing a few feet ahead of them. This is you, when you were still *almost* a family. This is you, when you thought there might still be a hope of putting things back together.

December brought a flurry of orders and Julian worked up until Christmas Eve. But it was a tiding-over, rather than a path out. They were still deprived of the oxygen that money and having just enough had once afforded them. January came with a lull that left him hopeless. Everyone at the Old Chocolate Factory felt it. Shops had closed, fairs were canceled, exhibitions permanently postponed. In April, a cabinet maker who'd moved into Orla's old studio a few years earlier took his own life. He was found in the woods, a note in his pocket. It seemed to make them all kinder, slower, for a while. "You all right?" they'd ask one another, stopping, making space for something more than "fine."

"You wouldn't do that, would you?" Orla had said, when he told her.

"What do you think?"

"That's why I'm asking. Because I want to know."

"I have you and the girls," he'd said, and she nodded—a short, clipped sort of nod—and he'd wondered if he really did have her, or if it was already over. But, either way, it wasn't an option for him. His mother's life had taught him that you do everything you can to cling to survival. He'd realized that perhaps his answer might seem manipulative, implying his perspective could change if Orla were to officially draw a line under things, and so he'd added, "But even if I didn't, the answer's no. It's not something I'd do." And she'd given a small smile, reassured.

But he'd carried on thinking about their conversation afterward. Because hadn't his mother's life also taught him you do everything you can for your children? That you'll fight—really fight—to give them the best life possible, to be there for them? He wasn't sure he was doing that. Not in the way his mum had. Not tooth and nail.

When Julian wasn't working, he began to return home more often. He borrowed a sander to strip the kitchen floor, repainted scuffed walls, and started to see their home through the eyes he'd had for it eight years ago when they'd first walked through the door. A chocolate-box house. Tiny cast-iron fireplaces and narrow alcoves, Victorian sashes framed by original shutters and window seats beneath. He could picture Orla and the girls all over it, hear their voices. And he wondered where they'd be if there'd been no pandemic, if they hadn't run out of money. If he'd found a way to be better, to do what was needed of him in time. If love weren't just two ordinary people, connected by gossamer-thin strands of silk, brushed away as easily as a spider's web.

He wasn't just devastated she was no longer there—the day-to-day tangible presence of her, of the girls—but by the reality that she could leave at all. He'd let himself believe she was his; he, hers. But perhaps that idea had always been too good to be true. Some days he woke and felt as though his head were being pushed backward through the pillow at the shock of it and he'd silently question if a room was a room, if his hand was a hand, if he was lying there at all.

And without warning, while he was in that odd place of rebuilding their house around the uncertain remains of their marriage, his mother's death hit him anew. As though his whole childhood had been a long, dilute glass of her absence, but now he was faced with the neat concentrate of it. The absolute nothingness of what he was left with.

Gardening had never been Julian's thing. Nor Orla's. But one day as he ran a hand over a small fir, wondering where to begin, it unleashed a scent richly familiar, casting him back to the garden of the England house. There, a thick trunk obscured most of his view, but as he peeped out, he could see his mother coming toward him, bending as she got nearer, reaching out with long, graceful arms. Her lips were moving, but it was her expression that told him she was coaxing, reassuring. Until, "It's okay, you can come out now." And then the vision was gone. And he was alone again, in the walls of his own garden.

He'd only ever had the same handful of memories, replayed so often, they ceased to move him. But here, the image was fresh, alive in his mind. Her voice surprising and real. He'd forgotten it.

In the days that followed, he worked in the garden whenever he could. Coming home in his lunch hour and hoping to find his mother there. He tried not to chase memories, anxious it might scare them away. Although sometimes impatience got the better of him and he would breathe in the scent of the fir as though inhaling Olbas Oil, only to draw a blank. Teasing a spade beneath tangled roots, emptying out terracotta pots, he tried to pretend his focus wasn't on the space behind him, wasn't crying out, *I'm here, I'm here. Please, just come to me.*

One evening, after visiting Orla and the girls, Julian unearthed a headtorch from a box of old camping paraphernalia in the shed. The beam mostly lost in shadow, he was hacking blindly at a large buddleia when he felt a tap on his shoulder.

For one irrational moment, he thought it might be his mother. But when he turned it was Maia. "Sorry, I didn't mean to scare you. I knew you must be home with so many lamps on."

"Oh, yeah, I was trying to throw a bit of light out here," he said, letting the blunt shears drop onto the pile of cut branches. It was a new thing, Maia letting herself in. Something she'd only done since Orla had left. But he liked it; the feeling it could be more than just him there.

They sat on the back step, mugs of tea between them. Maia in her winter coat, even though it was mild for mid-April. And he told her about hearing their mum's voice. "Oh, yes, the fir trees," Maia said. "They were at the back of the garden. She sent us there so we'd be out of the way if she knew he was going to lose it. Do you remember the Tupperware bowls?"

"Tupperware bowls?"

"Yours was blue; mine was yellow. She always had them made up with snacks, ready to go. Raisins and dried apple rings. Stuff that would keep. *Picnic Time*," Maia said, her voice heavy.

"That was Picnic Time? I remember it." Another memory. "I hadn't known that was why, though." He wanted these fragments of his mum back, but they were steeped in so much sadness. Even the bits she'd tried to make nice for them. "She really loved us, didn't she?"

Maia looked up at the sky, dark and inky but empty of stars. "Sky father," she said.

"What?"

"Your name."

"Oh, yeah," he said. He wasn't sure how he knew its meaning, perhaps from his grandmother or a book.

"Imagine if you'd been called Gordon. Like he wanted."

Julian looked up, stopped winding his teabag string around the cup handle. He hadn't known this.

"That was the plan. But on the day she went to register you, she couldn't bring herself to do it. Afterward, she told him *sky father* was a tribute to him. I even made these little moon and star decorations to go around his plate at dinner. But it wasn't a tribute. It was her way of saying you'd never be like him. That you'd rise above him."

Julian didn't say anything, just let out a long, slow breath. A breath it felt he'd kept held in for a lifetime. Maia reached for Julian's hand in the darkness and neither let go. They just stared up, both tracking the blinking lights of a plane as it crossed the sky.

"Me too," Maia said, when she saw him use his free hand to wipe his eyes.

"How come you never told me?" he asked.

"I'd forgotten. Well, not forgotten. I just hadn't thought of it."

"Do you remember anything else?"

She looked at him then, his face half lit by the room behind. "Oh, Jules. Loads of things. I was fourteen. I've just never known how much you'd want to know."

Over the weeks that followed, Maia unpacked her memories of their childhood when she came over. Without Orla, without Maia's girlfriend, Meg, they fell into their old rhythm of being together. As they stripped flaking paint from window frames or cooked dinner, he learned that their mother grew herbs on the kitchen windowsill; wore silver, not gold; made up stories about a gecko who lived on the bathroom ceiling to encourage him to keep his head tipped back at hair-washing time. *Do you see him? Can you hear him chirping?* Sometimes it was hard to know if Maia's words jogged a real memory, or if he was just imagining himself into whatever scene she painted, but he felt sure he could remember warm water trickling down his back as his mother rinsed the suds from his hair with a plastic jug. He also learned about *him*, the man whose name he didn't bear. At first, he worried the more he knew, the more he might feel tormented by the genetic link, perhaps risking embedding its code even more deeply in his DNA. But each memory Maia revealed only seemed to highlight their differences.

They skirted around the edges of their mother's death; Maia not offering anything, Julian not asking. Until he could wait no longer. "Can you tell me what happened? That night?"

He cried as she told him. For his mum. And for them. "Shall I stay?" Maia asked.

"I think I'll be on my own a while," he said. They hugged at the door. And then Julian had climbed the stairs of the small cottage and, not bothering to undress, pulled the bedcovers over him and slept for two days straight, waking only to gulp down a glass of water or to use the bathroom.

He was aware of the phone ringing. Of Maia coming in to check on him. But he doesn't remember speaking. Months later, Maia told him she'd worried to Meg that she might have broken him. During those past few weeks, it had seemed as though she'd been doing something essential, something long overdue, but then, she'd doubted herself.

On the third day, when he woke, the bedside clock showed it was 7:30 a.m. As though he'd never strayed from routine. He sat on the edge of the bed, feeling dazed, struck by his own stench, his furred tongue. In the bathroom, he dropped his unwashed clothes to the floor and, standing in the shower, hot water pricking at his skin, the room obscured by steam, it came to him. He was not his father. He'd thought he walked a narrow line, at any moment ready to tip over into likeness. But the line wasn't narrow after all. It was a great, uncrossable chasm. Julian could never be like him. Even if he allowed his anger to unfurl—raised his voice in an argument—he would never be capable of the cruelties his father had inflicted. Not even close. He could finally see that now. He leaned against the shower wall and sobbed until he was empty.

IT WAS A chance meeting that brought Meg into Maia's life again. A friend from homeopathy college had invited Maia to a summer barbecue, but when it began to rain, people moved inside, and it was Meg who sat down beside her on the sofa. "Oh! I think we've already met. I came to you a few years ago. For hay fever?"

It had just been a few appointments, but Maia had warmed to her. She wore a lot of blue, the same shade as cornflowers—was wearing it that day too—and she had an open, generous face. "Meg?"

"Yes, good memory." She nodded to the open patio doors. "People always say the rain sticks pollen to the ground, but that was never the case for me; the moment it rained I could barely breathe. But I'm here now, breathing. Proof of your brilliance." She smiled. "I've actually sent a few people your way over the years. Just a moment, let me fetch us a drink."

When she returned, Meg flipped off her shoes and sank into the sofa cushions, feet tucked up beneath her skirt. An intimacy that seemed to suggest she was there for the long haul, that she wasn't about to claim needing the loo or spotting a friend across the room. "I don't know about you, but I think there's an imbalance. Like, you know all this weird stuff about me—*and is it more of a nasal drip, or like you've got cotton wool in your nose?*—and I know absolutely nothing about you."

Maia laughed at how word-perfect her impression was. "Are you planning on coming back to me at any point? For treatment, I mean?" she asked, instantly regretting her question.

But Meg brushed it away easily. "Oh, God. Never. Absolutely never." She laughed. And she leaned over, her hand glancing Maia's knee as she spoke. Just the fingertips. Just for the briefest moment. But Maia felt something.

"Twenty questions, then?" Maia suggested, surprised by her own impulsivity. But Meg had only grinned.

"Okay, let's start with a simple one. Eggs: scrambled or fried?"

"Scrambled," Maia said, grateful to settle into a conversation that, for now, had a predictable formula. Something she might be contained within.

"Ireland or England?"

"Ireland. I came across when I was a teenager and never really picked up an accent. My younger brother is full Irish, though; he was only five. Sorry, that was more than a word."

"Oh, we never said it was one-word answers. Morning or night?"

"Morning. I like the sense of possibility."

"Town or fields?"

"Fields. My grandmother's house where I grew up is surrounded by them." Maia thought of her own flat down in the town, not too far from Julian's place. It had taken several years for it to feel like home, the transition softened by the bits and pieces her grandmother left behind each time she visited—a favorite vase, a well-used baking tray; by Cian stopping in to fix things. "We miss having you with us, but we're so proud," Sílbhe had whispered into her hair as they'd gone to leave one evening. It was a fierce sort of pride. Something that made them hug one another more tightly.

Meg put a hand over her glass as a man in a county jersey bumped into the sofa, but her gaze remained on Maia's face. "Summer or winter?"

Maia smiled. "Summer's my favorite day in Ireland."

"Past or present?"

"Present." It was the truth, although the answer pained her; it felt like an erasure of her mum. She glanced up, ready for the next question, and caught Meg's pause. As though she'd been able to read the turmoil on Maia's face.

"Dishes: before bed or the morning after?"

"Oh, God, before. But I'll leave wine glasses; they're best done sober." Although something in her felt compelled toward honesty and she added, "I don't actually drink that often, though." She felt sure Meg was someone who always had a bottle of red wine on the kitchen counter.

"Sorry, I should have checked. Is this okay?" Meg asked, tilting her glass.

"Oh, yeah, it's not that I don't drink. Just that . . . it would probably be misleading. To suggest I come down to a party of wine glasses in the kitchen sink every weekend."

"Good to know," Meg said, mischief flickering across her features. "But anyway, walking: fast or slow?"

"Slow. More time for conversation. Fast says I'm late."

"Fiction or non-fiction?"

"Fiction, although if there's a choice, I'd take poetry." Meg raised her eyebrows and Maia wondered if she'd sounded pretentious. Or if it was meant to indicate they had that in common.

"Logic or instinct?"

"Oh, always instinct."

"Happy or sad endings?"

"I want to say happy, but . . ."

"Agreed. Predictability or excitement?"

"Probably predictability." Maia cringed at how serious she must sound.

"Commitment or fling?"

"I think my last answer covers that," she said, hoping flippancy might lighten things.

"Regret or doubt?"

Maia thought for a while. "Mm, regret. Probably better to live and make mistakes."

"Guard up or down?" Meg put her head to one side and held Maia's gaze, not looking away even as a group over by the patio doors burst into raucous laughter.

"Right now? Being lowered one question at a time," Maia said, trying to keep the smile from her face.

"Cherished or respected?"

"Oh, cherished," Maia said, enjoying how the word had sounded as Meg said it. Like something gorgeous. Plump and ripe like a cherry, the stain of it coloring her lips as they formed the sounds. "I think respect would come with that anyway," Maia added, unsure how she could keep giving such sensible answers, when she was giddy inside.

"Straight or gay?"

A change of tempo, a pause, an intake of breath.

"Gay," Maia said.

"No qualifier for that one then?" Meg asked, her eyes laughing.

The rain must have stopped, because the group who'd been straggling were moving outside into the sunshine, leaving the room quieter and Maia's words more exposed. "I only came out a few years ago. Back in 2015, with the referendum. But I'm . . . sure."

Meg nodded, smiled. "So," she paused, seeming uncertain for the first time, "is this twenty questions at a barbecue, or could it be something more?"

"Is this the last question?"

"I've not been keeping count," Meg said. "But I think there's at least one left."

"Do you know what it's going to be? The last question?"

"It depends on your answer to this one."

"Oh, more then. Please," Maia said, moving her hand so her fingertips brushed Meg's.

"Come home with me?"

Meg is Maia's first serious relationship. And it works, even though Meg leaves the dishes until the morning after, even though she finds the countryside claustrophobic, hemmed in by too big a sky and endless green.

They sit beside one another in bed, reading bits out from their books. And Meg has adopted Julian as though he's her own; sometimes when he rings it is she who listens and dispenses advice, astute but delivered with more sarcasm and direction than Maia's. Paint samples gather in the hall beside their shoes, as they try colors on the walls of Maia's flat. They decide on a warm blue called Juniper Ash. In the bathroom cupboard there is a communal box of tampons, and this companionable distribution of things makes Maia feel oddly whole. Maia tells Meg the things she's never spoken out loud—not even to family—and Meg says, "Oh, you poor darling," and holds her, and somehow that is enough. And on Sundays, they drive to the beach and walk along the wet sand hand in hand, wind whipping at their coats, hair tangling, as Meg takes Maia's face in her hands, cherished.

ON A TUESDAY in June, Cian comes around the corner of the house, a handful of feathery-topped carrot spears in his hands where he's been thinning them out, and through the window he sees Sílbhe lying on the living-room floor. He runs to her, wanting to find her just grazed, soon patched up. But, instead, he finds her slack-jawed, her gentle face at rest. He kneels beside her, does the things we instinctively do: lowers an ear to her lips; checks her wrist for a pulse. But it only confirms what he knows. He brings her still-warm hand to his cheek and weeps. Because they have not had long enough. Because he is not ready for their shared life to be at its end.

He sits with her as the light fades, as the chill starts to creep in through the open door, as her cooling body sets in place. He sits with her through the night, not ready to move into the next phase he knows must come. One of phone calls and condolences. And her absence. For now, for just a little longer, it will be just the two of them.

JULIAN IS READING an email thanking him for the samples and confirming a large order when he answers his phone. He has never heard Cian cry before.

When he arrives at the house, it breaks something open in him and they cling, arms tight around one another.

Inside, Cian pours two large measures of single malt, and they quietly toast Sílbhe's life as they wait for the sound of Maia's car coming up the track.

That evening, it is just the three of them. Orla and Meg offer to come, but it feels right this way. They sit at the table until the early hours, talking, laughing, crying. Cian still hasn't slept, but when he thinks of going to bed, he cannot face Sílbhe not being there beside him. And so he stays in the kitchen with Maia and Julian and the warmth of traded memories. A clarity exists amongst them, that they have shared their lives with someone quietly magnificent.

When the coroner's report comes, they learn she'd lived with a hole in the heart. That she probably never knew, but that, still, it is a miracle she lived to see eighty-eight. And they wonder again at what she gave to them. How she lived for them, and because of them. And in spite of everything.

Now, JULIAN WALKS back into his empty studio, having said goodbye to his first wholesale consignment bound for England. He sits down at his workbench, puts on the glasses he's still getting used to wearing, and, without any kind of plan, spends the day just playing. Seeing where the metal takes him. It's ages since he's done this. For the last few years, when he's sat down to design, the anxious question of what might sell has always been whirring in the back of his mind. But now, he's smoothing the outline of a heart. It's like the birthmark on his forearm, he realizes. Both gently misshapen. He thinks of his mum, as he often does lately. Thinks of how she must have once looked on—touched, even—this raised part of his skin. Smaller and darker then, but still. He's surprised to find there's a comfort in this tangible link with his past. With her.

As he works on, thoughts of Orla drift into his head. He remembers her manhandling one of her giant tessellating artworks down the stairs, bubble-wrapped for a courier collection. He can't recall the exact timing, but probably in the years between telling her about his mum and finally getting together. "Will I give you a hand with that?" he'd said, trying to step in to take some of its weight. But she'd breezed past him as though it were nothing, and as he'd continued up the stairs, he'd looked over the banister to check she was still managing on the flight below. "You think I can't tell when your eyes are on me, Jules? Don't you be doubting me now. She may be small, but she is mighty," she'd called out. He could hear her smiling, even with her cheek pressed up against the height of the package. So Orla. So fearless in being exactly who she was.

She's teaching the girls to be that way too. On her first World Book Day, Niamh had gone into school dressed as a giant hot-air balloon from *A Voyage in the Clouds*. A brown cardboard box around her middle and a tier of long, sausage-shaped balloons gathered between two circular frames suspended above her head. Julian had worried some kid might burst them, but Orla had said, "It'll take more than a burst balloon to bring that girl down." And Julian had thought, *But there are twenty-four. Twenty-four balloons in that costume that could pop.* In the event, most of them had burst on impact while Niamh was playing football in the playground. "You tell Daddy what the score was, though!" was all Orla had said.

As he files down the silver he's working on, Julian can almost see her sitting on the sofa—*their* sofa, not the sofa at her parents', where she most likely is now—with Aoife on her knee, Niamh beside her, tickling them, kissing them, rapping lightly on the tops of their heads, "Who's going to get covered in Mummy's love?" and then spreading out her fingers, "Splat!" as she pretends to crack an egg, love trickling down through their hair.

He takes his phone out of his pocket, goes to check the time, and sees her name. **Popped home for a bit—do you have time to meet?** She has never stopped calling it home, he notices.

Are you still there? I can be back in ten, Jx, he types, already halfway out the door.

As he locks up the studio, he glances at his phone and sees the "..." of a reply coming.

Great. I've waited for you. Ox

He has always loved that when she signs off with just her initial and a kiss, she's a creature that's strong and unbreakable. Ox. His ox.

He wishes he'd told her about the Liberty order, so she'd know he's changing. He stops on the stairs, gets out his phone, hovers over the image of the consignment, then presses send, as if dispatching some sort of carrier pigeon to race ahead of him. Outside, he starts to jog down Dooley Street. He knows she'll still be there, but suddenly he doesn't want to waste another minute. He doesn't understand why—how—the strangeness of this time has torn at the threads that once bound them so tightly, but he's sure there must still be time to restitch them.

As he jogs, he feels his own hope catching like a kite on the wind, and he runs faster, wanting to send it higher, wanting to believe in happy endings. Wanting every grandiose, heartfelt thing he's seen in films to course through his life with Orla, and to feel it all. To really feel it. He wants to serenade her with a boombox. To stand in the rain for the moment when they come together, water tracking down their faces. But then—like a stylus being pulled across a vinyl record—these thoughts screech to a halt and he feels suddenly ridiculous. He can almost hear Maia's and Meg's laughter. But then there is Cian's voice willing him on, "Pack it in. Just go for it, son!" And Julian smiles and picks up the pace again, because, yes, he wants to live a big and fearless life. He wants to argue because they have something worth saving. He wants to kick a skirting board in protest, and for both of them to laugh at his stubbed toes and petulance, because neither of them is scared. Because he is nothing like his father and these things will not unleash a monster hidden deep inside. Instead, he is love, and fury, and sorrow, and euphoria, and all the things that will make their story continue together.

He runs past the shop where he'd once hunted down her pregnancy cravings. Julian, or ginger snaps? *Eejit*, he thinks, realizing she has always been choosing him. It was *him* who'd left things hanging: Orla, or history? Orla, or the risk that he might hurt her? He feels it now. That there was never a choice to make. He's sold to England, and it hasn't killed him. Hasn't changed a thing, except lift the stone in his chest. He sidesteps two council workers in protective clothing carrying a wasps' nest from the stairwell beside the dry cleaner's, dodges a woman who has paused in the middle of the pavement for some reason only she can know, and keeps going, rounding the corner by the phone box, home finally in view.

Inside the house, Orla paces. All these months Jules must have been working away on this house, on that order—overcoming his fears, for her—and she hadn't realized. She wonders what it's cost him to sell to England. If she's forced him into it. Or if, perhaps, this shift came from him. She studies the spines of their books, takes in the ornaments on the mantelpiece, and wonders if they're still charged with that thing—that essence—of their life together. Something to them, and nothing to anyone else. She pauses at a glass paperweight that holds a world inside and runs a finger across its surface, leaving a trail in the dust.

Outside, she hears footsteps thudding down the street. Hears them stop at the front door. Hears the pant of ragged breath. A key in the lock. She looks up. Jules stands in the doorway looking like he's just sprinted a marathon, hands on his knees, catching himself for a moment, grinning up into her uncertainty. He straightens, exhales. "Orla, I feckin' love you, all right. Come home. You're meant to be here, with me."

She feels an apple bob of surprise in her chest—at his words, at this more certain version of the Julian she knows—and she smiles, dimple-cheeked.

It takes only three strides for him to cross their small front room, but somehow, she feels as though he's moving in slow motion, as though with each step she has time to absorb every detail. Then his arms are around her. "Will you be coming back to me?" he says into her hair. And she nods against his chest, the dust already falling from her finger, its particles dispersing around the room, as she grips the fabric of his jacket, feels the warmth of his neck, the spring of his hair, the glorious burn of being fully loved.

Gordon

In the quiet hum of the office, Gordon eats lunch at his desk and considers the day's Wordle between bites of his sandwich.

"What's your starting word?" Amy asks.

"EARTH," Gordon says. He offers up a new five-letter word every time Amy asks, but really his word is always SOBER. "What about yours?"

"AUDIO," Amy replies, not looking up from her screen. "Someone said it's a good one, but what are you meant to do with all those vowels if you get anything from it."

Gordon puts the lid back on his empty lunchbox. "Hope you figure it out. You've three to beat," he says, sharing his own score. "See you in a bit."

He walks over to the main wing and, as he does every day, enjoys the moment of emerging from the staff-only door and crossing from one world into another. The cold echo of a concrete stairwell, out onto the polish and hush of the gallery, ruffled only by the shuffle of a school party or a gaggle of noisy tourists. Sometimes he takes a pair of headphones and listens to an audio guide as he walks through the rooms; other times, he sits on one of the benches dotted throughout the gallery, eyes traveling around the painting in front of him. He knows it's illogical—he's read *The Goldfinch*—but he feels as though nothing bad could happen while he's held within the quiet of these rooms.

His sponsor got him the job here. One day—when Gordon was starting to feel able to return to work, but not quite sure he was ready for the adrenaline rush of the City—Rob had phoned and mentioned a gallery was looking for someone to manage the digital team and its website. It doesn't engage Gordon's brain in the way masterminding trading algorithms once did, but he enjoys being part of this world and knowing that, in some small and hidden way, he is bringing art to people. Not like Rob with his paintings—or the curators—but still. It's enough.

GORDON MET COMFORT in the summer of 2019 on a broken-down train stuck somewhere just outside London Victoria. She was sitting opposite, fanning herself with an exhibition program from the Dulwich Picture Gallery.

"What did you think of it?" he asked, and she'd looked confused for a moment, before telling him it had been left behind by another passenger. But they carried on talking and when the carriage finally juddered to life again, she looked disappointed.

As the train pulled into the station, she typed her number into his phone and said, "You seem nice. Please don't be one of those guys who doesn't call."

Comfort is a few years older than Gordon and has a teenage daughter, Ida, from a previous relationship. Ida looks like a miniature version of her mum, with the same thick, dark curls and the same habit of widening her eyes when someone is talking, as though listening through the whites of them. Ida calls him "Gord," which she manages to make sound both derisory and vaguely affectionate. "Oh, you're here, are you, Gord?" she'll say, adopting the censorious tone she reserves for adults. At first, it needled—a reminder of who he'd been at school—but gradually he's come to associate it only with Ida and the person he is now. Ida is funny and more interesting than Gordon remembers himself being at fourteen. She likes Manga comics and watching YouTube videos of people doing odd things. One day she shows him a car being shrink-wrapped in vinyl until its whole body is a brilliant reflective gold. It's mesmerizing and he has a sense he is learning the world anew.

When the pandemic hit, Gordon had been seeing Comfort for less than a year, but it was Ida who'd raised the possibility of him staying with them. "Is Gord going to try to muscle in on our ark to see out whatever this thing is? Or will he be staying home all alone?"

He'd smiled at the way she made it sound like it was his own exhausting idea that she should endure his company through lockdown. Weeks into their confinement, she would delight in walking into a room and saying, "Oh my God. Are you *still* here?!"

"I can see I've totally outstayed my welcome, but if you could just see your way to a few more days, I think Boris is on the verge of lifting things," he'd say, wearing a pained expression and raising his hands in feigned helplessness.

They enjoy this even now, nearly three years on, when he has given up the lease on his own place and pays half the rent on their garden flat.

"Oh my God! Are you *still* here?"

"I know, I know. I only dropped round for a cup of tea, and here I am still stewing away."

Ida's presence meant things moved from the headiness of the first few dates straight to old married couple, but Gordon's happy with that. Films made it seem as though love was hidden in the petals of red roses and a view of the Eiffel Tower, but he's relieved to find it sitting side by side in the trapped warmth of a glass potting shed in Willesden, nestled in the steeped scent of compost and the first green globes of fruit on the vine.

He'd told Comfort about his breakdown early on. And she'd listened, eyes wider than usual, as he described the situation he'd grown up in.

"I was an awful child. Horrible to my mother, but I couldn't see how I was being manipulated. It's no excuse . . . but—"

"When Ida was little, she believed in the Tooth Fairy and Father Christmas. She wrote letters to them because I encouraged her to. Do you think she should have known better?"

"But Maia understood what was going on."

"And one kid in every hundred doesn't believe in Santa; Maia was that child."

This had always been his stumbling block—the reason he'd found his childhood self so hard to forgive—but somehow Comfort's logic seemed simple. It didn't excuse the person he was in those middle years, but it helped him to understand how he'd ended up in that place.

CORA SITS IN the darkness of the Royal Opera House alone, as *Swan Lake* nears the end of Act Two. It is "Dance of the Cygnets," four women moving as one in perfect synchronicity, hand in hand, arms overlapping in flawless Xs. Cora watches, her own calves and thighs held taut, as on stage they execute shimmering bursts of *entrechat quatre, relevé passé*. Their footwork is clean, precise. Their movements light. Cora feels a lift in her chest; she knows this soaring feeling, of being the one performing the magic. The dancers look this way, then that, curious, serene, while beneath the plumage of their tutus, their legs beat imagined water. She recognizes the choreography. It is a chorus part, but one with the potential to earn bigger roles. The quartet must move in relation to one another to avoid upsetting the spacing. They must share the same musicality, the same tempo; a count for every step, until finally, in the last moments, they break apart and attempt to fly, before falling to the floor.

She looks at the women's faces, trying to pinpoint who is the star, who has the determination needed to set themselves apart from the rest. They are so young! Cora likes to imagine them off-duty, gossiping, stretching, discussing the male dancers. She wonders if they still smoke between practice. If they still subsist on cigarettes and coffee as so many of her peers once had.

Echoes of that time reverberate unbidden across the stage with the *pit-a-pat* of feet she can hear beneath the music. *You'll fly higher if it's from the heart;* the voice of her teacher, rising above the *plink-plonk* of a piano. The ritual softening of new pointe shoes. Trapping the toe box in the hinge of a door; slow rises through demi-pointe to break in the arch. And then, looking at the clock, as she pushed through pain, feet already bleeding, another six hours to go.

Her marriage, Cora realizes, was like a magnified, more awful version of her ballet career. Hopes. Dreams. Then agony and disappointment. Sacrificing herself for an ultimately unattainable thing. She's sixty-eight now, and although she knows the idea of being *put out to pasture* is a phrase others associate with obsolescence and redundancy, for her it conjures lush green fields filled with buttercups where she's free to roam.

She lives in a small Victorian terrace in West London, not far from Maia and Gordon. Her house has window boxes that she changes with the seasons. There is a small walled garden. She has planted pots with shrubs and standard trees and is gradually learning their names: *Salix integra*, bay, dwarf Korean lilac, hebe, broom, hibiscus, hypericum. This year, she's introduced fresh herbs and salad leaves shielded by a cold frame. Watching them peep out as small shoots and grow to harvestable food seems like the real joy, and as she produces too much to eat herself, she leaves string-tied bundles on her front wall with a handwritten note encouraging passersby to help themselves. The first time, she'd worried people might not want them, but felt a silent rush of love from the empty street when she opened her door and found them all gone.

On Saturdays, she buys fresh bread from the local bakery and picks up two thick weekend newspapers. She reads slowly across the course of the week, enjoys leaving the supplements on a side table in the living room, or by her bed. These signs of life, this trail of her own self inhabiting a space, with no need to clear away the evidence, still makes her sigh with unexpected contentment. So, too, does the sound of the Roberts radio she has in the kitchen. It is the female voices she wants to hear—their stories, their take on life. These women, with so many different experiences amongst them, finding their way into her home, opening the door to a wider world with their humor, their insight, their passion.

She still jumps when a car door slams outside or if there's an unexpected knock on the door. Her body bears the scars and creaks of one that has not been well looked after. She tries to soften it with yoga and Pilates, but there is no escaping the arthritis that has crept into broken bones never properly set. She feels the weight of her children's concern and the responsibility they feel toward her. During lockdown, they made pavement visits, left sanitized gifts on her doorstep.

"Are you sure you're doing okay? You could come and stay with one of us? You don't have to be alone." Although they all knew that couldn't work, with Maia and Kate working at the hospital; Ida going into school.

"I'm fine! I have books and podcasts. The whole of the internet for company!" These things still feel shiny and new, even now.

They'd looked skeptical, as though she was trying to make the best of things. Somehow unable, even having witnessed the daily reality of her life, to truly understand that she had endured a much more draconian lockdown for over forty years. Covid-19, she could do; this one, for her at least, would be easy.

And she had Gordon—the child she'd struggled to bond with, the young man she'd once found so unknowable—to thank for this liberation. When he'd first moved back home, after the car accident, he'd kept his distance in the house, as though relearning his place within it. But she remembers the night things changed. He'd come in from meeting Maia for dinner. Cora had been in the kitchen, folding clothes still warm from the dryer. She'd heard him at the front door, kicking off his shoes, hanging up his coat. One foot on the stairs, two. But then he'd appeared in the kitchen doorway, his hair wet with rain. "I was thinking on the train back tonight, you must miss her. Maia."

Cora had looked up, surprised. The bare truth of his words was disconcerting; she so rarely allowed herself to miss her girl.

"Oh, yes. Yes, I do," she said, smoothing the creases from a shirt.

"I think she misses you, too," he said. "Did you know she's taking a sabbatical soon? A month in Australia with a friend."

She'd let the clothing drop. Because, no, she had no idea; she knew none of the details of her daughter's life. A rush of questions hovered at her lips, but then his father appeared beside him, and she returned to her folding.

"Good evening?" he asked.

"Yes, a gallery and then we went to a restaurant at the bottom of Long Acre."

"It's all right for some. I've been stuck here with only your mother's burned offerings."

And her son—her strange and inscrutable son—had replied, "Do you know, you always say that, but I can't actually remember Mum ever burning a meal."

She hadn't dared look up, hadn't dared acknowledge the exchange, but she heard her husband clear his throat, and from the corner of her vision, saw it was *his* shoes that turned to leave the room first. Then Gordon, a few moments later.

One afternoon, when her husband was still at work, Gordon had come home and found her in the dining room watering the house-plants. "I thought you might like this," he'd said, putting a bar of chocolate down on the table. She'd looked at him, unsure if it was a trap. He must have seen her uncertainty because he said, "It's okay. I won't tell." And so they'd sat across from one another, the bar open between them, and had each taken a piece or two. She can still re-member how that first square had softened against the roof of her mouth, how its flavor had spread across her tongue, sweetness like a warm towel after a bath.

"It's good stuff, isn't it?" he said. "It's from this little shop that's opened up in town, just past the common. It does cards and stuff too. You'd like it." She was touched. That he'd imagined her enjoying vis-iting that shop. Any shop. "They had samples. Almond and salted caramel, I think."

"That sounds nice," she said.

He nodded, then added, "They only offered me one on the way out. Otherwise, I would've got you some."

"No, no," she said, keen not to upset the delicate balance of what-ever this was. "This is amazing. I can't imagine anything tasting better than this. How did your sight test go?"

"Oh, they just said to get some off-the-shelf glasses for reading." He fumbled around in his bag and brought out a case. "What do you think?"

Cora smiled, said they suited him, realizing that her son—her child—was aging. That in a few years he would be thirty-five, then forty, quickly fifty—might even begin to lose his hair or go gray.

Gordon folded the wrapper back into his bag, then swept the table clean with the side of his hand, the other out flat to catch any crumbs. "Thank you," Cora said. And she wondered if he knew she meant not just for the chocolate, but for taking care not to leave any trace.

At dinner, Cora was on edge, unsure if her son would give her away, but he didn't. And after that, it became a regular thing to share those forbidden treats.

Gradually, they began to talk. Cora would ask how his day had been, or how Maia was. And he'd tell her about something that had interested him at Rob's studio, or a painting he'd seen.

"You know, Michelangelo, he wasn't just an artist. He did all these dissections, and when you really study his paintings, you can see he's hidden anatomical images in them. Look, I'll show you," he said, taking out his mobile. He passed her the phone, and she held it—tentatively—as though it might explode in her hands. "That's right, like this to zoom in. Yeah, like you're pinching the screen."

She'd laughed then. At the oddness of seeing the image growing larger beneath her fingertips.

"It's a ceiling in the Sistine Chapel. Can you see where—" he said, pointing.

"Oh, yes! Isn't that incredible?" she said, as she realized God and a posse of angels were emerging from a kidney, rather than some indistinguishable shape. They sat in silence as she zoomed out, then in again. "Wow," she breathed, her amazement extending far beyond the painting.

On the night Gordon told his father he'd got the job at the gallery, Cora had looked on as the older man gave a dismissive sniff and asked, "Does it pay as much?"

"As banking?"

"What else might I be referring to? That was your last line of work, wasn't it?"

"It doesn't, but I'm unlikely to find that salary—or the bonuses—anywhere else."

"And you think you'll be able to cope? Without your flashy car and £300 dinners?"

Cora had winced to hear him refusing to acknowledge their son was a different person now. But rather than lob a grenade back, she'd seen Gordon's shoulders visibly loosen, watched his hands raise in submission, as if to say, *I don't know. You've got me there. You win.* There was a subtle power in bowing out. It left his father empty-handed, the stick he'd been about to beat him with disintegrated.

A few months later, their son announced he was ready to move out. Cora had been expecting it. He'd stayed longer than she'd anticipated, and she suspected that might have been for her sake. She tried not to let her disappointment show, but she could already feel herself missing him beside her in the kitchen as she cooked, clearing up around her, ready to absorb whatever error or mistake she might make—*No, it was me who chipped the plate*—his presence easing her isolation.

"I've left a phone and some money in a plastic box buried under the hydrangea. For emergencies," he'd said, on the morning he was due to leave. And she realized that must have been what he was doing when he went out to the garage for gardening tools a few days earlier. "You'd only notice the earth's been disturbed if you knew to look for it."

It was the most explicit he'd been in discussing her situation and his sensitivity made her eyes fill. "Thank you, but I'll be fine," she'd said, even though it felt like her mother leaving her on the first day of school. Cora had turned back to cleaning the cupboard doors then—thinking about her mum, their lack of goodbye, that she didn't get to go to her funeral; it still hurt—Gordon leaving was already pain enough to bear for one day.

It was only hours after he'd left that the lid on the pressure cooker blew off, hitting the kitchen wall, releasing a hiss of scalding steam. She spent that week sleeping on the floor beside the bed with nothing to cover her. Was yanked awake by her hair. Had her face pushed into a plate of food he insisted was cold, even as it burned her cheeks.

When the doorbell rang around lunchtime a week later, she was surprised to find their son on the doorstep. "Oh," she said, instinctively lifting her hand to cover the split in her lip, which she'd felt reopen as she'd smiled hello. "Oh, look at me. I hadn't realized you'd be coming." She was flustered, unsure how to conceal the change in her appearance in the days since he'd left. "I fell," she said, as she ushered him into the hallway. "That damn rug. The corner curls up and—"

"Mum, don't. I know it was him. But it's okay, you're going to be safe now." He held out his palm, and in it were two keys.

"Oh, you don't need to give those back. Or did your father ask you to return them?"

"They're not mine. They're his."

And he told her then. How he'd just come from visiting his father at the practice. How he'd shown him video footage uploaded to a secure server online. Footage he'd collected from their house, on tiny hidden cameras planted before he'd left.

"I wanted to make sure there was enough evidence; I'm sorry I had to leave you all week. I know how bad it's been."

"You've been filming us?" She looked around the room, at a photo frame, at a table lamp.

"They're in the smoke detectors."

"Oh," she said, feeling her eyes grow large as she gazed up. She remembered him replacing the batteries in them all recently, but most of the time they seemed to disappear unseen into the fixtures of the house. "Is it still filming us?" she asked, putting a hand to her hair, suddenly self-conscious. Then she remembered herself. "And you told—But—What did he say? Is he coming here now?"

"He's not coming back. I told him he could go immediately and avoid a public scandal and prison sentence. Or I could send the footage to the other partners at the practice and the police . . . So these keys, they're yours now," he said, handing them to her. "He'll sign over the deed of the house to you later this week."

She sat down on the sofa then. Hands in her lap. Looking about her—at the sideboard, the TV cabinet, the wooden coffee table. Into the kitchen. Out into the hallway—these rooms, which for so many years had been her world, already shifting in her vision. Such a peculiar emptiness. Such an absence of anything to suggest it might be a place she'd call home.

Cora can still remember the mix of independence and fear she felt each time she used those keys to let herself back into that house. She'd not stayed long—just a few weeks; a part of her always feeling he was about to come up behind her.

She'd only seen him once more, on the day of their divorce. Maia and Gordon had both booked the day off work and stayed close to her side as they'd walked into the solicitor's office, as they sat across a table from him. Neither exchanged words with him. They had, Cora felt sure, barely looked at him.

Her eyes had met his, though. Only for a second. And he'd been the first to look away. She remembers that, because it had surprised her. And because in the next moment she'd noticed a small stain on his shirt. Two orange dots, as if a pan of tomato soup might have spattered up at him. She thinks of it often. Of the things it seems to tell her: that it had escaped his notice; that he was alone; that he was fallible. And it somehow makes her less afraid.

It's summer now. Gordon is in Spain with Comfort, Ida, his mum, Maia, and Kate. The others want to go to the boating lake, and no one objects when he says he might head off to a nearby gallery instead. He works his way through the rooms at random, wanting to be surprised by the painting he knows he'll find there. The one he'd last seen all those years ago, when it was on loan in London.

Eventually he arrives at a room that's smaller and darker than the others. And where the paintings that came before were in gilt surrounds, these are framed in onyx. The space is almost empty: just a young couple and a child with her grandmother. His own footsteps echo between their whispers and the silence. He makes his way methodically around the room, studying each of the paintings in turn. They are dark, heavy, macabre. The voice in his headset tells him they are known as Goya's "black paintings," applied directly to the walls of his house, only transferred onto canvas posthumously. It's hard to imagine anyone painting these horrifying images on their living-room walls.

Gordon moves slowly, not allowing his eyes to skip ahead, but knowing he is drawing closer. And then it is there, halfway around the left-hand wall. *Saturn Devouring His Son*. He stands. Looking. Listening.

The audio explains how contemporary art movements—even literature and cinema—have roots in this work, created in isolation, without self-censure. It goes on to discuss how the mythological god—Saturn—can be seen as the personification of feelings such as the fear of losing one's power; that he is said to have consumed his children out of a terror of being overthrown. And then, almost as an afterthought, the narrator says that one of Saturn's sons—Jupiter—escaped. That Jupiter's mother protected the child, kept him safe. And that as an adult, he returned and made good on the prophecy. That the boy did indeed overthrow his father.

He studies Saturn's features. He remembers feeling terrified by this face the first time he saw it, recalls the hopelessness he felt that night in the restaurant discussing it with Maia. But he sees something different in the figure now. Where once he'd seen power and rage, now he sees desperation. Fear.

Gordon crouches down, touches his hands to the cool black floor and breathes in the scent of oil and aging canvas that permeates the space. He's not sure why the painting resonates so much, or why he's so willing to draw parallels with his own life. But he feels relief in discovering the more recent part of his story—that freedom, for him, for his mum—was hidden in it all along.

Gordon stands, turns from the painting, and heads back through the rooms of the gallery. Past Sorolla's days at the beach and walls filled with shrines to other stories and alternate endings; maybe some of them his own. And finally, he steps out into the brightness of the day and turns to walk across the park, ready to meet his family.

Epilogue

July 29, 2022

The pain in his chest had been sudden when it came, but he recognized it instantly, like a familiar face in a crowd. Its markers etched in his mind, despite the years since medical school. A sensation not unlike heartburn. Pain spreading out to his neck and jaw. A feeling of impending doom.

Now, as he lies on his kitchen floor, spilled coffee seeping into his sleeve, he bears the pain, holding steady, ready to observe the symptoms that will usher him toward the end. But then comes the flash of Cora's face. His own hands, not shaking and useless as he'd believed them to be, but solid, brutal things. Pushing, pounding, the pain in his chest now doing the same.

He tries to summon his patients, the people he'd once helped, though can conjure them only fleetingly before it's Cora's bruised face again. His daughter not meeting his eye. The wails of his infant son. And this is the truth of it. The people he was meant to love, he has only hurt. He cries out then, a guttural sound. Because it's so clear. He had one life. And he could have spent it differently.

He will not find peace; his final realization is too fresh, too stark, to be smoothed away. But still, he snatches at a moment, plucks it from the air. A time when he could have set them on separate paths.

As his last breath escapes him, he is walking through Embankment Gardens with Cora. She wears a surgical boot on one foot, but his own feet are bare. He can almost feel the grass around his toes. They reach the gates on Villiers Street and an odd sensation travels through him, like seawater permeating his skin and rushing in. They slow. He likes her, yes. But this time, he lets her hand drop. They say a few words, and then she smiles, turns, and walks away. He watches her reach the end of the road, watches as she fails to become familiar to him, watches as she rounds the corner and disappears from his view.

As his body cools, the air quivers with unspent possibilities of how else their fates might have become untied, what other paths their lives might have taken.

There is a child. She stands outside a church hall beside her mother, who studies a noticeboard, ads pinned behind the glass. There is a ballet class on a Tuesday afternoon or Irish step dancing on a Saturday morning. The mother weighs it up and decides it would be a rush to get to ballet straight from school. She looks down at the child, who is wrapping the stem of a dandelion around her finger, and begins to explain what step is, tells her about the special shoes they'll need to buy. The girl lets her dream of wearing ballet slippers fall from her grasp with the picked flower, and a few years later, she drops step too, more interested in working alongside her dad as he tends his vegetable patch.

There is a young man. Just starting out, in his first year as a qualified GP. He listens as a salesman talks up a gleaming new car with a pop-up sunroof, cassette-tape stereo, ABS. But before he can explain the anti-skid system, something causes them to look up. That's when the young man catches sight of a soft-top two-seater in the corner of the forecourt. *That's for sale?* he asks, already walking over, taking in the character and refinement of the older, classic design. Six months later, in heavy rain, its brakes fail. The young man's father is performing surgery in the same hospital when, two floors down, they call the time of death.

There is a girl. On the cusp of fourteen, when a new boy joins her class. He has long hair, flared jeans. Lips like the singer from the Rolling Stones. From the bus, they walk the same ribbon of tarmac, their houses a quarter of a mile apart. With each day, their pace slows to eke out their time together. *I'll come to the end of your track*, he offers. But when they reach her gate, fingers smudged with blackberries, they're not ready to part, so they wander back toward the road again. And somewhere in the gentle to-and-fro of these days, the trappings of girlhood—ballet, cartwheels, plaiting her best friend's hair—fall away. Almost unnoticed.

There is a boy. Ten years old. He glides along hospital corridors at his father's side, seeing the way people defer to him, the way his colleagues appear anxious not to drain the precious resource of his time. Later, when he's dispatched to the canteen, he imagines himself bathed in his father's glow, as though he, too, might one day be a surgeon, might command that same respect. Until, coming up behind two white coats, he overhears their conversation. Sees the man he's always revered through someone else's eyes. He retreats to a toilet cubicle, locks himself inside, burning with shame. And then emerges, determined to be nothing like him.

There is a woman. She pushes a pram, her nine-year-old daughter at her side. They go into a building, leaving a wind-torn street behind. When the registrar looks up and asks what the woman would like to call her child, she hesitates. Then finds herself saying her late father's name, Hugh. She doesn't know where the idea comes from. She hadn't thought of it before. But the moment the word is out of her mouth, it feels right.

Character Names

(official meanings in italics)

Cora — the core of the story

Gordon — *great hill*, immovable, looming; a hard climb to reach the other side

Bear — soft, cuddly, brave, strong

Julian — *sky father*; Jules, jewels, jeweler

Maia — *mother*

Atkin (surname) — kin meaning *family*; to be "at kin" can be read as being at peace or at war

Vihaan — *dawn*, representing the beginning of a new age

Sylvia/Sílbhe — silver-haired

Cian — *enduring one*

Orla — *golden princess*; all

Lily — *purity, innocence*; traditionally, a symbol of both virginity and grief

Pearl — *precious*

Mehri — *kind, sunny*; merry, joyful

Fern — provider of shelter and shade

Roland — *famous throughout the land*

Felix — *lucky, fortunate*; associations with a popular brand of cat food

Kate — *pure*

Charlotte — *free*

Meg — *pearl*

Comfort and Ida — together, an eiderdown

Aoife — *warrior princess*

Niamh — *radiance*

Eileen — I lean; a name that suggests dependence, yet invites a similar confession in the mouth of another

Author's Note

Although this novel is a work of fiction, some of the artworks described are inspired by those of real-life makers. If you're interested to find out more: Orla's huge tessellating artworks, made from reclaimed yardsticks, are based on the exquisitely beautiful work of **Rose Vickers**—you can find her on Instagram at @rosevickers.studio • For several years, I've loved and worn jewelry designed by the German goldsmith **MANU**, and this is what I had in mind when I wrote about the pieces Julian creates (@manu_schmuck) • When Julian and Orla are in the pub with friends from the Old Chocolate Factory, the paper artist whose work they briefly discuss I imagined to be **Matthew Shlian**—I've always been captivated by the way he plays with shadow (@matthewshlian) • When everyone gathers around Bear's doorway after he's left home, his room is referred to as a *still-life*. This idea comes from the poem "Empty Nest" by **Carol Ann Duffy**, found in her eponymously named anthology, a collection that comforted me endlessly when my own children first left home.

If you're holding an edition featuring an illustration at the head of each chapter, the artist who created them is **Sam Scales**. I fell in love with Sam's drawing style long before my novel found a publisher, so it's a privilege to have his beautiful illustrations sitting alongside my words. You can find him on Instagram at @samscales.

Finally, the living artwork that appears on the cover is by **Jennifer Latour,** captured in Donegal, Ireland. Jennifer's organic sculptures fuse individual flowers to fleetingly create new species. Looking at the meanings associated with those that make up the hybrid plant on the cover, each seems to reflect a particular narrative (I'll leave you to decide which is which) while sharing the same stem. It feels like the perfect cover for this edition. You can find more of Jennifer's gorgeous work at @bonjourlatour.

Acknowledgments

Most joyful and heartfelt thanks to **Karolina Sutton**, agent of dreams. While I've kept my hope in a small jar with the lid firmly on, your belief in this novel has always seemed capable of filling entire swimming pools. I am just so grateful for this, for your editorial insight, your warmth and humor, and for being the most reassuring voice on the end of a phone. To borrow some words from Bear: you are a swarm, and I adore you • Thanks to **Anna Stein**, my brilliant US agent, for being there at all the right moments—whether diverting your holiday to join us for that very first meeting, making magic happen in North America, or bringing everyone together for the best sort of food and conversation—I'm grateful for every bit of it. You are a wonder • Thank you to **Jake Smith-Bosanquet and Zoe Willis**, for ensuring this novel reaches readers in so many different languages—it's hard to imagine two rights agents more lovely, yet tenacious. And Zoe, huge thanks for selling the very first rights to *The Names* anywhere in the world (yes, even before the UK)—hearing you'd found a home for my novel in Greece will stay with me as a magical moment • So many thanks to **Michelle Weiner**—you only ever seem to appear bearing good news, and I'm so grateful for all the work you do behind the scenes to make that happen • Finally, thanks to **Izzy Redfern**, for being such a welcoming presence at CAA and for organizing . . . well, everything.

Oh, **Francesca Main**. If I were reading this aloud, you'd hear the sigh of happiness in my voice, and we could just leave this right here, as it would tell you pretty much everything you need to know about what a wonderful privilege it feels to have you as my editor here in the UK. I've been delighted by both your exquisite line edits, and your dedication to understanding my characters and their motivations in considering every change. Your kindness, thought, humor, and care shine through in everything you do, both on and off the page. So too, **Pamela Dorman** at Pamela Dorman Books at Viking Penguin US, and **Lara Hinchberger** at Penguin Canada. Thank you, all three, for loving the manuscript that first arrived on your desks so wholeheartedly, and then helping me to shape it into something that feels even better. I'm grateful for your warmth and enthusiasm, and for your wisdom in encouraging me to make big changes. It's a richer, more nuanced novel for your involvement, and it's been a joy to work with you all.

Thank you to the wonderful art department at Orion for your tireless creativity in designing a cover I adore: **Nick Shah**, **Steve Marking**, **Dan Jackson**, with thanks in triplicate to **Chevonne Elbourne** for coming up with the concept of "three-shadows man." I could not love this beautiful cover more.

And to **Jason Ramirez** and **Elizabeth Yaffe** at Penguin US, thank you for creating such a gorgeous cover that so perfectly reflects each strand of this story. It's everything I'd hoped for.

Thanks to **Susie Bertinshaw, Holly Kyte,** and **Jade Craddock** for copyediting and proofreading my novel with such care and cross-referencing so many tiny details for accuracy. I'm grateful to you for rescuing me from countless errors and for allowing me to refuse to be saved when it came to hanging onto certain quirks • Also at Orion, I'm indebted to: **Anna Valentine** (an excellent name and an excellent woman), **Katie Espiner, Sandra Taylor, Lindsay Terrell, Jen Wilson, Virginia Woolstencroft, Cait Davies, Javerya Iqbal, Leanne Oliver, Sian Baldwin, Esther Waters, Eleanor Wood, Karin Burnik, Paul Stark, Louise Richardson, Hannah Cox,** and **Alice Graham.** And, not least, **Sam Eades,** for all the thought you put into looking after debut authors • At Penguin US, I'd like to thank **Marie Michels** and **Natalie Grant,** along with **Brian Tart, Andrea Schulz, Kate Stark, Molly Fessenden, Carolyn Coleburn, Yuleza Negron, Patrick Nolan, Mary Stone, Rebecca Marsh, Andy Dudley, Rachel Obenschain, Chelsea Cohen, Claire Vaccaro, John Francisconi,** and so many more besides—I've been bowled over by your enthusiasm for *The Names* and feel so incredibly lucky to work with you all.

To my **publishers** and **translators** around the world—it's the most magical privilege to reach readers in languages I don't speak myself—thank you.

Huge thanks to: **Henu Cummins,** for your generous advice and professional insight, which was instrumental in shaping Gordon Sr.'s character and the family dynamic that forms around him. I'm so grateful to you for giving up your time to discuss my novel when it was just an idea, and later, for your encouragement and cheerleading on reading the finished manuscript. The world is a kinder, safer place for having you in it • **Peter and Guy Jenner**, for being so helpful in considering my questions around goldsmithing • **Geoff O'Sullivan** (via **Anna Stein**), for answering my questions around Irishisms with such generosity and good humor. Any inaccuracies are entirely my own.

While no name in this novel is drawn from life, a few characters share their names with family and friends' children, although they've been chosen only for their meaning or because it evolved naturally. But either way, to real-life **Bea**, **Maya**, **Felix**, and **Pearl**, you have the very best names and I hope you won't mind that my characters also wear them for the telling of this story.

To the **Merry Women's Book Group**: Thank you for challenging me to read books both plotful and plotless, for the shared feasts and the raucous laughter. Collectively, you are a joyful bottle of anti-allergy prosecco; individually, you are **Donna**, **Emily**, **Maria**, and **Marieke** • And to my other equally glorious book group: **Shauna**, **Michèle**, **Pippa**, **Sue**, **Audrey**, **Jennie**, **Fiona**, and the many dogs who read with us. Thank you for your friendship, for your incredible kindness, and for sharing in my delight over all this book stuff.

To **every friend** who generously welcomes me back into your orbit whenever I emerge from writing, who has said something encouraging, who has shared in my happiness over *finally* having this dream come true . . . thank you • Especially large hugs and gratitude to: **Joanne** and **Jenny**, for your advice in matters of librarianship and French language respectively (and so much more besides); **Shauna**, for encouraging me to pick up a pen again; **Kathryn**, for your gentle encouragement in whatever I try to do; and **Samson**, **Charlotte**, **Ben**,